MW00772903

Strike Team Two - Book 3

HOT JUSTICE

A Hostile Operations Team - Book 14

LYNN RAYE HARRIS

The Hostile Operations Team® and Lynn Raye Harris® are trademarks of H.O.T. Publishing, LLC.

Printed in the United States of America

First Printing, 2019

For rights inquires, visit www.LynnRayeHarris.com

HOT Justice
Copyright © 2019 by Lynn Raye Harris
Cover Design Copyright © 2019 Croco Designs

ISBN: 978-1-941002-42-1

Prologue

HAYLEE JAMISON RUSHED THROUGH THE DOORS OF the hospital and into the bright emergency room waiting area. Panic throbbed in her belly as she skidded to a stop in front of the desk. The receptionist looked up.

"Nicole Montgomery," she said. "She was brought in a few minutes ago?"

The receptionist glanced down at her paperwork. Then she looked up, a blank expression on her face. "They're working on her, Miss...?"

"Jamison. Haylee."

"Are you family?"

Haylee gnawed the inside of her cheek. "If you mean is she my best friend and roommate who I've known for the past five years then yes, we're family. If you mean are we blood related, then no."

The woman—her name tag said Brandy—smiled. "If you want to have a seat, we'll let you know as soon as we have news. I can't promise you can go back, though. I can't even promise I can give you much information."

"She called me…" Haylee swallowed the knot in her throat. Nicole had sounded so out of it. Like she was drunk. Though stoned was a better term. High on prescription pain pills. "I have a list of her medications."

She took out her phone and opened her notes. Brandy gave her a clipboard with some paperwork. "If you could fill this out—just write it all down here, please. I'll see it gets to the right place."

Haylee's hands trembled as she clutched the clipboard to her chest. "Thank you. Please… anything I can do, I will."

"Just fill that out as soon as you can."

"Right. I'll do it now." Haylee retreated to a chair and began to methodically write in the answers on the paperwork. She thought of Nicole this morning, the way her friend had seemed so jumpy and upset. Nicole'd had surgery a year ago to repair shoulder damage from her teenage years when she'd been a gymnast. After the surgery, her doctor gave her Percocet for the pain. That was a normal course of action, but when the pain didn't ease, Nicole asked for more. And more. Until she couldn't function without the pills. She'd begun doctor shopping, seeing different ones to get her fix when the previous one wouldn't prescribe them anymore.

Haylee sniffled and wiped her eyes, then kept writing. *Dammit, Nicole.* It wasn't her friend's fault, she knew that, and yet it angered her so much that a beautiful, promising life had suddenly been afflicted with the evil that was opioid addiction. Haylee didn't know how to make it stop, though she tried to help Nicole however she could. She took her to appointments, took her to rehab, carried the burden of paying the rent and doing the grocery shopping when Nicole lost her job.

She'd gotten another job three months ago, after being clean for six weeks. A good job with benefits working for a PAC with offices in DC. But this morning, when Haylee had been at the coffee shop working on a writing job so she could turn it in and get paid, Nicole had called her. It was a Saturday, so it wasn't unusual for Nicole to be home. But Haylee's blood ran cold when she realized what was happening.

Nicole was high. Worse, something was wrong because Nicole was sobbing that her skin burned. Rather than scream at her friend for succumbing again, Haylee called 911. Then she'd shoved her computer and notes into her bag and raced over here.

She swiped her eyes again, kept writing. When she finished, she took everything to Brandy, who thanked her and told her to take a seat. Haylee found a chair in the corner of the packed room and scrolled through her phone, gazing unseeing at her Facebook feed. Nicole's last update popped up. A photo of her with a guy she'd met through work. Tony Davis, who looked exactly like the young up and coming DC lawyer he was. Worked for Senator Watson of Arizona. Nicole had found that such a cool coincidence because she was from Arizona and her parents still lived there.

Oh God, Nicole's parents. Haylee froze as she wondered whether or not to call them. She looked up at the packed waiting room, her gaze sliding over the faces there. The children with their parents. The elderly people in wheelchairs. The people in obvious distress, but not life threatening distress.

Yes, she had to call Mr. and Mrs. Montgomery. They needed to know that Nicole had ODed, even if Nicole would be mad when this was all over that Haylee had told them. It wasn't the first time, though Haylee prayed it was the last. But she'd prayed for that before, and it hadn't worked out.

While Haylee was rehearsing what she'd say to Nicole's parents, the doors to the ER opened and a man in scrubs walked out. "Haylee Jamison?" he asked, reading the clipboard in his hand.

Haylee's heart dropped but she stood and made her way toward him. He turned his head, met her gaze, and the look on his face caused her breath to stop in her chest. She forced herself to keep walking.

"Are you Haylee Jamison?"

"Yes. Is Nicole okay?"

He tried so hard not to frown—or at least she thought he tried. He didn't quite manage it though. He motioned for her to follow him. They didn't go far, just to a little nook off the waiting room with chairs and a small table. She sat when he did. Then he looked at her, and the sorrow wasn't gone. Her belly twisted.

"Miss Jamison, I'm really sorry, but your friend… We tried. Her body shut down. I'm so sorry."

Haylee blinked as disbelief socked her between the eyes. "I… She's gone?"

"Yes. I'm sorry."

Oh my God… Nausea crashed into her. Her knees grew weak even though she was sitting. She wanted to scream. But she had to hold it together. Had to make sure he was right. "Can I… can I see her?"

He frowned. And then he nodded. "Come with me."

It would be an hour before Haylee walked out of the hospital, nerves frayed, heart broken, tears streaming from her eyes. She had to call the Montgomerys. Had to find out what they wanted to do about the arrangements. Haylee already knew that Nicole didn't have a will. They were in their twenties, two girls living in DC, working to make the world a better place. Or so they'd always hoped.

They'd had plans. Live together, have fun, meet the right guy, get married, have kids, live in the same neighborhood and be besties for life. Girls' trips. Wine and gossip and life issues. But it wasn't going to happen that way because Nicole was gone.

Haylee stood on the sidewalk, trying to process everything that had just happened. Life threw curveballs. She knew that. Had known it since her parents sat her down when she was eight and told her they were divorcing. She'd been so upset that Daddy wasn't going to live with them anymore. But he'd promised he'd see her often. And he had at first. But then he got a new wife, new kids, and she saw him once a month. Then once every couple of months. Then once a year.

Yeah, life threw curveballs. You swung, you missed, you kept trying.

Haylee vowed then and there that she wasn't going to let Nicole's death be for nothing. She was going to write about this. If she saved one person, kept one person from getting addicted to pain meds, it would all be worth it.

"I promise," she whispered. Then she punched the button to dial Nicole's parents.

Chapter One

DEAN "WOLF" Garner waited for the jump command. He was standing nut-to-butt with his team-mates, all of them suited up and ready to go. This was a HAHO jump where they'd fall out of the aircraft one behind the other, open chutes about fifteen seconds in and then coast for forty miles to the landing zone. Cade "Saint" Rogers was team lead and he'd be first out the door. Wolf was second. Echo Squad would stack up behind the leader while they were airborne and follow Saint's lead as he guided them using GPS and landmarks.

The C-130 Hercules doors were open and they'd switched over to oxygen bottles. HAHO jumps were hell on the body, whether from the minus-zero wind temps, the lack of oxygen and threat of hypoxia, or the incredible snap of the harness when the chute deployed. It was a necessary evil when trying to sneak up on the enemy, though.

They were currently at T-minus two. The PT had cleared them all to jump and the jumpmaster was about to give the signal.

"You bastards stick with me," Saint said into their earpieces. "Let's go get those hostages and get the fuck out."

Seconds later, Wolf was free falling into the sky behind Saint. Wolf deployed his chute, grunting as the harness snapped him hard against the restraints. *Jesus.* He was carrying a hundred pounds of gear and weaponry, which made the experience even more fun.

He sighted in on Saint and lined up. The rest of the team followed, everyone checking in, and then they were gliding under canopy toward the LZ.

The sun perched in the sky behind them, sinking quickly toward the horizon. Everything below was bathed in golden light that faded into darkness the farther east Wolf looked. It was a beautiful sight and he never took it for granted.

The terrain here was mountainous and green and a river cut through the landscape, marking the border. This was the area where the Mexican cartels got their rocket-propelled grenades and grenade launchers as well as other military-grade equipment they used as they fought each other for territory. It'd be fine if all they did was kill each other, but unfortunately civilians often got caught in the crossfire.

Sometimes those civilians were American, and sometimes they were held for ransom. Like now. A group of dentists and dental assistants on a mission to provide services to an impoverished village had been swept up in the raid and HOT had been tasked with getting them out.

It took twenty minutes, but the team touched down and shrugged out of their chutes. They buried them, along with the special jumpsuits and oxygen canisters. Then they slung their M4 rifles across their chests and started the trek toward the camp where the Juarez cartel was holding the hostages.

HOT had pictures of the camp from drone photography and they knew the layout and the approximate number of people who guarded it. Echo Squad wasn't just there to extract hostages—they were also there to take out the cartel members who were in the camp. At last count, that had been twenty.

Wolf didn't feel sorry for the men. They were rough, evil, nasty men who terrorized innocent civilians. They killed indiscriminately, and they left messages in the form of headless bodies dangling from bridges and trees.

No, Wolf had no problem with killing them.

It took Echo another forty minutes to reach the camp. It was dark by then, and the cartel men were drinking. The camp was illuminated by battery-powered lights that spilled over the ground, picking out shapes and highlighting positions. The hostages were nowhere to be seen, but HOT knew they were being held in a rough concrete structure in the center of the camp. Ten men and women from somewhere in Alabama, on a religious mission to help the poor. They were no doubt terrified and probably dehydrated and hungry.

"Like we planned it," Saint said into their earpieces. The team split up and fanned out around the camp. Wolf and Noah "Easy" Cross slipped silently toward their target. They waited for the signal, then glided toward the men they'd marked, shadowed in darkness until almost the last moment. A quick slip of the knife and two cartel members would never harm anyone again.

A man emerged from the building where the hostages were being held, dragging a woman. Wolf and Easy dropped back into the shadows. He was too caught up in what he was doing to notice his people weren't at their stations. The woman was small and dark-haired and she fought mightily, twisting and tugging and slapping at the man's hands. Wolf stiffened as the man wrenched her forward and thrust her against the side of the building. He put his mouth on her neck and she cried out *"No!"* She wrenched her head to the side and tried to hit him but he caught her wrist and pinned her to the wall while she continued to writhe.

Wolf's blood boiled. He signaled Easy. This one was his. Easy nodded, lifting his rifle to provide covering fire if necessary as Wolf crossed the distance. He was focused on his objective, but he could hear through the mic that the cartel members were falling quickly as his teammates took them out. Soon, Echo would converge on the building and the hostages would be freed.

The woman was fighting hard when Wolf slipped up behind her attacker. Before Wolf could grab him, the man grunted and stumbled backward. His hands dropped to his crotch and Wolf nearly laughed. Smart girl. Brave girl. She'd kicked with all her might and bought herself a moment.

Wolf yanked the man back and stabbed him in the kidney, dropping him to the ground. The woman didn't wait. She sprinted for the darkness. Wolf caught her in two strides, spinning her back to him. Her dark eyes widened as her fists balled up. She was wearing a stained white button-down shirt that had been torn open and jeans with tennis shoes. Black hair whipped around her head in silken waves and his heart thumped once before he clamped down on the reaction. What the hell?

"It's okay," he said quickly. "You're safe." He was clad all in black, face grease-painted, and he wore no distinguishing markers to tell her who he was with. For all she knew, he was from a rival cartel. A well-equipped one, but still scary after what she'd been through.

As soon as he spoke, though, her shoulders sagged an inch. As if she knew she could relax.

"You're American?" she asked in a soft southern accent that vibrated with emotion. "You've come to rescue us?"

"Yes," he told her, turning to place her behind him as he scanned the camp for any stragglers. Someone shouted in the distance and a shot rang out.

"Got him," Jax "Gem" Stone said in Wolf's ear. "Fucker."

"Status," Saint ordered.

"All clear," Malcolm "Mal" McCoy replied. The rest of Echo squad followed suit.

"Let's get the hostages," Saint said.

Wolf turned back to the girl, knowing that Easy had his back and that his teammates were converging on the building to extract the rest of the hostages.

"You okay?" he asked, dropping his gaze over her body, back up to her eyes. Dark, fiery eyes. Angry eyes. Her skin was golden in the soft light of the lanterns. She trembled, but she didn't cower. She was exquisitely pretty now that he got a good look at her. Interest flared deep inside.

Down, boy. Not the time or place.

She lifted her chin as she pulled her shirt together. "I'm fine."

"What's your name?"

"What's yours?" she shot back, not impressed or intimidated.

Wolf grinned in spite of himself. "Wolf."

She blinked, taken aback. "Is that really your name?"

"No, but I like it better than my real name. Which is Dean, by the way."

"Dean." She paused for a moment. Then she thrust out her hand. "I'm Haylee. Pleased to meet you."

He took her hand in spite of the silliness of such formality out here in the jungle. A sizzle of something electric rolled through him at her touch. "You always so polite in dangerous situations?"

She sucked in a breath and stared steadily back at him. "I don't know. This is my first kidnapping."

The team rushed in from the dark corners of the camp. Haylee dropped his hand and quickly tied her shirt beneath her breasts so it would stay closed. She wouldn't look at him now and he wondered if she was embarrassed that he'd seen her like that. He hadn't let his gaze drop below her chin on purpose, other than that quick assessment for injuries. The fucker who'd attacked her had ripped the buttons off when he'd jerked it open, exposing her white lacy bra. Haylee pressed herself against the wall, her gaze flicking uncertainly over his teammates. He didn't know why that made him feel protective, but it did.

"Hello, ma'am," Saint said. "How many are inside?"

"Ten," she replied.

Saint frowned. "So there are eleven of you?" He motioned to the men behind him and they hurried inside to retrieve the other hostages.

"Yes."

"We were told there were ten with the mission trip."

Haylee's tongue darted over her lips. "I'm not with the mission. I'm, uh, a tourist."

There was something in her tone that caught Wolf's attention. If Saint noticed, he didn't comment.

"We weren't aware you were here," Saint replied. "Was there anybody else with you when you were taken?"

"No, just me." She shrugged and reached up to push her hair behind her ears. She projected an air of bravery, but Wolf could see her fingers trembling. She was still processing everything and trying not to fall apart over it. He admired her strength. But he wondered what the hell she was doing here if she wasn't with the Alabama mission. Had she come alone? Why?

His teammates came rushing out of the building with the hostages. They were a sorry sight, disheveled and dirty and more than a little bit scared. Four men and six women. One of the men had an arm in a sling, but otherwise they seemed in decent enough shape except for some bruises and cuts.

"We ready?" Saint asked.

"Ready," Easy replied.

"Wolf," Saint said.

Wolf took over the explanation about what was happening. "Ladies and gentlemen, we're getting you out of here. We'll divide up into the boats the cartel used and take you downriver to the rendezvous point."

One of the women whimpered.

"Don't worry, you're with US soldiers now and we aren't letting anything happen to you. We're getting you out of here, ma'am."

The woman nodded. Haylee hadn't moved from her spot against the wall, though she watched him intently.

"It won't take more than a couple of hours and then you'll be on a helicopter and on your way home. We've got you, don't worry."

"Let's move out," Saint said.

Echo Squad hustled the hostages out of the village and toward the river half a mile away. They knew the cartel had boats because they'd been on the satellite photos. And the boats had still been there a couple of hours ago, according to HQ, so that was the plan. If they reached the river and the boats were gone, they'd move on to Plan B. That one involved a swim across crocodile infested waters and a trek over mountainous territory. Wolf hoped that wasn't the option they had to take.

Wolf and his teammates fanned out to surround the hostages. They had to stay on alert, looking for any other cartel members who might show up. The ones they'd encountered in the camp were only the tip of the iceberg. Wolf slipped his night vision goggles into place and held his rifle at the ready as they started to move.

Bodies lay strewn across the ground, the light from fires illuminating sweat-soaked clothing and dark pools of blood that seeped into the ground. Most of the hostages turned away. A couple of the women cried. Not Haylee. If anything, she stood taller when they passed the bodies on the ground, as if giving them one last *fuck you*.

Once they were out of the camp and into the darkness, they pressed the hostages to move faster. It wasn't easygoing in the dark. The hostages stumbled over the jungle floor. Sometimes they fell. Wolf was right behind Haylee when she tripped, a little cry escaping her as she started to fall.

He caught her around the waist, wrapping an arm around her and tugging her backward. She landed with an *oof* against his chest.

"Sorry," he said as he let her go again.

"No, no. It's okay. Thank you." Her voice was soft and breathy and he wondered what it would sound like if he tugged her against him in different circumstances.

No, don't go there.

"Where are you from?" she asked as they started to walk again.

"Iowa," he said, and then wondered why he'd said it. She wasn't asking where he hailed from, she was asking where he'd deployed from. And he wasn't obligated to answer her questions anyway.

"What base is in Iowa?"

He decided to be obtuse. "That's where I'm from. That's what you asked."

"Oh—no, I meant where is your team from?"

"Not important, Haylee. Where are you from?"

"You mean where did I grow up or where do I live?"

"Both, actually."

"I'm from Mississippi originally. But I live in DC —ouch, dammit, I can't see a thing. Can't we have some light?"

"Unfortunately, no. Your eyes should adjust."

"Why aren't you tripping over these roots?"

"Night vision goggles."

"Oh. Got any extras?"

It sounded like she was joking—but before he could reply, a caravan of engines revved to life in the camp behind them. Men's voices reached them, shouting in Spanish. Someone fired a weapon.

Shit.

Reinforcements had arrived. This mission just got harder.

Chapter Two

Haylee clamped down on the inside of her lip so she wouldn't scream. She'd been doing her best to hold it together for the past couple of days. Tonight, when that disgusting guard had jerked her from the dank room she'd shared with the others and dragged her outside, she'd known it was all over.

He'd been planning to rape her. He probably wouldn't have killed her, because the people she'd been with kept talking about ransom, but he wouldn't have made it easy for her either. She'd have been torn and broken from his assault—and she was sure she'd have wanted to die after that. No matter what she'd promised Nicole about getting her story out there and helping others.

But the man standing so near now—the big man in an assault suit with a helmet, a rifle, and goggles that meant he could see like a cat in the darkness—

had materialized out of the night and saved her. Perhaps luck was still with her after all.

She was tired and hungry and achy, but she was also filled with hope for the first time in three days. Her computer was gone, her notes, everything she'd brought with her to Mexico, but it was in her brain. She could recreate it—and she would. For Nicole and for others who were desperate for relief.

Provided she got out of here alive, she amended. There were gunshots coming from the camp and the shouting was growing louder.

The military commandos suddenly launched into action. One second she was staring back in the direction they'd come and the next Wolf dropped in front of her. Haylee barely had time to squeak before he lifted her and tossed her over his shoulder.

He sprinted through the jungle like a cat while she dangled in the air. It was a shock to realize he moved much faster carrying her than she'd been going on her own. She clung to him, her body bouncing as he ran, her teeth jarring with the impact of his booted feet on the jungle floor. She wanted to insist she could do it herself, but that was a lie. Her life depended on letting him do his job. He reached the edge of the water much faster than she thought he would—she could tell by the sudden smell of fish and rotting vegetation that's where they were—and plopped her down.

Some of the other women were there too. The commandos—what else could they be?—had snatched them up and ran to the boats all at once.

Haylee blinked. The moon emerged from behind a cloud bank, shafting light down onto the ribbon of water. Two boats sat at anchor. For a drug cartel, they certainly weren't fancy. Stripped down tin can fishing boats. Because gleaming cabin cruisers would be too attention-getting out here in the deep jungle.

Two of Wolf's teammates leaped onboard the boats and started helping people climb onto the deck.

"Get on the boat, Haylee," Wolf ordered as he turned away.

"Wait," she called. Because she was grateful to him and she didn't want him to go away without saying thank you. She hadn't done that yet.

"What?"

"Thank you, Dean. Thank you for saving me." If she was honest with herself, that wasn't the only reason she'd called him back. She wasn't quite sure why, but she was drawn to him. He made her feel safe. She hadn't missed that he'd kept his eyes on hers back there, when her shirt was torn open and her skin was exposed. It had been so sweet. So unusual. Men stared. They ogled. They made comments.

Wolf had not. Though maybe he wasn't attracted to her? She didn't like the way that thought pricked her pride. Though of course it was possible. She wasn't a beauty in the classic sense. She wasn't blonde and perky. Not like Nicole had been.

His teeth flashed in the darkness. "You bet, babe."

Before she could respond to the fact he'd called her babe, he was running back the way he'd come.

She didn't know if he was fetching more of the hostages or if he'd gone back to fight. Either way, she hoped he'd return soon. She climbed onto the fishing boat, trying not to gag at the smell, and listened hard in the darkness for the sounds of gunfire. More men emerged from the jungle then, carrying the remaining hostages. And then they all scrambled onto the boats.

She searched for Wolf among them. It was hard to distinguish who was who when they wore helmets and assault suits and painted their skin with grease-paint to avoid being seen. The boats powered up and started inching down the river. Rancid fish assailed her nostrils and she pressed a hand to her mouth so she wouldn't gag. She leaned her head over the side, trying to gulp in fresh air, but the river wasn't much better. It had a smell all its own.

"You can barf over the side if you need to."

Haylee looked up—right into Wolf's sparkling eyes. They were blue. Or maybe gray. But they were definitely piercing. Not that she could see their precise color right now. She remembered they were light, however, from the moment he'd dropped her attacker in a heap on the ground and asked if she was okay. The camp lights had illuminated pale eyes in a grease-painted face, and they'd seared themselves into her memory.

"I'm trying not to," she told him.

He sank onto the bench beside her, bracing his rifle in his lap. Ready to take aim and fire if need be. "Don't hold it in if you really gotta. Trust me."

The boats powered up a little bit faster now, the wind rushing across their bodies and pulling the smell of fish with it. Haylee slowly lowered her hand. "I think I'm all right."

"That's good."

She strained to hear any noise from the jungle, but the only sounds were night sounds. The camp sounds had faded. Still, she didn't feel entirely safe just yet. She'd come so far and gotten so little. Frustration hammered into her in spite of the danger of the situation. If she'd just been able to get a small piece of the information she'd been looking for, maybe all of this would be worth it.

"So how'd you get here, Haylee? You weren't on our list."

She wasn't sure she should tell this stranger what she'd really been seeking. "I, uh, I was on vacation."

"Kinda far from the usual tourist locations."

Her skin heated. He wasn't stupid, this man. "I like the road less traveled."

"Robert Frost. *Two roads diverged in a wood and I / I took the one less traveled by.*"

A shiver skittered down her spine. Handsome and literate and able to quote poetry? Oh dear heaven. If only Nicole were here. She'd laugh. Haylee's heart ached. "Keep a book of Frost in your locker at the base, do you?"

He laughed. "No. My mom's an English teacher —or was. She retired last year. I know more lines of great literature than I should probably admit."

"Wow, so's mine. We could have a quotes war."

"No shit?" He laughed, and she liked the way the sound warmed her.

She nodded. "My mom teaches creative writing at the local community college."

"Mine taught AP English classes to high school juniors and seniors."

"So I bet you've read your fair share of the classics."

"A few."

"Do you have a favorite?" She could hardly believe she was having this conversation, but at the same time maybe it was good to keep her mind off of what had almost happened to her tonight. The more she thought about it, the shakier she got.

"*To Kill a Mockingbird.*"

"Good one," she said, twisting her hands in her lap. "One of my favorites, too."

He was silent for a moment. The boat chugged and the water splashed as they glided down the river. "So how about you tell me what you came here to see, Haylee."

"Mayan ruins," she said without hesitation.

"How did you get grabbed?"

"I paid someone to take me to a site I'd heard about. They kidnapped me instead." She shrugged. "I ended up in a cell with these people."

It was mostly true. Except for the Mayan ruins. She'd been paying someone all right. She'd learned at Nicole's funeral that her death was actually caused by *fake* opioids. Nicole's mom had told her that. Haylee hadn't even been sure what fake opioids were, so she'd researched it. She knew more now than she cared to know, and it was disgusting.

Fakes were pills made with ingredients from China, pressed by Mexican cartels in the jungle and smuggled into the US where they were sold to people desperate to feel better. The pills that had killed Nicole contained a high degree of fentanyl, in addition to a bunch of stuff that wasn't even legal to give to humans. Nicole died because she'd fallen off the wagon and taken pills that weren't what they appeared to be. Where she got them, Haylee still didn't know. But she would never get over Nicole's death, and she would never stop trying to find out where the drugs had come from.

It had taken her months to track down a lead. She'd come to Mexico and she'd paid someone who said they could put her in touch with a person who knew where the fake opioids were being made, as well as how they were being funneled into the US. Once she knew that, she could expose the pipeline and cut off the supply. Maybe it was like trying to kill cockroaches—there were always more—but at least she could make a difference in one small corner of the world.

"You know," Wolf said softly, cutting into her thoughts, "The truth is easier to keep up with. When you make stuff up, you can't always remember who you told what."

Haylee's heart flipped. How did he know? And what did it matter anyway? He was one of the good guys, not one of these cartel scum who cared more about money than people. She could tell him the truth. Or some of it, anyway. She made a decision—and the words tumbled out.

"Okay. Did you know that the opioid epidemic in the US is getting worse, not better? That people get hurt and then they get addicted to pain pills because it's the only way they can function? They lose their jobs, their families, everything that matters. But they can't stop using, and when their doctors cut them off, they buy pills on the street. Pills that are sometimes fake and filled with harmful substances, because nobody gives a shit about addicts. Some of those pills come from Mexican cartels. And what they do to a human body is something you don't want to know."

Stroke, sepsis, multiple organ failure. If Nicole had had a slightly smaller dose, she'd probably still be alive. But she'd been a small woman and the drugs had overwhelmed her body.

Wolf seemed very quiet. And angry somehow. Well so was she, dammit. Angry and sick over what had happened to Nicole. To those like her. Good people who'd taken the drugs they'd been prescribed for procedures in good faith. And then found out they couldn't live without them when it was time to stop. Needing those drugs to feel alive was what put them on the road to disaster.

"Jesus," he said. "You traveled to Mexico to hunt

down a drug cartel—and do what? Ask them questions? Or something more?"

Oh, he was perceptive. Too perceptive.

"I wasn't trying to *question* the cartel. Or get revenge." Not that it wouldn't have been nice to do so, but who was responsible and how the hell did she take revenge on them? She was one woman in a foreign country, not a team of military commandos like this one. Haylee shook her head. She'd charged into this trip with a lot of anger and conviction and not much thought about the potential complications. "I just wanted information."

"Information. About a drug cartel." He tilted his head and she knew he was thinking about something. "What do you do back home, Haylee?"

"I'm a reporter." Not for a paper that could really make a difference with this story, though that was a bridge she'd cross when she got to it.

"A reporter. So what did you plan to do with this information you were trying to get?"

She clenched her hands into fists on her lap. "I planned to write about it. People need to know."

"You think that's wise? Cartels like this one have a lot of reach."

Anger filled her. And despair, because dammit, if she didn't get this story out there, how many more people might die? It was unconscionable what some people would do for money. They didn't care about the end user when they were pressing their fake pills and shipping them off for sale. They didn't care that

Nicole had died. Nobody cared except for her family and friends.

And they were going to miss her forever. "I don't know, Dean. But somebody has to do it."

He studied her in the darkness. Then he nodded. "I guess you're right. But maybe don't try to do it alone, huh?"

Haylee swallowed. She didn't know how else she was supposed to do it. "I don't want to do it alone. But I don't have much choice really."

He blew out a breath. "You know, I see far more of this kind of shit than I like. There are evil people in this world, and they don't care about ideals or truth or morals. They only care about what they can take for themselves. Be careful when dealing with those types."

She was trying to be careful. "There's more to this than just a cartel and fake pills. I know there is. And I intend to find out who's responsible. They need to pay."

For lives cut short. For lives ruined. For families torn apart. For Nicole, who would never fall in love or have kids or grow old.

"Yeah, they do."

She'd expected him to argue with her but he didn't. Before she could ponder on that too much, a sudden burst of gunfire sprayed into the night, making her squeak and jump. It was much closer this time—in fact, she swore she'd seen what looked like a bunch of fireflies on the Guatemalan side of the river. She couldn't figure it out though because Wolf leapt in front of her, pushing her down onto the dirty floor of the boat. He pressed her hard into the metal. Water seeped into her clothing. Fishy water. She tried not to gag.

"Don't move, Haylee," he commanded.

There was screaming suddenly and the piercing sound of rapid gunfire spitting all around her. She clapped her hands to her head and closed her eyes. Hot metal dropped onto her body but it cooled so fast it didn't burn. She forced her eyes open, looked up. Wolf stood over her, legs braced apart, gun nestled against his shoulder, flame bursting from the barrel as he returned fire.

It was loud and scary and somehow exciting too. She didn't know how long they went on like that, men cursing and returning fire, bullets raining down on the occupants of the vessel. Magazines dropping as new ones got shoved into the rifles.

She noticed that the fishy water in the bottom of the boat seemed to be creeping higher with every passing minute. Almost as if…

"We've gotta abandon ship," one of the commandos shouted during a lull in the firing. "We're going down."

Chapter Three

GODDAMMIT.

Wolf slung his rifle over his shoulder and reached for Haylee. The fucking boat had been hit and it was sinking in the middle of the Rio Usumacinta. Gem had been steering them toward the north bank, which was Mexico, but they were still a good distance from shore. If they'd continued on the river, they'd have reached Mexico when it turned north, but that wasn't happening today. They had to abandon ship and swim for it.

The Usumacinta wasn't terribly wide or deep, but they were in a remote area and there'd been a lot of rain to the region lately. There was also the threat of crocodiles, but hopefully they were well-fed and uninterested in the tasty humans about to descend into their waters.

"Can you swim?" he asked gruffly.

"Yes." The whites of her eyes showed brightly. "Is it safe in there?"

He snorted as he pushed her toward the side of the boat. "Probably not, but it's safer than staying here. You ready?"

They stood at the edge. He could hear his teammates splashing into the water, hear the shouts of the other hostages as they followed the lead of their Echo Squad member and plunged into the murky river.

Haylee whimpered. He squeezed her hand, ignoring the jolt of electricity that zapped into him. "Yes," she said. "Please don't leave me alone in the water," she added in a rush.

He held on tight. "Honey, not happening. Trust me. This is what I do." He tugged her to the edge, up onto the lip of the bow. "On three."

She nodded.

"One… Two… Three." He fell forward, taking her with him. He twisted, making sure to land first, cushioning the fall for her. It wasn't an Olympic worthy dive, but it didn't need to be. He flipped onto his side and tugged her with him, sidestroking his way toward shore. "You okay?"

"I… Yes."

The water wasn't cold this far south, but it wasn't exactly a bathtub either. He didn't know what lurked below them and he didn't want to know. He'd deal with that if he had to.

"I can swim," she said as he continued to tug her toward the shore.

He hesitated. They'd get there faster if he let her go, but he didn't want to do it. She was small and light and she'd been a captive for a few days. She had to be hungry and tired. Yet he had to give her the chance.

"Can you follow my lead?"

"Yes."

"I won't leave you behind, Haylee. I promise."

"I know."

He let her go and struck out for the shore, keeping an eye on her as he swam. She stayed by his side, cutting through the water somewhat efficiently if not as smoothly as he did. But he'd had a lot of training, especially loaded down the way he was. He wore a pack and a rifle, but they didn't give him any trouble. Because he'd trained for this. Over and over and over again, until it was as ingrained as taking a piss or walking across a room. Instinctual.

The rifle fire from the Guatemalan bank was sporadic now, but still dangerous. The cartel wouldn't give up. They needed to get these people to the extraction point as soon as possible. A Black Hawk would meet them there and fly everyone out of the jungle. But first they had to make it.

Wolf lifted his head to study the shore. A couple of his teammates were emerging, dragging hostages with them. The rest would be there soon. He glanced back at Haylee. She was laboring but still swimming. He stopped where he was and waited. When she reached him, he hauled her into his chest and struck out again.

"Hey," she said between puffs of air. "I'm fine."

"Of course you are. But you aren't fast enough. I'm faster."

She didn't fight him and he knew she was tired. She could swim, but when you didn't swim often, you lost the stamina it took to cross a couple of Olympic-sized pools. He knew he'd reached the shore when he struck out and his hand hit ground. He lifted them in one smooth motion. Haylee stumbled forward, her body soaking wet with muddy water. He followed, ready to pick her up and carry her if she needed it.

Saint stood on shore, waiting for him. Waiting for everyone. "Wolf," he said in acknowledgement.

Wolf turned to gaze at the center of the river. One boat sat there, abandoned, listing to port. The other boat—the one he'd been on—was sinking quickly beneath the surface.

"Both hit?"

"They got the engine on the second one."

"Any causalities?" There'd been no radio communication since they'd hit the water but that's because they'd all been working to reach the shore.

"A couple of hits. Mal got winged. One of our dentists took a shot to the shoulder."

"Shit."

"Yeah. Easy's got Mal. Muffin and Hacker are taking on the dentist."

Wolf stepped in close, away from Haylee. "They aren't giving up, Saint."

Saint nodded. "Yeah, I know. But maybe this was

the last stand for them. Maybe we've seen all we'll see of the Juarez Cartel."

God, he hoped so. "Five miles to the extraction point. Over a mountain," Wolf said, looking up at the dark shape rising above them.

"No choice," Saint replied. "Unless you've got a better idea?"

Wolf gritted his teeth. "No."

"Didn't think so." Saint jerked his head. "Best get moving."

Wolf turned on his heel just as Gem rose up out of the water. He was hauling a short stocky woman with him. Her sides heaved and she sucked in air, sputtering and coughing. Zane "Zany" Scott followed, tugging a slight male who stumbled to the ground and touched his forehead to the sand. "Oh God," the man said. "Thank you, Jesus."

"Let's go," Saint said gruffly. "No time to waste."

Wolf put a firm hand on Haylee's back and pushed. "Go," he told her as gently as he could.

They headed inland, seeking the others. The rest of the team and their charges waited just inside the jungle. Echo had their weapons out, ready to do battle if necessary. The dentists and assistants were mostly silent, though there were definitely some chattering teeth that clacked over the sounds of frogs and other night creatures.

"Five miles to go, ladies and gentlemen," Saint said grimly. "We've got a mountain to climb and no time to waste. We need to be there by 0500 at the latest. That's seven hours from now."

"What happens if we aren't there?" one of the civilians asked.

"They leave without us."

A few of them gasped. "But we're American! They can't leave us."

"Yeah, well they can. We aren't supposed to be operating inside the Mexican border. American military helicopters draw attention. They'll be back after nightfall tomorrow—provided we don't get caught before then."

Beside him, Wolf felt Haylee stiffen. He wanted to reassure her, but there wasn't really any way he could. Either they reached the extraction point and got the fuck out, or they stayed a full day in the jungle, trying to avoid capture by the cartel. It wasn't really anything that worried him—or his teammates— because they were elite warriors and more than capable of holding off a bunch of drug runners for a few hours.

But civilians in the mix complicated things, that's for sure. They weren't as quiet, or as capable. They were liabilities in a firefight, but there was nothing to be done for it other than make sure a firefight didn't happen.

Or not another one anyway.

They'd hit some of the men shooting at them tonight, but it was hard to say how many. Or how many more would come looking for them.

"Time to move out," Saint said. "We've got a long way to go."

"I can't," someone said. The woman Gem had dragged from the water. Her voice shook. She sounded tired. Stressed. Emotional. "I need to rest."

"Ma'am, I'm sorry, but we can't rest," Saint told her. "It's not optional."

A sob escaped her. Haylee pushed past Wolf before he knew she was moving and went to the woman's side. "I'm sorry you're tired," she said, putting her arm around the other woman's shoulders. "I'm tired too. It's not just you. But I think we have to keep going. I think if we don't, those men across the river are going to take us back to that camp."

The woman sobbed. A single, wretched sound that escaped her throat. "I can't go back."

"No, you can't," Haylee said firmly. "And you won't. Do you think you can walk a bit further tonight?"

"Yes. Yes, I can do it." She didn't sound certain though.

Another woman came forward then. She held out her hand. "Come on, Cindy. You can do it, honey. I know your arthritis is flaring up, but there'll be a hot tub and plenty of booze at the end of this thing. And maybe a hot guy or two. We'll get Dennis to take off his shirt."

A younger man in the group snorted, but it wasn't a derisive sound. "Hey, if we get a hot tub at the end of this, I'll take off as much as you want me to."

Cindy laughed brokenly. The other woman squeezed her hand. Haylee smiled too. "Simmer down, Dennis," Cindy said. "I'm not that kind of girl."

The hostages laughed then and the tension broke. Cindy and the other woman started walking together, holding hands while Cindy limped and tried her best. The woman glanced behind her at Haylee. "Thank you," she said softly.

Haylee's teeth flashed white in the darkness. "You're welcome."

The tension in the air quieted to a slow boil and everyone started walking. Wolf caught up to Haylee in a few steps. She peered up at him and smiled. Remarkable girl. Except for that part where she wanted to take on a drug cartel.

"That was nice," he said to her, keeping his voice low enough so the others didn't hear.

"Everyone was annoyed with her. But nobody tried to empathize."

"Saint was polite but firm."

"Yes. But polite is distant, you know? She needed more than that. She needed someone to feel like she felt."

He understood what she meant. She'd broken the tension in the air by empathizing. She'd made it possible for the other woman to remember Cindy's weaknesses, and to help her. Which meant the whole group found their empathy—and Cindy didn't create enmity by refusing to move.

Not that Saint would have let her hold them up. Gem would have carried her if he had to, but that would have slowed him. All of them, because they'd have had to take turns. Hell, they still might. Best to save it until necessary though.

"We wouldn't have left her."

"Are we going to make it, Wolf?"

It was the first time she'd called him Wolf. He liked it. "We'll make it."

"Thank you."

"For what?"

"For telling me what I need to hear. Even if it's not true."

He reached for her hand, squeezed it. Ignored the thrill that zipped into his balls at the touch of skin on skin. Now was *not* the time. And definitely not the place. "It's true. Trust me."

She squeezed back. "I do."

———

THEY HIKED through the thick jungle, moving steadily higher, until they were climbing what seemed straight up the side of a mountain. The jungle didn't thin out up here. It just kept growing. Thick trees, buzzing mosquitos that drank their blood leisurely, bugs Haylee didn't want to imagine. She just kept moving, following the person in front of her. Knowing Wolf was behind her. The trail had narrowed and they were moving single file through rock and vegetation. Her heart pounded with the effort.

Cindy, bless her heart, hadn't stopped again. Though she did cry. Haylee could hear her sobs in the night and it broke her heart. But the others kept encouraging her, and she kept moving. Eventually they reached an area that was clearer than what they'd come through. It seemed as if they'd come out on a plateau.

"Break," someone said from the front and the entire line stopped. Haylee's blood pounded in her ears. She swatted at a mosquito and dragged air into her lungs. It was fresher up here. Cooler. Thank God.

Even the mosquitos weren't quite as plentiful. She had no idea how high they'd climbed but her leg muscles ached, her feet throbbed, and sweat dripped between her breasts. Wolf offered her water and she took it gratefully.

"Not too much," he told her.

She took a couple of swallows and gave it back, wiping her lips as she leaned against a rock.

"We'll rest for half an hour," he told her. "Might want to sit while you can."

She sank down against the rock until her butt hit the ground. She worried about bugs, about snakes, about all manner of creepy crawly things, but she was so exhausted that she did as he said.

He rummaged in his pack and tossed something at her. She caught it, her mouth watering when she realized it was an energy bar.

"Be right back," he said. "Eat that. I'll give you more water once you do."

He strode away, toward the front of the line, and she leaned back against the rock and tore open the package. The bar was delicious. She hadn't eaten much in three days so even if it tasted like cardboard, it was still the most wonderful thing she'd ever had.

She could hear the others ripping off wrappers and she knew they'd all been given food. The cartel had fed them, but only once a day. Beans and tortillas and water. Nothing else. The energy bar was heaven.

Wolf returned and gave her his canteen again. She drank carefully before handing it back. He slipped onto the jungle floor beside her and stretched out his legs.

"Is everything okay?" she asked.

He turned to look at her. "Fine, why?"

"We stopped."

"For you, Haylee. For all of you."

"Oh." Her muscles took that moment to ache forcefully. Her feet hurt. Exhaustion dropped over her like a blanket.

"Just a few more hours and it'll be over," he said. "We'll fly to a base in El Salvador, you'll all be checked out, and then you'll board a transport for home once you've rested a day or so."

It sounded like heaven to her. "And what about you? What happens to you and your team once we get to El Salvador?"

"We'll rest and regroup, then we'll be sent home."

She twisted the tails of her shirt that she'd tied at her waist. "You must do this kind of thing a lot."

He laughed softly. "Yeah. You could say that."

"How did you get to the camp? I mean since we had to take the boats and now we're hiking to where the helicopters will be."

"Parachutes."

"Oh." So he'd jumped out of a plane tonight. In the dark probably. She couldn't imagine what kind of strength and bravery that took. "That sounds terrifying."

"You get used to it."

She gazed at his dark shape looming so close and her belly tightened. A wave of heat washed over her. Her breasts tingled. Her center grew hot and achy. Haylee blinked. Was she really doing this right now? Getting horny over a military commando with the most piercing eyes she'd ever seen? She hadn't really seen his face. Had no idea what he looked like, or what color his hair was. He had nice eyes. Didn't mean he was the kind of guy she was usually attracted to though.

She liked them safe. Tall and not too muscular, but self-assured and kind. This man was anything but safe. He was big and bold and full of violence. Because he had to be. Haylee shivered a little and sucked in a breath.

"So tell me," he said, and she tried to focus on his words and stop thinking about his raw masculinity. "Why is this personal to you?"

Haylee blinked. Heat flared in her cheeks and she thanked God he couldn't see her face right now. And then it hit her what he was talking about. Mexico. The cartel. Why she was here. *Not* why she was taking a personal interest in him.

She pushed trembling hands down her jeans, smoothing fabric that didn't need smoothing. "My best friend. She got a hold of some fake opioid pills—and she died."

"I'm sorry to hear that."

Haylee sucked in a breath. Why had she told him? But it didn't feel wrong. Not at all.

"Thank you. Nicole was a good person. She had shoulder surgery and she got addicted to the pain pills when it didn't heal quite right. Not because the surgeon did anything wrong. It was just her physiology. She'd get clean, then she'd start using again. But the doctors stopped prescribing the pills to her—so she found another way."

His hand entwined with hers. Squeezed. She liked it.

"She had everything to live for, Wolf. She shouldn't have died. And she wouldn't have if the pills had been normal."

He squeezed again softly. "You don't know that. Opioids are dangerous even when they aren't fake."

Her throat ached. "I know. But she'd beat it before. She could have beat it again."

"Maybe so." He sighed. Let go of her hand. She felt the loss much more sharply than she would have liked. Why did his touch matter? She hardly knew him. "My sister is a user," he said, surprising her. "She hurt her back getting thrown from a horse and then she had a baby and injured it further. She's in and out of rehab. Her husband left her. Just fucking disappeared. The kids are in state custody, though my parents keep trying to get them…" He shook his head. "Sorry. Shit, that's not what you wanted to hear. This isn't about me."

She rushed to reassure him. "No, it's fine. Really. And I'm sorry, Dean. Sorry you know what it's like to have a loved one addicted. It's not easy."

"No. My parents—their whole focus is those kids. Taylor and Jack. They're six and four. But my parents are older, and Cheryl lives in California, so getting the kids isn't just a matter of being their closest relatives and being willing to take them. There are a lot of hoops to jump through."

It was her turn to reach for him. She squeezed his arm. "I know it's difficult. You must be so angry."

"Fucking pissed. But there's nothing I can do about it."

"You feel helpless."

"Yeah. And considering what I do for a living, it's not something I'm used to feeling."

No, she didn't imagine that was easy for a guy like him.

"All right, everybody up," the guy Wolf had called Saint said as he got to his feet. "We've still got some ground to cover before the night is over."

Chapter Four

Wolf didn't know why he'd told Haylee those things. Talking about his sister and her addiction wasn't something he did. It was too personal, too painful. He and Cheryl were only a year apart in age and they'd been close growing up. He was older and he'd taken his big brother duties seriously. Cheryl had been so tiny that he'd felt protective of her, even when they were small and he was supposed to be picking on her instead. He'd saved his aggression for the neighborhood boys and guarded his baby sister like a bloodhound.

Fat lot of good it had done since he ultimately couldn't save her from herself. Cheryl had been so petite and pretty that she always got her way. Even with his parents. She'd had scarlet fever as a child and she'd nearly died. From then on, his parents indulged her more than they disciplined her. She'd always been so sweet-natured that it hadn't seemed to matter.

But then, when she got old enough and wanted to start riding horses, they'd told her no. They simply couldn't afford it. So Cheryl had put that dream on hold until she'd started working as a teen and could pay for her own lessons. She'd done great and she'd been so excited when she'd started riding barrel racers.

Then came the ugly fall when a horse landed on her during a run and broke her back. She'd only been nineteen. He'd been in the Army by then and hadn't been home when it happened. She'd gotten through with painkillers and rehab, but she hadn't ridden again. Then she met her ass-wipe of a husband and got pregnant, and her back pain flared up once more. She'd had such a hard time going to term. As if once wasn't enough, she'd done it again.

Wolf still didn't know where the breakdown happened. He didn't know when she'd started using or what'd happened between her and Bo. He only knew that Bo was a deadbeat dad and Cheryl was too lost to pull herself out this time. He hadn't known it was happening, and he'd feel guilty about that for the rest of his life. She hadn't told him.

The first he'd heard of her relapse was when his parents called to tell him a month ago that the state had taken the kids and Cheryl was in rehab. She'd been using meth of all fucking things. In front of her children. She wasn't the same girl he'd known. They'd grown apart when he'd joined the military and left

Iowa. He wasn't there to protect her anymore, and he didn't know how to get that girl back again. Or even if he could.

He'd consulted a military attorney who'd explained there was very little he could do. So he sent money home to his parents, who'd hired a lawyer of their own to help them get custody of the kids. Wolf made good money with combat pay so he could afford it. He didn't buy things for himself. Why would he? His needs were few and he had enough. Clothes, food, a roof over his head, his truck. His medical care was courtesy of the US Government.

He still had enough discretionary income to go out with his friends. And sex was free—or no more than the cost of a couple of drinks or a meal. He was content with his life. He didn't need more. He didn't have time for more.

The team moved through the darkness of the jungle with the hostages, not turning on lights in case the cartel was tracking them up the mountain. In truth, Echo didn't know where the cartel might have men stationed, or how determined they were to regain the hostages. They'd lost twenty men in that camp, and they'd probably lost a couple more in the gun battle on the river. How much risk were they willing to take? Maybe none, but it was hard to know that.

Wolf and his teammates stayed on alert as they started down the other side of the mountain. Saint called another halt for a few minutes once they were on the downhill side. Cindy moaned as she fell onto her rear and Gem hunkered down beside her, saying something in a low voice while she nodded. Then he reached into his pack and withdrew a syringe of painkiller, injecting her with it while she turned her face and cried softly.

The rest of the hostages were holding up. They talked in quiet voices and some went over to sit with Cindy once Gem finished with her. Haylee dropped to the ground and stretched her legs in front of her as Wolf sank down beside her.

"You okay?"

She looked up at him, the moonlight catching her eyes. They glistened with what he thought might be tears. His heart clenched. Odd reaction to have for a woman he didn't know.

"Yes, fine. Just tired. How much farther?"

"Two hours to make the drop zone in time. More than that and we'll shelter in the jungle until nightfall."

She smiled at him and something kicked him in the gut. What the hell was going on here?

"That's a pretty good non-answer, Dean."

He snorted. "It's not a non-answer. Two hours to make the pick up. If we don't, we're stuck for another twelve hours."

Which wasn't ideal. The sooner they got these people out of there, the safer they'd be.

She stretched her arms forward, grabbing onto

her feet and pulling herself downward. Flexible. Hmm…

Stop.

"Two hours sounds better than three miles through dense jungle. That's what I meant. You phrased it in time rather than distance."

"Honestly? Distance isn't the important part of the equation. Time *is*."

"Will we make the distance in two hours?"

He glanced over at the knot of people around Cindy. "Maybe."

Haylee was smart enough to know what he meant. "She's done incredibly," she said, pitching her voice low. "For someone suffering so much."

"Yes. She's not a quitter. That's the most important quality she needs right now. It's more than some people have."

"Is this what you do all the time? Go and get people out of bad situations?"

"Not all the time." They also went after terrorists, drug dealers, and human traffickers. Not that he was going to tell her that. It was too much information for a civilian—a reporter—to have. "We go where we're sent."

"Well, I'm glad they sent you here tonight. I don't think we'd have lasted much longer."

No, they definitely would not have. The religious group the dentists and assistants came from was big by church standards but not so huge they could afford to pay a large ransom. When the demand came in, the church had gotten the authorities involved. How HOT got the assignment Wolf didn't know. But it was good they had.

"So what are you going to do when you get back home?" he asked.

Haylee brought her knees up and hugged them. "I don't know… but I do know I'm not giving up on this story yet."

He didn't like that. "Don't come back here, Haylee."

"I won't. But there's so much more to know, and I'm not quitting. Nicole deserves better."

"That's your friend?"

"Yes." She let out a sigh. "I miss her. She got cheated out of so much in life."

Wolf put a hand on her shoulder. "I know. And I'm sorry."

She put her hand on his. He liked the feel of her warm palm on his skin. "I'm sorry about your sister, too. I hope she gets the help she needs. I hope she can break free."

Wolf didn't let the despair get to him. Not out here. Not now. But it was there, simmering away like a cancer. "I hope so too."

Saint stood and Wolf levered to his feet and held out his hand to help her up. "Come on, Haylee. Time to get moving again."

She put her small hand in his and he closed his fingers around it, feeling a wave of protectiveness toward her. He tugged her up, resisting the urge to tug her against his body and place a quick kiss on her forehead. Since when did he give in to sickly sweet gestures like that anyway?

Before he could do anything idiotic, he let her go. They stood there in the dark, breathing each other in, saying nothing. Then the column began to move and the spell was broken. Wolf shouldered his rifle and doubled down on his determination to get this group of people to the pick up zone on time. Once that happened, this mission was over. He'd never see Haylee Jamison again.

———

HAYLEE TRUDGED through the darkness with Wolf behind her. In front of her the column moved steadily. Behind her too. But it was only Wolf she was aware of. What was this fascination she had with the guy? Deprivation, maybe?

She hadn't dated in so long now. The last guy she'd gone out with was more than a year ago. She'd just been so focused on her work and on building her reputation as a writer. She wanted to work for a major newspaper. It would make her mom so proud. And it would be the fulfillment of a lifelong dream.

She'd been focused, building her portfolio, working for the paper who'd hired her to cover Hill affairs, taking on freelance jobs. Anything to get the experience she needed to apply to a place like the Post or the Times. She'd tried them when she'd arrived in town, but they weren't impressed with her resume at that point.

She'd dated a couple of guys here and there, but no one seriously. She couldn't even remember the last time she'd had sex. In fact, in spite of her body's obvious interest in Dean, aka Wolf, she didn't think she'd ever had truly memorable sex with anyone. It was always vaguely disappointing, even if she did manage to get off.

And yet her body was incredibly attuned to the man behind her. He touched her to offer comfort and her skin tingled. He occasionally caught her when she stumbled, and her entire body went up in flame.

Seriously, her hormones must be out of balance. That was all it could be. Because Haylee had never in her life had sex with a man she'd only just met. She'd never even wanted to. But she thought, if the circumstances were different, she wouldn't mind being naked with Wolf even though she didn't know him.

In fact, it was those thoughts that kept her going. She didn't know how far they walked, or how long it took, but suddenly they were on a plateau. The moon shone down, illuminating the vast field of rock and scrub, which was so different from the jungle they'd emerged from. The sky was beginning to lighten off to the east, the first fingers of pink starting to creep above the horizon. Haylee's heart leapt into her throat as she spun to Wolf.

"Did we make it?"

He grinned, his teeth flashing white in the gloom. "Yeah, we made it."

"Oh holy cow. Thank God."

The former hostages milled about. Saint told them to rest and they plopped onto the ground with groans and sighs. She noticed the commandos didn't drop their guard though. They kept their weapons at the ready and turned in steady circles, scanning the area. The group wasn't completely exposed, as there were rocks and small trees, but it felt more open than what they'd come from.

It only took fifteen minutes before the faint sound of something stirring the air reached them. It didn't sound like an aircraft at all. And yet the military men looked up and began to urge them to rise.

"Are they coming?" Haylee asked. "To rescue us?"

"Yes," Wolf told her. "Two Black Hawks. Just a few more minutes and we'll be airborne."

Haylee chewed the inside of her lip. Once they were on those helicopters, that was it. They were out of here and she might not see him again. He might get on a different helicopter than she did. And why not? They weren't on a date. He'd done nothing except talk to her throughout the night. It meant nothing more than that.

"Thank you," she said, her heart throbbing in her chest.

"We aren't there yet, Haylee," he said, sounding slightly amused. Teasing.

"If I… If I don't see you again," she began.

He tilted his head to the side. "We're getting on a helicopter together."

"Yes, well… I mean this is it, right? We'll be safe and you'll go rescue somebody else."

"Yeah, we'll go rescue somebody else. But not right away. Still, when we get to the base in El Salvador, that'll probably be the last time we see you."

There was a knot in her throat. How silly. "I just wanted to say thank you. You saved me—not only in general, but also from the man who attacked me. If you hadn't been there…" She didn't like to think of it.

He skimmed his fingers along her cheek and she bit back a gasp. "I was there. Any of us would have done it, but it was me and I'm glad. You're lovely, Haylee. You deserve to be cherished by a guy who knows how to do that, not attacked by a rapist asshole. Later, once you've thought about everything that happened for a bit, you might be sickened by what I did to him."

She shook her head vehemently and then regretted it because his hand fell away. "I won't. Really, I won't."

"That's good."

The helicopters were closer now. They weren't loud, not at all. Not like she'd expected. But they disturbed the air around them enough that if you knew they were coming you'd notice it.

And then the first one was there, dropping out of the sky and hovering just above the ground. The second one dropped down as well, staying clear of the first.

"Follow your leader to the helicopter he takes you to," Saint directed. "Do exactly as he tells you and we'll be on our way in moments, ladies and gentlemen. Stay in the same orderly line you've been in. No running toward the craft. No scrambling onboard. Do as you're told."

Haylee saw the guy with Cindy bend down to pick her up. Her arms went around his neck as he sprinted toward the helicopter. The rest of the group followed the men they'd been with, splitting evenly between the aircraft. The helicopter was higher off the ground than Haylee had expected. She halted, unsure of herself, but Wolf's hands closed around her waist and then she was being tossed up to the man who hung over the side, waiting for her. He grabbed her wrists and pulled her in and then Wolf was up, falling onto the seat beside her. Haylee trembled as her gaze slipped over the metal interior, the soldiers in uniform, the pilots up in the cockpit as they controlled the craft and kept it hovering.

A few moments later, the rotors began to beat faster and the helicopter pitched forward, lifting into the air with startling speed. Haylee turned her head to look at the landscape below, the plateau and the jungle, the mountain they'd crossed. It was still dark over the terrain, but the higher they went, the more pink filled the sky from the bottom up. Her heart beat fast and tears sprang to her eyes as the enormity of everything she'd been through hit her.

She could have died. She was still alive, thanks to these men. Thanks to the man beside her. She focused on his profile, studied the hard line of his nose and chin. His face was still hidden, covered in greasepaint, but then he turned and those pale eyes speared into her.

"You're welcome," he shouted over the thwopping of the rotors.

Chapter Five

THE FLIGHT TO EL SALVADOR DIDN'T TAKE LONG. Haylee thought they must have been in the air for an hour or so. She didn't have her phone or computer anymore so time was kind of relative. Her luggage was lost forever, which made her sad because her mother had given her the set as a college graduation present. But the sun steadily rose in the sky and the fingers of pink turned to flame as the sun slipped over the horizon. Considering she hadn't been sure she'd ever see that again, she was overcome with happiness.

She didn't realize how exhausted she was until they landed. She hardly remembered the trip from the helicopter to the clinic where they were checked out and then shuttled to a building where they were given rooms. She'd thought they would head back to the States immediately, but a storm had moved in after they arrived and rain lashed the windows. Haylee had a room to herself. It was inevitable, she supposed, given as there were seven women and four men in the party. She was the odd person out since the rooms had two beds in each one. She went into the bathroom, turned on the shower, and left her clothes in a pile on the floor as she stepped inside to let the water sluice over her and wash away the past few days.

After scrubbing herself clean, she dried off, slipped into an oversized T-shirt that'd been left for her, and then went and fell into the bed. She was asleep in moments. When she woke later, she wasn't quite sure where she was. She lay in bed and blinked at the ceiling. It was dark and gloomy and she couldn't quite remember what had happened.

And then she did. It all came rushing back—the jungle, the man who'd tried to rape her, Wolf as he'd rescued her, the night escaping from the cartel—the river, the gunshots, the swim for shore, the hike up a mountain, and the blessed arrival in time for the helicopters.

Haylee lay on the soft mattress, warm and safe— but hungry—and felt the despair wash over her. Despair because she'd liked Wolf and she knew she wouldn't see him again. He'd done his job, saved her from certain death, and now she was alone. Why had she told him so much about why she'd gone to Mexico? About Nicole? She wished she hadn't done so. Wished she hadn't listened to his story about his sister. Because he was gone and she wouldn't see him again.

The end.

She swiped at the tears gathering in her eyes and sat up. She was dizzy with hunger. But she didn't have any clothes—she seriously didn't want to put the ones she'd been wearing back on again—and she didn't know what to do. Was there room service? She somehow doubted that.

She sniffed and pushed the covers back. The room she'd been given was more of a small suite. There was a bedroom that connected to a living room with a television, a bathroom, and a very small kitchenette with a coffee maker and a microwave. She slipped out of bed and padded into the living room—where she found a pile of clothing on the coffee table. It wasn't anything stylish. Only T-shirts and military camouflage with a pair of basic tennis shoes. She remembered the nurse asking her questions about clothing and shoe sizes. It all made sense now.

She picked up the stack and donned the underwear, pants and button-down shirt that hung to her thighs. There were socks and shoes and she put them on too. Maybe there was food if she left this room.

Haylee pocketed the key card they'd given her and opened the door, peeking first one direction and then the other. The smell of food wafted to her nose and she closed the door behind her, went in the direction of the smells until she found a common room with pizzas and people. She stood in the entry and blinked. But no, there were men and women and food.

And not just the dental group, but some of the

commandos as well. Her heart kicked higher as she searched for Wolf. She didn't see him at all. Had he left? Or decided not to join them? But then a man who'd been standing at the far end of the room with two others turned, his gaze meeting hers. For a moment she didn't know who he was—his face was chiseled, handsome, his hair short, blonde. He was incredibly gorgeous—and his eyes. Oh God, those eyes.

Haylee's belly flipped. Those were Wolf's eyes. Her Wolf. *Her Wolf?* He gave her a sort of half grin. She was frozen in place. But then he started to move, sauntering toward her with the easy grace of a sleek predator, and her heart hammered harder than before.

"Haylee," he said as he reached her side. "Did you sleep well?"

"I… Wolf?"

He laughed. "Yeah, it's me. You okay?"

Was she okay? Oh hell no. She was *not* okay. This man was freaking gorgeous! Nothing like the guy who'd swaggered into the jungle and rescued her a few hours ago. Not that he hadn't been appealing, but she hadn't known. Hadn't suspected that he'd look like *this*.

"I… yes, I'm fine."

He ran his fingers over her cheek. A shiver rolled down her spine. Into her center. Her skin prickled with heat and longing. *Longing?*

"You hungry?"

Hungry? It seemed such a base need compared to the feelings swirling inside her now. But she had to eat, right? As if her stomach was afraid she'd say no, it chose that moment to growl. Loudly. Wolf arched an eyebrow.

"Um, yes. I could definitely eat."

"There's pizza. Some fruit. Might be a salad somewhere if you want that."

Her belly threatened to turn inside out. "No, not a salad."

He snorted. "Good girl." He led her to the table laden with boxes. "Pepperoni, sausage, cheese, and supreme. It's from the pizza joint on the base, in case you were wondering."

He made her feel giddy inside. "I'm not even questioning it. Would you think ill of me if I said all the above?"

His eyes danced with laughter. "Nope, not at all."

She picked up a paper plate and some napkins. Then she attacked the pepperoni and the sausage. "Okay, I know I said all, but maybe I'll start with this."

"Find a seat. You want a beer? Or something else? Water, soda—you tell me."

She didn't know whether to be embarrassed or flattered that he was still talking to her. That he planned to get her a drink. But that didn't mean he was interested. She needed to stop thinking those things about a guy she didn't really know and would probably never see again after tonight.

Except he was just so damned gorgeous that she couldn't help herself.

"Uh, I think a beer sounds good." She wasn't much of a drinker, but after the ordeal she'd been through, alcohol sounded good. Just one to take the edge off.

"Be right back."

Haylee found a seat at a table against the wall. Most of the dental group was there and they were talking intently about things. The commandos looked so different without their greasepaint. In fact, she had to acknowledge to herself that it was entirely possible not all these guys were the military team who'd rescued her and the others. She wouldn't recognize any of them, other than Wolf—and she'd barely recognized him.

Wolf was back in a few moments with two bottles of cold beer. He handed her one and she took it, her fingers brushing his for a brief moment. Just that single touch and her skin sizzled along all her neural pathways. She dropped her gaze as heat flared in her cheeks.

What was wrong with her?

"Thanks," she said.

"You bet." Wolf flopped into the seat opposite and took a slug of his beer.

Haylee sipped hers, welcoming the icy coolness

and the tangy aftertaste. She didn't know how she was going to eat with him sitting there.

"You sleep okay?" he asked.

"If by sleep you mean did I fall into the bed and not hear a single sound for the past ten hours, then yes, I slept well. You?"

He shrugged. "I got a few hours."

Her stomach rumbled again and she picked up the pizza to take a bite, because if she didn't she was going to pass out from hunger. The cheese and sausage were like an explosion of nirvana on her tongue. Haylee closed her eyes. She may have moaned.

Wolf chuckled and she snapped her eyes open again. He was watching her. Grinning. Her stomach flipped. Dear God he was pretty.

"I moaned, didn't I?" Might as well brazen her way through this.

"Yeah. Not that I blame you, understand."

She took another bite, swallowed. The raging hunger in her belly was still there but getting better by the bite. "I love Mexican food, but I may never eat another tortilla again. That was all they fed us. Tortillas and beans. Once a day."

"I'm sorry."

"If it'd been as good as the tortillas and beans at my favorite Mexican restaurant, I suppose it would have been okay. Who knew you could screw either of those things up and make them taste bad?"

She ripped into the pizza and polished off a slice.

Then she took a healthy swig of beer. The liquor warmed her, crawled into her veins and took away her nervousness. Which apparently she needed with this guy. Every time her gaze met his, her stomach did a somersault. *Those eyes.*

It turned out they were either steely gray or blue depending on the light. But captivating. The rest of him was too. His hair was blond, a combination of dark and light, and short. His face looked as if it were carved from the finest marble. He wore a black T-shirt that clung to his muscles like a second skin. His dog tags hung on the outside of the T-shirt. The shirt was tucked into gray camo pants. He wore black boots with laces and moved like a panther. Graceful. Sleek. Oh so assured of his power.

"Haylee?" He snapped his fingers. "Earth to Haylee."

She shook herself. "Uh, yes?"

His brows were drawn together but he was still smiling. "You okay? You seemed a million miles away."

"Um, yes, fine. Sorry, just thinking. Trying to remember everything that I'd written in my notes. I need to recreate it." It was a tiny lie but she wasn't going to tell him she'd been thinking about him. Drooling over him in her head.

His smile faded. "You still planning to write about this?"

"Yes. I have to do it. For Nicole."

He nodded. "You'll get a debrief soon, but they're

going to tell you not to write about any of this. *Us,*" he added as if clarifying.

"The commandos. Got it."

He grinned again. "Special Operators, but what- ever. Just don't write about the rescue or any aspect of it."

"It's not really what the story is about. The drugs are the story. Not me or you or any of this."

"That's good. Though be careful there too. Cartels can have a long reach. Longer than you think sometimes."

"I will be." Though she didn't really know enough to anger anybody. She'd been following a *very* tenuous lead in the hopes it would equate to something. Some- thing she'd heard on the Hill from one of Senator Watson's staffers. Watson was very anti-drug and he was leading the charge to make it more difficult for people to cross the border in his home state of Arizona. His stance was a bit of a political bandaid since most of the drugs came by ship into various ports, or through tunnels beneath the border. There were too many cartels to keep up with, but the one that kept cropping up in regards to the fake pills was the Juarez Cartel.

"You want more pizza?"

Haylee looked down at her plate, surprised that she'd eaten two slices already. "I do. I shouldn't, but I do. Am I wrong?"

Wolf snatched up her plate. "Nope. What do you want?"

"Supreme this time. Thanks."

"Got it, babe."

Haylee watched him walk away, her heart thumping in her breast, her skin prickling with heat. His ass was made of perfect. His back was wide and the T-shirt stretched across those muscles like it was painted on before tapering down to a narrow waist.

If she was a different kind of girl, she'd want to jump him. Okay, she *did* want to jump him—but she wasn't spontaneous like that. Nicole had always told her to just go for it, bang the hot guy and worry about regrets tomorrow, but she'd never been that way. She'd always wanted to know a guy first. It felt… safer.

"Haylee, for fuck's sake," Nicole would say if she were here, *"you need to get laid. And that guy is gorgeous. If you don't want him, I'll take him."*

Haylee hated the stab of pain in her heart, but she was also used to it by now. Her bestie was gone. But her spirit lived on. Hell, her spirit was giving advice, apparently.

Haylee snorted a laugh to herself. Wolf sauntered back toward her—and she just went with it. Let her gaze roam over his hard body, his perfect face. Those soul-searching eyes that could destroy a woman if she weren't careful.

Sexy man. Gorgeous man.

Dangerous man.

Her breath stopped in her throat. Oh yes, he was definitely that. She had to be careful here.

"Stop it, Haylee. Just let yourself go. If he wants to take you to bed, let him. Then get up in the morning and go back to work." And there was Nicole again. Haylee frowned. She'd heard Nicole's voice in her head a few times since her friend had died, but never in regards to a man.

Like there'd been any men. Haylee had thrown herself into work for months now. There'd been no men. Well, except Tony Davis, who she'd talked to on a few occasions. But even if she'd been attracted to Tony, she wouldn't have gone there. He'd been interested in Nicole. And she in him apparently, though she hadn't said much about him to Haylee at the time.

Wolf set Haylee's plate down with two new slices. "You need another beer or you good?"

Haylee picked up the bottle. She'd drank three-quarters of it. She shouldn't drink another. "Maybe one more."

"Got it. Eat, babe."

The skin on Haylee's neck prickled as she picked up her pizza and took a bite. Of course she studied Wolf's ass again. She'd asked for the beer just so she could watch him walk away from her. He was back a few moments later, setting a cold beer down next to the one she was still drinking. He had a fresh one for himself as well.

"I kind of thought you'd be gone already," she said to him in between bites.

"Rough weather in the Gulf. It'll clear out tonight and we'll be gone tomorrow."

"You never told me where you were stationed."

His gray-blue eyes sparked. "Didn't I? We're a special detachment out of DC."

———

WOLF WATCHED her as she took in the information. Her eyes widened slightly, though he thought maybe she didn't want him to know that judging by the way she darted her gaze away. Was she interested?

He hoped she was. Because he was interested in her. He didn't know quite why he was digging her so much, but from the moment she'd kicked her attacker in the nuts—even though it had been a risky move considering she'd had nowhere to run—he'd admired the hell out of her. Haylee Jamison didn't take shit lying down. The way she'd gone to Cindy's side when all of Cindy's coworkers—or whatever they were— had stood silently by and glared because the woman had the potential to slow them down had notched his admiration a few pegs higher.

Haylee Jamison was made of stern stuff. It didn't hurt that she was pretty. Her long black hair hung in a silken wave down her back. She had dark, sparkling eyes, a high forehead, and a nose that wasn't quite perfect. Her lips were pink, her mouth wide. He imagined kissing her and his groin tightened.

Proper. That was the word that he would use to describe her if asked. Haylee was proper. He'd bet his last paycheck she wasn't a one-night stand kind of woman. Too bad, because he really wanted to bed her. Not that he couldn't call her again. Of course he could. Maybe he would. He thought of his teammates with girlfriends. They didn't seem so unhappy, did they? Saint was stupid over Brooke Sullivan. Hacker was planning to remarry his ex-wife. Hell, even the CO—Colonel Mendez—had a wife. Alpha Squad were all married or getting married. The SEALs were heading to the altar in frightening numbers too.

Wolf took another pull of his beer. Seriously, he needed to clear his head. Just because some of his teammates were in long-term relationships didn't mean he needed one. Or wanted one. He just thought this woman was cute and he wanted to get her naked. Nothing wrong with that.

Haylee took a sip of her beer. He didn't miss the way her fingers trembled as she reached for the bottle. *Score.* He'd bet money she was attracted to him. Good.

"No, I don't think you mentioned that at all."

"Yep, live in Maryland."

"I live in Bethesda."

"You don't say? Huh, guess we're practically neighbors."

"Guess so." She finished a slice of pizza and wiped her mouth delicately on a napkin. He figured she'd call it a done deal, but she picked up the next one and bit into it. Then she smiled. "It's a small world, right?"

"It is. In the military, we never say goodbye. We just say see you later."

"That's nice."

He shrugged. "Can be."

Mal came strolling over, beer in hand, eyes roving over Haylee. Wolf's gut tightened. He didn't know why. Mal flopped down on a chair nearby, stretched out his legs, and grinned at them.

"Hey," he said.

Haylee frowned adorably, shooting Wolf a puzzled look before turning and meeting Mal's gaze. "Hey," she replied.

"Mal," he said.

"I'm sorry… what?"

Wolf rolled his eyes. "His name's Mal. Malcolm McCoy, better known as Mal. Occasionally known as Captain Tight Pants."

Haylee's brows lifted as she grinned. "*Firefly.*"

Wolf smiled. "Yep. You a fan?"

"Are you kidding me? Nathan Fillion in those pants—uh, yeah. Definitely easy on the eyes."

He liked that she was a fan of *Firefly.* It was an old program now, but it was iconic. If she liked *Doctor Who* as well, then hell, she might be marriage material. Which was a joke but also kinda not.

"Hey, I'm over here," Mal said to the two of them, waving his beer.

"We see you, Tighty."

Mal snorted. "Keep trying, Wolf. You aren't changing my call sign. I got it fair and square."

"Yeah, whatever. Tighty would be so much better."

Mal stretched indolently. "I am a man of many talents. You can't define me with a word."

"Riiiiight," Wolf drawled. "What do you want, Mal of Many Talents?"

"Nothing. Just came over to see what you guys were chatting about so seriously."

"Interrupting," Wolf replied.

"You aren't," Haylee interjected. "Don't listen to him. We were just chatting about living in Maryland."

Mal perked up. "Hey, you live in Maryland?"

"Bethesda."

"Cool. We're more, uh, Laurel. Sort of."

"Oh, you mean Fort Meade?" Haylee asked a touch too innocently.

"Not precisely," Wolf said. "But close." Haylee had finished her pizza by now so he stood, beer in hand, and tipped his head toward the pool table at the other end of the common room. "Do you play?"

Haylee turned to look at the table where two of his teammates were currently embroiled in a match. "Actually, yes I do."

"Want to play a game? Pass the time?"

"Sure. Why not?" She unfolded herself from the chair and stood. Her head didn't come above mid-chest on him.

"I'll even give you the break," he said, feeling generous.

She stopped and arched an eyebrow. "Maybe you shouldn't do that. What if I'm a shark?"

His senses tingled. Nah, she couldn't be. She was

just teasing him. Flirting. He liked it. "If you're a shark, then maybe you want to make a friendly bet on the game? Winner take all?"

He'd know in a moment if she was bluffing. Instead, she looked gleeful. Her smile spread across her face like she had a secret. A really good secret. "Absolutely, Dean. But why don't we make it interesting instead of friendly?"

Chapter Six

Haylee shouldn't have drank that second beer. Not that she'd drank it all yet but she was about a third of the way through. It tasted good, dammit. And she felt looser than she had in weeks. Almost happy, in spite of herself.

Wolf towered over her, beer bottle in hand, big hard body relaxed and tense all at once. He looked surprised. "Seriously? What did you have in mind?"

The one named Mal was still sitting. Still watching them. He was attractive too, big and hard and pretty in that masculine I-could-rip-something-in-two-without-breaking-a-sweat way that these men had about them. Geez, if she'd had any idea that hanging around a military base would have netted her guys like these to stare at, she'd have hopped over to Laurel and its whereabouts more often.

Not that Bethesda didn't have its share of military men and women. But not *these kind* of military men.

Not commandos. *Special Operators*, she corrected. Delta Force. Green Berets. Navy SEALs. The kind of men that made a girl shiver—and want to throw her panties at him at the same time.

She shrugged. "I don't know. What do you have to offer?"

Wolf seemed to recover his equilibrium. He grinned and stepped in close. So damned close, until the heat of his body hit her like a wave. His scent— steely, woodsy, masculine—slammed into her. His damned gray-blue eyes bored through her soul. Her limbs felt liquid. "Whatever you want, baby. Tell me."

Uhh, were they still talking about pool here?

She took a step back so she could breathe. She could feel Mal's eyes darting between them. Maybe he was safer. Maybe she should be flirting with him instead.

But she didn't want to flirt with him. She wanted to flirt with Wolf. And she wanted him to flirt right back.

"Let's start simple. For every shot I sink, you owe me five bucks."

He reared back, studying her as if she'd dropped in from Mars. "Five bucks a shot? That's what you want? That's a potential forty bucks. Not very high stakes."

Haylee took a step closer to him. He didn't back away. She felt the danger rolling through her. The excitement. She hadn't felt this carefree in months.

This crazy. "Okay, smartass—make it twenty a shot. That better?"

She'd been trying to take it easy on him, but he wasn't having any of it. He had no idea how good she could be. How natural shooting pool was for her. Then again, what if he was more than just a guy who played pool with his buddies to let off steam?

"Twenty a shot. Fine. Best of five for the championship?"

"Sure, hotshot. I'll take those odds."

Mal bounded up from his chair, waving his arms. "Whoa, whoa, whoa, *amigos*. That's not interesting enough, is it? I mean a hundred and sixty bucks per game? Big deal. What else you people got?"

Wolf didn't take his eyes from her. "Stay out of this, Mal. That's eight hundred if somebody wins all five."

"Yeah, but make it *more* interesting."

"What did you have in mind?" Haylee asked without looking at Mal.

"A kiss," Wolf said before Mal could add anything. "With tongue."

Haylee's heart skipped a couple of beats. Her nipples tightened. *What the hell?* Mal laughed. "Now that's some stakes. Though they seem to benefit you the most, Wolf," he added.

"Go away," Wolf growled without looking at his teammate. "Haylee? Got another suggestion?"

"Deal," Haylee said, throat closing tight because

she couldn't think of anything else except the possibility of kissing this man. "If that's what you want."

"Yeah," he murmured, gaze dropping for half a second, skimming over her collarbone, her chest, and then back up to her eyes. "It's what I want. For every shot I sink."

Haylee wanted that too. But it was too easy. She couldn't give it to him. "No. If you win a game, you get the kiss."

"And the ultimate prize?"

Her heart thumped. "There is no ultimate prize, Wolf. Five kisses are up for grabs here. Or a hundred and sixty bucks per game. Unless you'd rather change your prize to money?"

He shook his head. "You know what, I'd say the prize is one-sixty per game *and* a kiss. *With* tongue. If you want to collect on one, you have to collect on the other."

Oh, he was good. Haylee's belly twisted. But dammit, she liked it. Liked the way he thought. "Okay, fine. One-sixty and a kiss with tongue."

"Winner has to collect both or forfeits both."

"Fine."

"Fine."

Mal snickered. "Hoo-*wee*, this is gonna be fun."

"Mind your own business, Captain Tight Pants," Wolf said without looking away from her.

"Naw, man. This is much more fun."

WOLF STARED at the pool table and the vision before him. He shook his head, wondering if he'd had too much beer. He hadn't. He knew he hadn't. Four beers in two hours wasn't too much for him.

No, the truth was that Haylee Jamison was a pool shark. He didn't know how. He didn't know why. He didn't understand a damned thing about it, but the girl was sinking shots like the Black Widow during her exhibition games in Vegas. Fucking hell.

"Where'd you learn to do that?" he asked as she chalked the cue and bent over the table, gaze intent on the cue ball and her target. Stripes. Girl had chosen stripes and she'd already sunk four of them. He hadn't even gotten a turn yet.

"Misspent youth," she said, lining up the shot and taking it. The eleven ball dropped into the pocket, the cue ball ricocheting across the table and missing everything else in its path. He hoped she'd sink one of his balls so he could have a turn and put the cue ball wherever he wanted it but so far it was a no go. "Three more to go, hotshot."

"You're a sore winner, you know that?"

Dark, dancing eyes met his. Fucking hell he wanted to kiss her. Which he would get to do even if she won. And that, he decided, made the whole thing less annoying. Win or lose, he still got to kiss Haylee Jamison.

"Haven't won yet." She sank her sixth ball in a row and he snorted.

"Only two to go, babe."

Mal stood on the sidelines, cheering Haylee on. Bastard wanted in her panties, Wolf was sure. Wasn't happening. He shot his teammate significant looks but Mal only hooted and urged Haylee on. The rest of the team filtered over, interested in the commotion. He and Haylee had waited their turn at the table. Once Gem and Easy were done, they'd taken over. Gem and Easy had melted away but now they were back. All eyes were on Haylee. Sexy, sweet, pool shark Haylee. Damn the girl was smooth.

"Fifteen in the corner pocket," she said, pointing at the far corner. She didn't need to say where she was sending that ball, but she did anyway. And then she sent it sailing, sinking into the pocket like it was magnetized to go there.

"Day-um," Saint said.

"Holy shit," Ryder "Muffin" Hanson added.

"Fucking awesome," Zane "Zany" Scott breathed.

Wolf didn't let the heat rolling through him rattle him at all. Was he irritated that this slip of a woman was about to beat him at pool without him even getting a chance at the table? Hell yeah. Was he upset that she was better than he was, at least for this game? Uh, no. It was pretty fucking fantastic to watch. And maybe he'd get a break on the next game.

"Eight ball, side pocket," she said, rolling around the table with the fluid grace of a cat. The room was silent, swear to God, when she lined up her stick and cradled it in her fingers. And then she shot it toward the ball—and the ball broke perfectly, gliding across the table and dropping into the pocket as if someone had pulled it on a string.

Haylee straightened and pumped a fist in the air. Echo Squad seemed to stare as one, silence reigning— and then they broke into laughter and cheers. Wolf stared at the table while Gem and Easy slapped his shoulders. "Man, she fucking *owned* you!"

Yeah, he wished she owned him. Privately. Completely. At least for a night.

Haylee met his gaze across the table. She smiled shyly. Then she shrugged. Wolf didn't care. Didn't care about any of it. He strode around the table to her side. She gazed up at him.

"You get a kiss," he said. "Fair and square."

He could see the pulse beating in her throat. "Later."

"Now."

She frowned. "Maybe I plan to save up and collect all at once. You ever think of that?"

"Nope. Now." Wolf snaked an arm around her waist, tugged her in close, oblivious to the pool cue still in her hand. She could gut him with it if she chose, but instead she gasped as their bodies came into contact. Full fucking contact.

"Wolf," she breathed, both hands coming up to press against his chest, the pool cue part of the picture as it lay between them. He thought back to the circumstances in which he'd found her and kept his hold loose. If she pushed, he'd let go. But if she stayed?

Hell, that thought excited him. "Part of the deal, Haylee. One-sixty and a kiss. I always pay up."

She tilted her head to the side, eyebrows lifting. "You paying the cash right now too? Or just the kiss?"

"Cash later. Kiss now."

"Doesn't seem quite fair," she said, but she didn't push him away.

"Does to me." They stared at each other for a long moment. And then he dropped his mouth to hers —and the world faded away.

———

HAYLEE'S HEART threatened to punch its way out of her chest. She'd been an idiot to agree to a kiss and twenty bucks a shot, but she hadn't thought he'd want to pay up right this second. She'd thought maybe she could put all of it off—and then she'd tell him she didn't really want the money, so he could keep his coin and his kisses. Even though she really wanted to kiss him.

She'd sorely misjudged, however. Not only his determination, but her desire to let it happen. She was in his embrace, bent back over firm forearms, his mouth on hers. She blinked once and then her eyes closed automatically. Wolf's tongue slipped along the seam of her lips. Vaguely, she heard cheering. His teammates. Whose side were they on anyway?

His tongue pressed lightly—and her heart hammered. She wanted to open to him—and she was scared to. Scared she'd like it too much. Scared she'd want more. He pulled back slightly, kissed the corners of her mouth. "Haylee," he whispered against her skin. "Let it happen."

"I—" she began. But the very act of speaking meant her mouth opened. And his tongue slipped inside, stroked across hers. Haylee shivered. Her body went limp. Simply folded up like an umbrella that someone had collapsed.

Wolf's tongue teased hers. Dipped and darted. And oh, she couldn't help but respond. Her arms slipped around his neck. She tilted her head. Sighed. Let him all the way in. A tingle settled between her legs, set up a regular rhythm.

His grip on her tightened. Her stomach somersaulted. Tongues met and tangled. His mouth was a revelation. Hot, sensuous, soft. He tasted like beer and determination. Like the sex she'd been lacking for so long. If they were alone… Dear God, if they were alone she'd jump him.

But they weren't alone, as the hoots and hollers brought back to her. They were here. In El Salvador, on a military base. This was a temporary reprieve from real life, and she wasn't about to let herself forget that. Real life waited. The Juarez Cartel waited. They needed exposing, and she was the woman to do that. Wolf was a distraction. Hell, it hit her then that she didn't even know his last name.

Haylee pressed her palms to his chest, pushed. He took the hint immediately, breaking the kiss even though he continued to hold her. Her body pressed close to his, her senses firing like ping pong balls from a cannon. His eyes—those incredible gray-blue eyes— stared down at her, questioning.

"I think that's enough," she said hoarsely.

His nostrils flared. Then his hands fell away, his arms, until she was standing there with no support. "Next game then. You ready to lose?"

Haylee reached deep for the ability to act unaffected. "Puh-*leeze*, GI Joe."

Curiosity flitted across his features. "Where'd you learn to shoot pool?"

She took a step back, relieved that he didn't stop her. "My mom was a single mom for much of my childhood. I spent far too much time with a neighbor who was obsessed with the game. She taught me."

"So you're telling me a neighbor taught you to shoot like a professional? And you just happened to remember those lessons tonight?"

Haylee couldn't help herself. She laughed. "Not quite. Yes, a neighbor taught me. But I was obsessed, so I practiced a lot—and I worked my way through college partly by making bets."

Wolf frowned. "You paid for college with pool winnings?"

"Uh, yep. Partly, I said. Once people figured out I was good, they stopped playing me."

"So I should forfeit the games and let you collect your kisses?"

Haylee snorted. "Aw, come on, Dean. I haven't

seen you shoot yet. I'll even let you break on the next game."

He shook his head. "Yeah, I'll do okay—but the second I miss a shot, you're going to cream me."

Haylee laughed. "I tried to hold you to five bucks a shot. Remember?"

"Yeah." He backed away and started pulling balls from the pockets, dropping them into the rack. "Not giving up, Haylee. Even if I should. Not my style."

"I'm glad to hear it," she said, thinking she hadn't had this much fun in, well, forever. "Even sharks have bad shots, you know. You might best me yet."

"I might," he said, eyes sparkling as he picked up his cue. "You want to check the rack?"

"Sure." She went over and peered at the balls, then lifted the frame off the triangle. "Go for it, Wolf. Make me sweat."

Belatedly, she realized what she'd said. Haylee swallowed as Wolf's mouth curved. "I intend to, babe. One way or the other."

Chapter Seven

"HEY, BABE," WOLF SAID, SHAKING HAYLEE'S shoulder. She'd sat down on the couch opposite the pool table and fallen asleep. He'd left her like that for a while but now it was getting late and they were the only two left in the common area. He didn't want to wake her, but he also didn't want to leave her sleeping out here in the open.

She blinked awake, her eyes unfocused and hazy for a second. But then she seemed to remember where she was because she jumped and scrubbed her hands over her face. "Oh, sorry, is it my turn?"

He laughed. "No, we're done. You beat me."

"Did I?"

"Yep, four games in and you won every single one. I don't think we need another one for the championship, do you?" Hell, they hadn't needed a fourth, but watching her play was so much fun that he'd racked the balls and took the opening shot anyway.

He'd missed the third ball and she'd taken over from there.

"Oh, no, I guess not." She grinned up at him sleepily. Damn she was pretty.

"So, I'm not exactly carrying cash on me at the moment, but I'll get the money to you." He really shouldn't have bet so much. It wasn't like him to be so reckless, but it was too late now. He still had plenty to send back to Mom and Dad. And he'd had fun tonight, so there was that.

She waved a hand. "Forget it. It was just fun to play. And I exaggerated the amount because you scoffed at five bucks."

"Big mistake on my part, eh Sharky?"

"Huge." She stretched big and he enjoyed the way her chest thrust out. She had a nice rack. Two good handfuls there. He imagined peeling off her clothing, kissing her pretty nipples. He wanted that pretty badly, but he also wanted to know her better. Not quite the usual from him, but then again he'd never met a woman he was this attracted to on a mission either.

He forced his thoughts to the present moment. "I always pay up, Haylee. Like I said… You've still got three kisses coming, by the way."

Her eyes sparked. He figured she'd deny those, but he hoped she wouldn't.

"Well," she said, dropping her gaze.

"Unless you don't want them." *Why the fuck did you say that, dude?*

Her head came up, dark eyes meeting his. "Do you?"

Not what he'd expected her to say. "Yeah, I do."

"Okay then. Though maybe not tonight. I'm kinda beat."

"Understandable."

She shrugged. "I thought I'd slept enough already, but I guess everything caught up with me. Though I'll probably be wide awake for hours now even though I still feel as if I've been run through a wringer." She glanced around the room. He could see the moment she realized it was empty. Her gaze darted back to his. "How long have they been gone?"

"About an hour. I thought you'd wake up on your own."

"You stayed here while everyone was gone? Because I was asleep?"

"Yeah. Is that a problem?"

She shook her head. "No, not at all. I think it's sweet."

"You ready to head back to your room now?"

She smiled up at him. "Guess I should."

"I'll walk you."

"You don't have to."

"I know I don't have to. But I'm going to." She stood and he waited for her to move. And then he realized what she might be thinking. "I'm not planning to collect on those kisses, Haylee. Just walking you to your room before heading to mine. I'm not a total dick."

"I didn't think you were. You've been more than decent to me. You saved me from that guy, and then you've been with me every step of the way. I think I know what kind of man I'm dealing with by now."

He liked the way that sounded, and yet if she could peek into his mind and see what he was thinking about her, she'd probably have a different opinion on his decency. Because nothing he was thinking was decent. More like hot and sweaty and dirty.

"After you," he said, waving a hand for her to precede him. He followed her down the hallway, around a corner, and into another hall. She stopped in front of a door and turned with her back to it as she took her keycard from her pocket.

"This is me."

"Then I guess it's time for me to say goodbye," he said softly.

Her brows drew together. "Goodbye? Not goodnight?"

He shook his head. "We'll be gone before they transport you out of here tomorrow. It's been nice hanging out with you tonight, Haylee."

"I… Yes, it has."

He couldn't stop himself from tucking a lock of hair behind her ear just so he could touch her again. "I'm still planning to pay up, don't worry. I'll find you back home."

"You promise?"

He grinned. "Found you this time. I'll find you."

She rolled her eyes mockingly. "You didn't even know I was there."

"Yeah, but now I do."

He started walking backwards down the hall. "Get some rest, Haylee. Go home and take care of yourself. I'll see you around. Promise."

He was nearly to the end of the short hall when she called out. "Wolf. Wait."

"Yeah, baby?"

"I… I don't want to say goodbye just yet."

His heart clenched tight in his chest. Neither did he. But he also didn't want to assume a damned thing where she was concerned. He returned to where she still stood with her back to the door, the keycard clutched in front of her, her eyes wide as they searched his face. He took the card gently. Reached behind her and slipped it into the slot. The door clicked.

"Then we don't have to," he said, pushing the door open behind her. Waiting for her to move. His heart rate sped up, but he didn't budge. Didn't push her.

Her gaze roamed his face, slipped down his body, landed about mid-abdomen and stayed there. Wolf sighed and tipped her chin up, made her look at him again.

"Not gonna lie to you. I don't know what this is or where it's going, but I'm not planning to force you to do anything you don't want to do. If all we do is talk, then that's all we do."

She gave him a soft smile. And then she stepped backward and entered the room. Wolf followed.

———

HAYLEE DIDN'T KNOW what she was doing. Not really. Her heart hammered and her palms were sweating and her senses seemed to be hyper-engaged.

Wolf was in her room. Standing just inside the door, his big frame filling it, making her belly throb and her sex tingle. She was crazy. Had to be. She didn't know this man, not really, and yet here she was. Letting him inside her room—no, *begging* him to come inside and stay. What must he think she wanted?

Hell, she didn't know what she wanted. Sex? Talk? What?

He closed the door softly behind him, plunging them into a darker environment than the brightly lit corridor. There was a light on in her room, but it wasn't very bright. She swallowed. *Now what, girlie? You brought him here.*

She wasn't sure if it was her voice or Nicole's talking to her in that moment. But, yeah, *now what?*

"I don't know what I'm doing," she said. And then she started because she wasn't sure she'd meant to say it aloud.

One corner of Wolf's mouth curved into a smile. *So sexy.* "So we'll figure it out together."

"What if I don't want sex?" she burst out as he took a step toward her.

He stopped. "Already told you I didn't expect it. Nothing's changed just because you've invited me in."

Haylee folded her arms over her chest. Was this guy for real? She didn't think she'd ever dated a guy who was so understanding. Not that they were dating, but the ones she'd gone out with always seemed to think they were owed something at the end of the evening. Wolf seemed perfectly content to hang out and not try to get his hands in her panties.

Was he gay?

Haylee nearly rolled her eyes. Was the man gay? Not likely considering the way he'd kissed her earlier. Sure, maybe gay men kissed women like they wanted to eat them for dinner, but she didn't think it was a typical reaction.

"I don't think there's anything interesting to drink in here," she said, trying to cover her nervousness with busyness as she turned and went into the small kitchenette. She tugged open the door and blinked. "Okay, strike that, there's beer. And water and soda."

She felt Wolf walk up behind her. His heat was so close, but he didn't touch her. "Probably a VIP room."

"Can we drink it? Or should we leave it alone?"

He reached past her, his body leaning into hers. Making her ache. She bit the inside of her lip.

"I think if they didn't want it drunk, they shouldn't have left it," he said in her ear. His fingers closed around two bottles of light beer. He pulled them from the fridge, straightening, his heat fading.

He twisted off first one top and then the other as she turned to face him.

"Cheers," he said, handing her a bottle. She took it and they clinked the glass. The beer was cold and smoother than she expected as she took a sip. Three beers in one night. She was turning into quite the party animal.

Wolf went over and sat on one of the chairs in the living area. She went and sat in the opposite. Then she dropped her gaze, uncertain what to say. And then she knew.

"Do you usually spend so much time with your rescues?" she asked.

"Nope. We're usually moving out pretty quick, and we go our separate ways as soon as we get them to safety. This time was… unusual."

"Why?"

"We don't typically have to go to Plan B like we did with this group. And then there are the storms in the Gulf which kept us from flying straight out." He shrugged. "So we get an extra night of R&R. Not a bad thing."

"No, guess not. Plus it means I got to beat you at pool."

He laughed. "Definitely that. You have some amazing skill, Haylee. The guys were impressed."

She felt her pride sit up just a little bit. "Were they?"

"Oh yeah. Mal thinks you should join us at the bar back home, be a ringer for us."

"A ringer? For what?"

"We've got this one guy—well, he's on a different team. Name's Cage, and he's so good nobody wants to play him for money anymore. Might be nice to send you up against him."

Haylee laughed. "Hey, there's no guarantee I'd beat him. Besides, how would you get this guy to play me? All of you pushing and laughing like fools, you think he's not going to figure it out?"

"Nah, we'd be cool. It's a great fantasy though."

Fantasy. Good Lord, just hearing that word on his lips made her mind go to places she wasn't sure she should allow it to go. "I might not win. What then?"

Wolf scoffed. "No way, baby. You're a fucking shark."

Haylee laughed then. She couldn't help it. His utter conviction was amusing. And sweet. "Well, I don't know about that. I'm a bit out of practice."

The look on his face was comical. "Out of practice? Hell, you could have gone to Vegas on those games."

Haylee laughed harder. "No, really. I'm good— I'm not *that* good. I know a few tricks. I pay attention. You play me a few more games, you'll spot my weaknesses."

"Yeah, you'd still blow Cage out of the water. He wouldn't even see it coming."

"Well then. Maybe one day."

He twisted the beer in his hand. "Yeah, maybe so." He was silent for a moment. "You know, I'd ask for your number, but neither of us has a cell phone right now."

She dipped her head shyly. "I appreciate that. I have to get a new one when I get back."

"What's your address?"

"You don't have to do that," she said, shaking her head. "You don't have to ask me. It's okay."

"I said I'd find you, and I will. But an address would make it easier. I'll remember."

She recited it. She could see the gears turning. Then he nodded. "Got it."

The conversation got easier after that. They talked about mundane things, about living in Maryland, eating the local seafood, taking visitors to the Capitol Mall and still being excited to see it all again, even though they'd seen it several times before. Haylee was tired, but she didn't want him to go so she kept talking.

And then, finally, he leaned back against the chair and sighed, eyes closing. "I'm sorry, sweetheart, but I think it's time to call it a night. I'm losing the ability to stay awake."

"Me too," she said on a sigh, legs curled in the chair, eyes drooping.

He stood. She stood too, not easily. And then he was at her side, tugging her against him, one hand spearing into her hair, the other curving around her back. "It's been great meeting you, Haylee. I've enjoyed every minute with you."

Her throat tightened. Her arms snaked around

him, held him tighter than she should have. "Me too."

"But I gotta go."

"I know."

"You want to collect a kiss now? Or save it?"

She knew the answer. Didn't have to think twice. "Collect."

It wasn't the answer he'd been expecting. She could see it on his handsome face. His eyes sparked. His nostrils flared. But then he seemed to make a decision. "Whatever you want, baby."

He was so much taller than her that she almost had to stretch up to him on tiptoe, but then his head dropped, slowly, and her eyes closed long before he arrived. She waited, her heart pounding, her senses on edge—

And then his mouth met hers, warm lips pressing to hers, and she shivered as a thrill rolled through her for the second time tonight.

"Haylee," he murmured against her mouth. She opened to him, tilting her head to give him better access, heart throbbing with excitement. He groaned as he took what she offered. Their mouths sucked and nipped and tasted, and her body began to tremble.

A moment later, he set her away from him. Gently. She blinked up at him. "Why did you stop?"

"Can't keep doing that, Haylee. Not without wanting more."

"Oh." She twisted his shirt in her fingers. What was this reluctance to let him go? Why was she so damned clingy with a man she hardly knew?

"I'd better go. Before something happens that we both regret."

That thought sobered her right on up. "What's that mean?"

"Means I don't want to push you into something. I wouldn't force you, not ever, but I'm this damned close—" He pinched his fingers together to show, well, *no* space at all. "—to using every trick in the book to convince you that sleeping with me is a good idea. Except I'm too fuckin' tired to do it right, which means I really need to go."

Haylee pulled in a breath. "I'm sorry. I didn't mean to make you uncomfortable."

"I'm not uncomfortable. In truth, I could lay down beside you and sleep all night so long as we didn't kiss. I could do that and be happy. Swear to God."

She searched his gaze. "Could you? Really?"

Even his grin was sleepy. She figured she was reflecting it back to him, tired as she was. What a mess.

"Yeah, really."

Haylee dropped her arms from around his waist. Took one of his hands lightly in hers. "I'd like that."

"You would? Just you and me sleeping together?"

She shrugged shyly. "Yes. You and me. Sleeping. I want to."

He didn't say anything for a long moment. And then he sighed. Shook his head. "So do I, babe. More than you know."

Chapter Eight

WOLF DIDN'T KNOW WHAT THE HELL HE WAS AGREEING to but he knew he didn't want to go. Could he lie in bed with this woman and sleep? Yeah, right now he could. He was exhausted. So he followed her into the bedroom and they lay down together, completely clothed, on top of the covers. He opened his arms and she curled into them, slipped her arms around his body. He lay there in the darkness and breathed in and out, forcing himself to think about what was happening.

He was in bed with a woman he'd just met—not unusual—and doing nothing more than holding her close—highly unusual. Her fingers splayed over his chest, her nose burrowing against his neck. Contentment dripped through him like melting wax, settling warm and sticky deep inside.

He closed his eyes. He had to be outta here before daylight, but he had her address. He'd see her again in DC. He ran his thumb absently up and down her arm, wishing he was touching bare skin instead of a camouflage shirt.

"This is the strangest thing," she said softly after a few seconds.

"What is?"

"This. Lying here with you. I don't even know you, but I want to be near you."

He thought about that for a second. "Yeah, me too."

She sighed. "You could just be saying that. I know it, and yet I feel like you aren't. Like this isn't something you usually do."

He frowned. "No. Not at all. I'm comfortable with you, Haylee. I like you."

"I like you too."

"I never met a girl in the jungle before. Never escaped a drug cartel with her. Just so you know."

She laughed. "It's a first for me too, I have to say."

He squeezed her softly. "You might have… issues when you get home. Don't ignore them, okay? If you need help, get it. Talk to someone. What happened tonight was intense."

"You mean the bodies in the camp?"

"Yes. And the man I, uh, stopped from hurting you." He'd killed a man in front of her. He'd done it quickly and he'd done it because it was necessary, but he didn't enjoy it. And he worried how she'd feel about it once she was out of here and memories of her captivity and rescue started hitting hard.

"I keep expecting to feel horror over it, but I don't. Is that wrong?"

He sighed. "I don't know. That's the kind of thing you talk to someone about. It wasn't wrong for me, but you're different. Only you know if something is bothering you or not."

"I'm not bothered right now. But I understand what you're saying."

"Good." A jaw-cracking yawn snuck up on him.

Haylee burrowed closer. "I can't keep my eyes open anymore. See you in the morning?"

"Yeah, morning," he said. And then he fell fast asleep next to a woman he hadn't had sex with.

———

IT WAS STILL DARK when Haylee woke. She was warm, burrowed against the hard body of a man. When was the last time that had happened? She knew where she was and who she was with, because the circumstances were unusual enough to stick in her mind. But she had to pee, so she gently disentangled herself and pushed away. Wolf didn't stir.

She escaped to the bathroom, did her thing, and swigged mouthwash from the small bottle on the sink. Just because.

Haylee blushed. *Not* just because. She did it because she intended to collect another of those kisses if he woke before she fell asleep again. She tiptoed back to the bed, pausing at the edge when bright eyes landed on her.

"Hey," she said, her heart skipping.

"Hey." His voice was gravelly, sexy. It thrummed deep inside her.

"Sorry if I woke you."

"You didn't." He put an arm behind his head. Yawned. "I don't sleep deeply on a mission."

"Oh."

He levered up and stood. "I'll be back," he said. Then he smiled.

"Okay."

She climbed onto the bed to wait, her heart pounding a little faster as Wolf headed toward the bathroom to do his business. What the hell was she thinking anyway? Swigging mouthwash? Wanting a kiss? This wasn't a romance. This was a tough situation creating a closeness that wasn't real.

And yet she still wanted to kiss him. Wanted to run her hands down his body, feeling all that hard muscle beneath her palms. He returned a few minutes later and her heart skipped at the sight of him. So sexy. So desirable.

"It's nearly time for me to go," he told her as he sat on the bed beside her. "Another hour, maybe a little more. They'll be looking for me."

Her belly tightened inexplicably. "Do you need to leave now?"

"Soon."

Haylee bit the inside of her cheek. She didn't

LYNN RAYE HARRIS

want him to go, and yet there was nothing she could do to stop it. She told herself she was just being clingy. That the circumstances of their meeting meant she felt a closer kinship with him than she should.

That's not it. Nicole's voice again. *You're hot for him. He's hot for you. For God's sake, Haylee, do something about it before he walks away.*

Haylee bit her lip. She didn't know that she could. That she *should.*

He reached out and skimmed his fingers along her cheek. Then he tucked her hair behind her ear. "Thanks for letting me sleep here."

Haylee swallowed. "You're welcome." Her skin tingled. Her body ached. Wetness pooled between her legs. It had been so long since she'd been touched by anyone but herself. Did she dare to risk more with this man? Or did it even matter? What if it was a one-night stand? Could she handle that?

You can. You know you can. For God's sake, let it happen. One good memory to hold onto.

"Before you go…" she began.

His eyebrows lifted. "Yes?"

"Maybe you could deliver on those kisses?"

He looked surprised. "I could. But Haylee, I need to know something."

"Yes?"

"Is there any possibility of anything more tonight? Or are those two kisses the end of it?"

Haylee swallowed. Then she put a hand on his chest and spread her fingers, feeling the hard muscle

98

beneath her palm. "I've never slept with a guy I just met."

He wrapped his hand around hers and lifted it to his mouth. Kissed her knuckles. "It's okay. I understand."

A sizzle of electricity rolled through her. "Kiss me, Wolf. I feel like, if you kiss me, I'd do anything you wanted."

She thought that would be enough, but he didn't move. Instead, he squeezed her hand. "Honey, no. Only do it if *you* want to. If I don't make you feel crazy with desire, don't say yes."

Oh God, she could fall in love with this man. He was a badass commando, but he was also a *nice* guy. Noble and honorable and concerned with her feelings. How many guys would care if she gave in and had sex because she was temporarily blinded by lust or if she knew deep down she really wanted it?

Not many, girlie. Not many at all.

I hear you, Nicole. Stop pushing.

Haylee gulped down her apprehension and her embarrassment and slid her body toward Wolf's, tugging him down until he lay across her, his gorgeous eyes gazing down into hers.

"You already make me crazy with desire," she whispered. It was the truth. He did make her crazy with desire—and she feared if she let him walk out, she'd never know what she'd missed.

His hands skimmed up her body, shaping her. Leaving fire in their wake. "I've never done this before," he told her in a voice that vibrated through her.

"You're a virgin?" she teased, trying to make light of the situation.

He snorted. "No. Not even close."

She ran her fingers over his chest, his collarbone, threaded them into his hair. "No way you could be, looking like this. And my comment was a joke, by the way. I know you're not a virgin."

"What I *mean*," he said, slipping his hands beneath her, slowly crawling them down to her ass as he rolled and tugged her with him. "Is that I've never rescued a woman from a bad situation, spent a lot of time with her, got to know her a bit and decided I liked her, lost a shitload of pool games to her, and then slept with her in a bed without any sex whatsoever. It's not what I usually do."

"What do you usually do?" she asked, fingers curling into his shirt.

"Usually I drop her off and say goodbye. No touching. No kissing. No pool games. And definitely no sleeping together, sex or not."

Haylee was acutely aware of his hard, warm body beneath her. Of the ridge of his cock riding the crease in her thighs. "So I'm different?"

Oh, way to go. Asking him if she was different. Rookie move.

"You're different."

"Bet you say that to all the girls."

His eyes were somber. "No, I really don't. I don't usually have to."

Her heart slowed for a second and then sped up again as she gazed into his eyes. No, he probably didn't have to.

"Kiss me, Wolf. Please."

He speared his fingers into her hair, cupped the back of her head. "With pleasure," he murmured before dragging her mouth down to his.

Their tongues met, tangling together with a desperation that surprised her. She wanted more of this man, so much more, but it was crazy to give in to this feeling.

He rolled them again, pressing her into the mattress. Dominating her. Haylee shivered, her arms wrapping around his shoulders, skimming down his back. She arched her body up to him, felt the hard press of his cock against her core, and shuddered deep inside.

He kissed her hard and deep and long. At some point, things went nuclear. He tore his mouth from hers and skimmed it down her throat, into the vee of her shirt. His hands found the buttons of the camo shirt the military had given her, popped them open one by one. And then he was shoving her T-shirt up, cupping her breasts in strong hands, his mouth closing over the lacy cup of her bra.

"Wolf," she gasped, arching into him as sensation exploded in her body.

He dragged the cups down, exposing her nipples.

"I want this so fucking bad you have no idea," he told her, his voice a low growl. "But if you tell me no, I'll stop."

Haylee's breath hitched. Her body hurt with how badly it wanted him. And yet her brain was trying to apply the brakes. "I'm not telling you no. Not yet. I can't guarantee I won't, though."

His eyes glittered in the light from the other room. "There's no point at which you can't tell me no. I want you to understand that."

"If that's true, you're an extraordinary man."

He frowned down at her. "What? No. You have the right to stop whenever you want to stop. Same as me. Nobody gets to keep going just because they want to."

Haylee felt as if somebody had knocked the breath from her. This man was too good to be true. "Don't stop, Wolf. Not yet. Please."

He shaped her breasts with his palms. Her nipples were hard and achy. Desperate for his touch.

He lowered his head and dipped his tongue to touch the point of her nipple. Haylee's gasp turned into a moan. She clutched his shoulders, arching her breasts up to his mouth. Wolf curled his tongue around first one nipple and then the other, licking and sucking each one into hard, tight, sensitive points. Her sex grew wet, swollen, needy. She couldn't remember the last time she'd wanted a man this badly.

Wolf licked his way down her belly, to the waist-band of her pants. Then he looked up at her, their eyes meeting in the dimness of the room. Her heart stopped.

"Do I keep going? Or is this enough?"

"Don't stop. Please don't stop."

He unbuttoned her pants and then, with her help, shoved them down her body before rising up and tugging them off, dropping them into a heap on the floor. Haylee lay there, fully exposed, her shirt open, breasts pressed together by the bra cups, the rest of her completely bare. What on earth was she doing?

Getting laid, girlfriend!

Haylee shuddered. She knew Nicole wasn't really talking to her, but that's precisely what her pretty blond friend would have said. Complete with a lilt and a saucy grin.

"Jesus, that's a pretty sight," Wolf said, gently pressing her legs open until she was completely at his mercy. "You're a gorgeous woman, Haylee Jamison— and don't take this the wrong way, but I want to fuck you until you scream my name."

Her stomach bottomed out as she imagined it. Her core ached. "I'm not taking it the wrong way. And I'm not saying no yet," she breathed. "I'm not sure I will ever say no."

His fingers skimmed along the top of her neatly trimmed pubic hair—thank God she kept that mani-cured—and then dipped into the seam between her legs. He found her warm and wet and ready.

"Oh fuck," he said on a hoarse whisper. "That's the most perfect gift you could give me. After everything, you give me your trust, your arousal, your body. I want to worship you." He dropped onto his elbows between her legs, his gaze meeting hers. Waiting for permission.

Haylee threaded her fingers into his blond hair and sucked in a breath. Seeing him between her legs was the most erotic thing ever. She nodded once, not really knowing if approval was what he needed, but then he spread her with his thumbs and touched his tongue to her clit.

"Wolf," Haylee gasped. "Oh God."

"That's right, babe. I'm gonna make you come." He flicked his tongue against her, sucked her clit into his mouth and tugged so sweetly while she moaned. And then he slipped a finger inside her, fucking her slowly, making her crazy with need until she gyrated her hips against his face. He chuckled as he pressed another finger inside her. And then he found her G-spot, his fingers hitting that magic place that she thought only she knew how to find. The pressure built to incredible levels before shattering into a million stars that exploded behind her eyes.

Wolf climbed her body while she lay there with her eyes squeezed tight, her body zinging with sparks and tingles. He kissed his way upward before plunging his tongue into her mouth, taking a kiss from her while she still sizzled with the aftermath of orgasm. He didn't do anything except kiss her. Somewhere in the corners of her mind, she marveled that he wasn't trying to shove his way into her body. Other men did that. They thought because they got her off it was their turn immediately, so they took it. They didn't give her any time to recover.

But Wolf did. He kissed her, her taste on his tongue, until she floated back down to earth. Until she reached for his cock and realized he had yet to take his pants off. Or his shirt. And then she was a mad woman, shoving his shirt up until he took over and yanked it off while she fumbled with his pants, finally getting the buttons open and shoving the camouflage down his narrow hips.

Until she could wrap a hand around him and feel his silken heat. He was hard and big and the way he groaned when she squeezed him was just about the sexiest thing she'd ever heard. She also heard Nicole's voice, encouraging her to go for it—and then there was her voice in the back of her head, asking her what the hell she was doing. Telling her she didn't really know this guy and she'd never see him again and she was giving him too much of herself.

But right now she didn't much care. He was vibrant and sexy and he knew how to make her feel alive. It'd been a long time since she'd felt that way and she wasn't ready to give it up.

"Hold on a minute," he said as she lifted herself up to kiss him. "There's gotta be a condom in here somewhere."

He lunged for the drawer of the beside table, rummaged through it, and came up with a box. "Fuck yes," he said, holding it up triumphantly.

"How is that possible?"

"It's the military for you. Prepared for everything."

He ripped it open and she grabbed the ribbon of foil packets, tearing one off and tearing it open. Before her mind could catch up to her heart and put a stop to this. Wolf caught her hand, stopping her from rolling it on him.

"Hey, baby—you sure about this? You're moving awful fast. Almost like you're trying to outrace your common sense."

Haylee gaped up at him. "Is that a bad thing?"

"For me, no. For you? Maybe."

Haylee shook her head. "Why are you so damned noble?"

"Am I? I just thought I was being decent."

Oh hell. He really *was* too good to be true. "You are. But let me regret this later. Not tonight, okay?"

"I'd prefer you don't regret it at all."

She didn't know what to say to that. "I… I don't intend to. I don't right now. And sure, I'm in a hurry, but you said you had to go soon. I don't want to regret that I *didn't* do this once you're gone. So please, Wolf. Please let's get back to feeling good together."

He seemed to hesitate, his eyes roving her face. And then he nodded as if he'd fought a battle with himself. She wasn't sure which part of him won, but she hoped it was the part intent on finishing what they'd started.

"Yeah," he said softly. "I want that too."

Chapter Nine

Jesus, this woman. Wolf could still taste her on his tongue. He wanted to shove his way into her body and fuck her hard until he came, but that wasn't his style. He didn't ever lose control. He believed that women were to be cherished, not used. Even when he fucked women he never intended to see again, he worshipped their bodies.

Women were perfect. Their bodies made for pleasure. He never forgot that. He never felt like they owed him or like their pleasure was dependent on his. He gave them the best he had, made them come, and then he took his pleasure while making them come again. And again.

Tonight, he wasn't going to get that chance with Haylee. He had to go, and soon. But damn how he wanted to be inside her. So why was he arguing about it with her?

Because he wanted her to be happy about her

choice. He didn't want her regretting it once he was gone. She'd have a lot of time to consider what they'd done, and he might not come out on the good end of it. But then she told him she wanted to feel good, and damn if he could deny her.

She rolled on the condom and he thought he might come unglued as her hands stroked over him. But then it was done and she lay beneath him, her body open for his pleasure. He grasped his cock and positioned it at her entrance. Then he pushed in slowly while her jaw went slack and her eyes dilated.

"Oh," she said on a gasp.

He throbbed deep inside her. She was tight and hot and so damned wet. Perfect. He held himself above her, gazing down at the perfection of her tits held high by the bra he hadn't removed. She'd shed the button-down shirt but the T-shirt was shoved up around her collarbone. He wound his fist into the fabric and tugged it upwards. She lifted herself until he could pull it off her, and then her hands found his shoulders, his biceps, stroking softly. Driving him wild with her sweet touch.

Wolf dropped down until he could kiss her. He held himself perfectly still for far longer than he thought possible, feeling his body throbbing deep inside hers. She quivered around him, and he took the time to really feel it. Then he began to move, slowly, so slowly. But he couldn't keep it slow. Not with Haylee. Their tongues tangled, bodies rising and falling faster and faster in a familiar rhythm. And not familiar, because something about it seemed so much more profound than usual. Or maybe that was just the situation. He'd never—not once—crossed a line with someone he'd rescued. It wasn't what he did.

But here he was, deep inside this woman, his body on fire, his balls aching with the need to release, his brain not wanting it to be over. Because then he had to leave. He would walk out of here and not see her again for days. Maybe weeks.

And even then, he couldn't really start to see her. His life was too chaotic. Plus he had to focus on doing whatever it took to help his parents get custody of Taylor and Jack. Hell, he already owed Haylee too much money for beating him at pool. He should have stuck to the five bucks a shot, but he'd goaded her into offering more. He could afford it, but barely. What he couldn't afford was to spend money taking her out and treating her right. She deserved to be treated like a princess and he wasn't the guy to do it.

No, he was the guy for a night of hot sex and no promises.

"Damn, Haylee—you feel so good," he groaned in her ear. "So good."

"Wolf," she gasped. "More. Right there. Faster. Please!"

His cock was on fire, his balls so tight they hurt, and still he kept pumping into her. Holding on hard. Trying not to let go until she exploded around him once again. It wasn't easy. Haylee was so sexy, so real, that he wanted to let go and fill her with his release.

He wanted to pump into her until he was spent, and then he wanted to roll over and take her with him, kiss her on the mouth and hold her tight until they fell asleep again. He wanted it more than he'd wanted anything in a long time.

He angled his body, slipped his hand between them, and rubbed her clit. She caught fire, her body stiffening and shaking beneath him as she came, gasping his name into the air between them. He pressed her knees back against the mattress and put his mouth to her neck, sucking the skin there. It was a primal need to mark her. He thrust harder now, deeper, until his balls exploded and he came in a rush of pleasure so strong he saw stars.

He lay on top of her, panting, trying to collect his thoughts and his strength. Her mouth was on his shoulder, soft and wet, and her arms wrapped around him. "That was amazing, Wolf," she said softly. "So amazing."

It was. He couldn't find his voice for long moments. And then he pushed himself up and propped his weight on an elbow. "You okay?"

Her smile was sweet. Dreamy. "Oh yeah. You?"

"Yeah."

"So when do you have to go?"

"Soon. Unless you want me to go now."

"No, I really don't. But I don't want to hold you up either. I know you have important things to do."

He dropped a kiss on her lips. "Nothing's more important to me right now than this."

Her palms pressed to his chest. "You shouldn't say things like that."

"Why not? It's true."

"For now."

"Now's what we have, Haylee. You should always live for now because there are no guarantees."

Her expression fell and he felt like an ass. "I know."

He dipped his lips to hers, kissed her sweetly. "Hey, hey. Don't be sad. I'm sorry. I shouldn't have said that."

"It's okay. I can't help but think about Nicole. She'd agree with you, by the way. I'm just sorry she didn't get more life to live."

"I'm sorry you lost her."

"Me too."

He kissed her again. "I gotta take care of this condom. But I'm coming back. And then you can tell me all about her, okay?"

She laughed, but the sound wasn't happy. "You're too good to be true, Dean. Much too good to be true. Nicole would have liked you."

"That's sweet of you to say." He kissed her again and then slipped from her body and went into the bathroom to dispose of the condom. He washed his face and hands, then looked at himself in the mirror as he dried off. His eyes were hard, troubled. He liked Haylee a lot, but he wasn't being fair to her. He had nothing to give her beyond tonight. So why stay and encourage her to share with him?

LYNN RAYE HARRIS

He tossed the towel onto the sink and turned, willing himself to go back in there and tell her he had to get back to his team. But when he walked into the bedroom and saw her lying there, her golden skin exposed, her limbs long and her curves lush, a new drumbeat of lust started hammering in his brain, his balls. His dick started to harden.

He needed her again. One more time before he left. But he'd told her he wanted to hear about her friend and that was more important. He climbed onto the bed and gathered her in his arms. "So tell me about Nicole."

Her hand splayed over his chest. "You know what, Wolf? I want to, but I can't help thinking that you're about to leave—and I want more of you and me right now."

He pulled her over until she was straddling him. His dick throbbed against her mound. "I want that too."

Her mouth settled over his and they lost themselves again. Somehow, Wolf found a condom and rolled it on between kisses. And then he was balls deep inside her again, thrusting into her silken heat. Telling himself it was great sex, but it was still just sex.

And when it was over, when he'd lost control for the second time and come hard inside her, he shuddered and pulled her close. "That was amazing, Haylee. You're amazing."

She curled into his arms, kissing his chest and

neck. "Thank you, Wolf. Thanks for everything. I don't regret a thing."

He hoped that was still true tomorrow when she woke up. He held her close, waiting until she drifted off to sleep. And then he gently disentangled himself from her arms and stood. He found his clothes, tugged them on, and then went back over to the bed to stare down at her. She slept peacefully, her dark hair spread over the pillow like a silken wave, her long lashes fanning across her cheeks.

Wolf bent and pressed a kiss to her forehead even though he told himself not to do it. But she didn't wake, and he straightened again, melancholy creeping through him.

"Bye, Haylee Jamison. You're one special lady."

With that, he turned on his heel and left the room. Then he slipped through the door, made sure it locked behind him, and went to join his team. Time to roll.

———

HAYLEE WOKE WITH A START, blinking into the darkness. It took her eyes a few moments to adjust, but she realized it was actually light outside. Probably just around dawn considering how dim the light was. Her body was languid and sated and she stretched indolently. What a delicious dream she'd been having!

Except it wasn't a dream. It took her only a few seconds to remember everything that had happened. Wolf, here in her room. In her arms. The two of them naked and sweaty and hot as they explored the depths of pleasure together.

Haylee pushed herself upright in bed. A delicious soreness throbbed between her legs. Wolf had been there, his thick cock taking her places she'd not thought possible. Her neck throbbed too and she realized he'd left his mark on her. A possessive mark meant to remind her of all they'd done.

As if she could forget. "Whoa damn, Nicole," she said into the empty room. "I really went there this time."

Her heart flipped and her belly dropped. Oh how she wished Nicole was really here to talk to. Her friend would love to hear *all* the details about Wolf and what he was like in bed. They'd shared those kinds of details before, though Haylee found herself imagining their girl talk and being reluctant to discuss Wolf as clinically as she'd done other men in the past.

As if there was something special about him. About what they'd done. There wasn't. She knew that. It was just sex—and yet it was probably the best sex of her life. Maybe that had everything to do with how quickly it had happened, how little they really knew each other—or maybe it was how dangerous he was, because he certainly was. Sure, he'd been sweet to her, and he'd treated her like she was important and special, but there was a hard man behind those soft caresses. The kind of man who could parachute into a war zone and slit his enemy's throat before returning home to make love to his lady as if nothing had happened.

Because that was pretty much an accurate representation of the previous couple of days. Except for the part where he made love to his lady because a) she wasn't his lady and b) she couldn't call what they'd done making love.

Wow, she'd had a one night stand. She blinked at the wall opposite and processed that. She'd never had one of those before, never fallen into bed so quickly with a man she'd just met, a man she knew she probably wouldn't see again. Oh sure, he said he'd find her back home. That he owed her money and he'd pay up. She didn't expect it because she hadn't been serious about the money in the first place. He knew it as well as she did. The bet had been in good fun. Besides, the most important part of the bet he'd paid up on. Kisses, and plenty of them. Delicious kisses she'd never get again.

A strange melancholy settled on her then. Wolf was gone and she was alone. The whole thing was like a fever dream. Not real. Brought on by stress. Haylee sucked in a breath, determined to get on with it. She got up and showered, then dressed again in the clothes she'd been given. The mark on her neck wasn't too apparent, but it was noticeable. She stood and looked at her reflection in the mirror, turning her head this way and that, pressing her fingers against Wolf's love bite. It wouldn't last, just like their night together hadn't lasted.

Haylee abruptly turned away, determined to put the night behind her. She wouldn't regret it, because she'd promised him she wouldn't, but she wouldn't dwell on it either. It was over and done. She'd had great sex with a hot military commando and it was over. Time to get back home and work on her exposé of the Juarez Cartel. Time to move on.

Chapter Ten

TWO MONTHS LATER

HAYLEE'S CELL PHONE RANG. She glanced at it, saw that it was Tony Davis calling, and frowned. She'd been talking to Tony a lot lately. He'd been dating Nicole right before she died, which Haylee hadn't known because they'd apparently wanted to keep it on the down low for the time being. Nicole hadn't been at her new job all that long, and the political action committee she'd been working for had been lobbying Senator Watson's office for regulatory action concerning opioids. According to Tony, Nicole had worried it might look bad if she were dating an attorney for the senator—and considering her own history with opioid addiction, she'd wanted to be doubly careful. It made sense even though Haylee couldn't help but feel a little hurt that her bestie hadn't confided in her.

Nicole had talked about Tony a little bit, and Haylee knew her friend had been interested in him, but the information that they were actually dating had not been something she'd shared, which surprised Haylee.

Tony was calling more often lately, and he asked more questions about Haylee's work. She got it—he was interested in her progress because it kept him connected to Nicole—but she didn't really like sharing what she was working on with anyone. Especially now that she'd found a new lead.

Still, Haylee picked up the phone and took a deep breath. "Hi, Tony. What's up?"

"Hey, babe. Just checking in. How have you been?"

Haylee leaned back in her chair. Her neck ached. Her temples throbbed with a dull headache. And loneliness wound itself into her days like a snake coiling around a tree. "Oh, you know. Good enough."

"How's the story coming?"

Haylee pinched the bridge of her nose and craned her head from side to side, stretching her neck. "It's coming. Nothing concrete yet."

But she was getting there. She'd written about her experience in the jungles of Mexico and Guatemala, minus specifics about the military unit that had rescued her and the others, and she'd been digging deep into the Juarez Cartel, tracing their supply lines as far as she could. It was tedious work but it was beginning to pay off. She'd found someone willing to talk, a drug courier with a grudge, and what he'd hinted at was nothing short of explosive. But he was too scared to give specific details, so she still lacked a smoking gun. She just had to be patient and keep trying.

For now, she had nothing she could use to take down the Juarezes or the man rumored to be profiting off the flow of fake drugs into the US. Billionaire Oscar Silva donated large sums of money to certain political candidates, including Senator Watson, and he owned a lot of land on the border. Not that the senator was implicated in any way, because so far he wasn't. Haylee still didn't know if the information about Silva was correct or if someone was trying to send her on a wild goose chase—but she wasn't giving up. She had nothing else to occupy her free time anyway.

Wolf had not gotten in touch. Two months, and she'd heard nothing. Not that she'd expected to. She'd almost gone to Laurel and started frequenting the bars there, especially the ones with pool tables, but she'd refrained. If he didn't want to see her, then he didn't want to see her. She'd thought the night they'd shared was special, but clearly he had not. And she wasn't going to embarrass herself by chasing after him.

"You may never get anything you can use," Tony said, bringing her back to the present moment.

"There've been no more deaths in the metro area from tainted drugs. I think maybe Nicole and the others got a bad batch."

Haylee's heart throbbed. It was true. Besides Nicole, eight other people had died that they knew of. There'd been a record number of overdoses in ERs lately, and many of those had fentanyl in the opioid mix, but Narcan seemed to work in those instances. It hadn't worked for Nicole, unfortunately, or for the others who'd died.

"I know. But I'm not ready to give up yet."

Tony sighed. "I know, babe."

She didn't like hearing babe from his lips but she didn't correct him. Instead she thought about Wolf calling her babe. Stroking her skin. Kissing her. Seriously, she needed to stop thinking about that man. It was a one-night stand and it was over.

"So what are you up to, Tony? Work keeping you busy?"

"When isn't it?" He laughed. "Hey, I called about something specific this time, believe it or not. I thought you'd like to come to the senator's fundraiser with me. You might make some connections you could use for your story."

Haylee's belly tightened. Oscar Silva might be there. Not that she could sashay up to him and ask him point blank if he knew anything about the drugs being smuggled into ports, but maybe she'd get something just by being in the same room with him. She didn't know what, but it wasn't the kind of opportunity she was going to turn down. Though she considered it for half a second.

"It's not a date, Haylee. I just want to help," Tony said when she didn't answer right away.

"Sorry, I was thinking about something. Yes, I'd love to go. Thanks."

Haylee leaned back in her desk chair, her gaze hitting a photo of her and Nicole that she kept on the shelf above her head. They were laughing hysterically about something. She didn't know what, she only knew she loved the photo.

"It's tomorrow night at the Ritz. Eight o'clock. I'll pick you up."

"No, that's okay. I can meet you there."

"You sure? It's no problem to swing by and get you."

Haylee bit her lip. It would feel too much like a date if he did that. And she wasn't going on a date with a guy who'd been seeing her best friend before she'd died. Didn't matter that he'd told her it wasn't a date. When a man picked a woman up at her house, the two of them dressed to kill, and then took her to an event—that was a date.

"No, no problem. I'll text you when I get there."

"Okay, great. See you tomorrow night."

"See you." Haylee hung up and sat staring at the words on the screen. Oscar Silva might not even be at the party. But if he was?

Haylee frowned. If he was, she needed to be the kind of woman he found irresistibly attractive. She opened a new tab on her browser and got to work finding out exactly what tripped the man's trigger. If she was lucky, he'd notice her—and then maybe she could learn a thing or two if she played her cards right.

———

HAYLEE ARRIVED AT 8:20. She didn't want to be early, and she didn't want to be too late, so she timed her arrival and exited the Uber she'd called to whisk her to the Ritz.

"Welcome to the Ritz, ma'am," a uniformed doorman said, opening the door with a flourish.

"Thank you." She passed inside, her phone in her hand, and texted Tony. The lobby of the Ritz was sheer elegance. A combination of sophistication and modernity, the white marble and elaborate moldings drew the eye.

A few moments later, Tony appeared, looking handsome in a black tux with a white shirt and black tie. His brows lifted at the sight of her, but then he played it off and opened his arms. Haylee went into them for a quick hug.

"You look wonderful," he said in her ear.

Haylee blushed. She'd worn a white dress that clung to her curves and tall black heels. She was uncomfortable as hell since she normally liked to wear yoga pants and tank tops or sweat shirts, but the mirror told her she looked fabulous with her curves on display. She'd done it because it's what Silva liked, and she hoped it drew his attention. If he took her into his circle, thinking her the kind of woman who frequented the places where powerful men gathered because she was looking for a sugar daddy, then he might not be so careful about what he said.

And yet her uncharacteristic clothing wasn't all that made her uncomfortable. It was Tony and the possessive hand on her arm. The way he curved his body around hers, the tickle of his breath in her ear. It had been seven months since Nicole had died—and Haylee had to wonder if Tony's motives weren't all that pure. He'd known Nicole for a month. He'd known Haylee for several more than that.

He stepped back, smiling, and a pang of guilt wracked her. Seriously, if he was hitting on her, why would he be so subtle about it? Especially after seven months? Haylee chastised herself silently. It was ridiculous to think so. Tony was affected by Nicole's death, just as she was. He swore that Nicole had been unlike any woman he'd ever known. That they'd connected strongly. Of course he'd still be feeling the weight of her loss if she'd been that important to him.

"Thank you," Haylee said, dropping her gaze. He didn't touch her again and she felt like she could breathe once more. "I'm sorry I'm late."

He offered her an arm, very proper like. She took it. "You aren't late. I swear I was bored to tears by Senator Carlson's chief of staff anyway. She cornered me and I was ready to stab myself to get away."

Haylee laughed. "Good thing I texted then."

"Definitely a good thing."

He led her to the ballroom where the event was taking place. The room was packed with Washington's elite, wining and dining and schmoozing, everyone looking for an advantage. Tony led her to the buffet table, snagging a couple of glasses of champagne along the way and handing her one.

He let her go and fixed a plate. She did the same and then they retreated to a table nearby. He stabbed a mushroom and popped it into his mouth. "Have you found anything new on the Juarez Cartel?"

Haylee's stomach squeezed. "No. Nothing useful anyway. They're pressing pills in the jungle and smuggling them into the US. But that's not a secret—or not a big one, anyway."

"But you don't know where they're entering?"

Haylee shook her head as she skewered a mozzarella ball. "No. And even if I did, I don't think that's the main story."

Tony frowned. "You don't?"

Shit, why had she said that?

"Not really. But I don't know what is," she added. It was habit to keep her ideas close to the chest. Just like a poker player. But in reality what she thought was that the Juarez Cartel had an inside track. They had to. Getting anything across the border wasn't exactly easy, especially with the tightening security there due to the drug trade, but someone was doing it. Was it Oscar Silva?

Tony frowned as he skewered another mushroom and popped it into his mouth. "Be careful, Haylee. There are powerful people with a lot of incentive to see things continue as they are. Don't get in the middle of something you can't handle."

Haylee flushed hot, but she lowered her voice. "Are you telling me to let it go? To pretend it's not happening?"

"That's not what I'm saying. Just be careful where you poke your nose in. That's all. The senator is working with law enforcement to put a stop to the flow of drugs, but it's not going to happen overnight. We *are* making progress, though. I promise we are."

Haylee's eyes stung. Her throat ached with all she wanted to say, but it would do no good. It wasn't Tony's fault that men like Oscar Silva literally got away with murder. He didn't like it any more than she did, she knew that, but it infuriated her that they couldn't make it stop sooner. That nobody had to pay for Nicole's death, or the deaths of the others who died because they took a drug they were addicted to, expecting it to be what they needed rather than a trip to the morgue.

"Nobody cares about addicts," she said bitterly, setting her plate down and twisting the champagne in her hand. "People think it could never happen to them, or that those who're addicted are lowlifes and criminals and deserve what they get. Nobody deserves what happened to Nicole—or the hundreds like her who may not get fentanyl in their drugs, but

LYNN RAYE HARRIS

still die because they're on the margins and nobody cares."

Tony's expression was sad. "I know, Haylee. I agree with you. And I'm working to fix it, I swear to you."

Haylee closed her eyes for a second and willed the anger and bitterness to subside. Not for the first time, she wished Wolf was here. That she'd open her eyes and he'd be standing in front of her, gorgeous gray-blue eyes filled with sympathy and understanding. He got it because his sister was an addict. She wondered if his parents had gotten custody of their grandchildren yet, and how Wolf's sister was doing.

Why didn't you call me, Wolf?

"Shit," Tony said, and Haylee opened her eyes. He was looking down at his phone. He smiled apologetically. "The senator needs me for a few minutes. Do you mind?"

Haylee smiled to reassure him. "Not at all. Do what you have to do. I'm fine."

He stood, gazing down at her with concern. "I'll be back as soon as I can."

"Take your time. I'm here to mingle, remember?"

He sighed. "Just be subtle with your questions, okay?"

"Subtle is my middle name." She made an X over her heart. "Swear to God."

He laughed. "Good. And Haylee…"

"Yes?"

"Watch out for other dangers, okay?"

126

"What's that supposed to mean?"

"It means there are men here who're already looking at you like you're their next meal. Don't let it happen."

"I can take care of myself, Tony. Don't you worry about that."

He nodded once. Then he melted into the crowd and she was alone. Haylee set her plate down and a waiter whisked it away. She took a swig of champagne for courage and then stood, keeping the flute in her hand but determined not to drink more than necessary. A slow spin around the room brought attention, as Tony had said, but none of them was Silva. Oscar Silva was five-eight, graying, pudgy—and not here. Haylee frowned as she retreated to a corner to watch and think.

Ten minutes later, a new arrival walked in with a woman trailing behind him, and her heart kicked up a few beats. Silva was wearing a tux and smiling broadly as Senator Watson strode over to greet him. Tony was nearby, watching the meeting but not a part of it. Watson and Silva shook hands and a photographer snapped a photo. Tony's gaze left his boss and searched the crowd—looking for her, no doubt. She smiled when their gazes met. He frowned.

But then she took a sip of her champagne and lifted her chin, sweeping her glossy black hair over her shoulder. Her dress was the stuff of wet dreams. Her shoes were of the Fuck Me variety. And she was definitely Silva's catnip. She'd made sure of it, from the extra makeup she'd donned to the tight dress and sky-high heels and flowing hair—he liked long hair, not short and not pinned up. Her lipstick was red, her nails matching. She started to walk, sashaying with exaggerated movements toward the place where Silva stood talking to the senator. The crowd parted as if she were Moses and they the Red Sea until she was nearly upon them.

Oscar Silva turned. She could see the moment he spotted her because his eyes widened and then traveled down her body and back up appreciatively. The woman who'd walked in with him stood nearby, glaring. She was blond and gorgeous, but maybe without the extra junk in the trunk that Haylee possessed.

"Senator," Haylee said a touch breathlessly when she reached them. Senator Watson turned, blinking, smiling automatically as career politicians did. "I just wanted to thank you for all you're doing to stop the illicit drug trade."

"My pleasure, Miss…"

"Jamison. Haylee Jamison," she supplied, offering her hand. He took it gently.

"Well, Miss Jamison, we're definitely doing all we can on that front. It's a great problem. Very great. But we're working on it."

"Yes, I know. Thank you soooo much."

"Have you met Mr. Silva?" the senator asked. "He's a great ally for the war on drugs."

Haylee turned to Oscar Silva, who did his best to look humble but couldn't pull it off if his life depended on it. "Miss Jamison," he said, offering his hand. "It is an issue I care very deeply about."

She put her hand in his, her stomach turning at the touch of his skin on hers. She didn't *know* that he was really involved with the Juarez Cartel, but her source had insisted it was true. And how else would the drugs make it across?

"As do I, Mr. Silva. Thank you so much."

He didn't let go of her hand. His thumb rubbed against her skin. "Perhaps I could buy you a drink and we could discuss it further?"

Haylee's heart throbbed. She didn't cut her eyes to Tony but she could feel his disapproval. "Yes, I would like that very much," she purred, even though her insides churned.

Silva drew her in closer, wrapping her arm around his. "Excellent," he replied, his heavy-lidded gaze dropping to her mouth and then to her breasts. "I think we should have a very long talk about this. Amanda," he snapped over his shoulder, "find us a table, would you? And then you may go."

Bastard, Haylee thought. But she let him lead her to the bar, smiling vacuously the whole way. If there was anything she could learn from this man, then she intended to learn it. No matter how much he made her skin crawl.

Chapter Eleven

WOLF DIDN'T MUCH LIKE THESE PRIVATE SECURITY jobs, but he took them whenever they came up because he made good money doing it. He needed the money if his parents were going to get custody of Taylor and Jack. They were close to succeeding, and he was determined to help. Tonight, the job was a fundraiser for Senator Frank Watson of Arizona. Wolf and Gem and Easy were working this one together. He stood in one of the back entryways to the hotel, making sure that the special cake the senator's wife had ordered was delivered smoothly and with no surprises.

Mundane, sure, but also important not to let some idiot protestor in the back door. His phone rang. It was Gem.

"What's up?" he asked as the last of the attendants brought the cake inside. The door shut and he made sure it was locked before following the cake down the hall.

"I think you might want to make it in here before too long."

Gem was in the ballroom along with Easy and several other security personnel. There were others stationed at different points in the hotel, all discreet of course.

"Why? Are there strippers?"

"No. But there's a really gorgeous girl who looks a lot like the one we rescued from the jungle a couple months back."

Wolf's insides went cold. Haylee Jamison? Here? It was possible. He hadn't stopped thinking about her since they'd returned, but he'd also not looked her up like he'd promised. Because there'd been a couple of missions and things had gone haywire for a while. Then there was his sister and her kids—and he'd decided that the last thing he needed was to look up a sweet girl like Haylee just so he could fuck her up by being emotionally unavailable to her.

Haylee was going through her own issues and she needed more than he could give right now. More than he wanted to give. But hot damn, what a night they'd had. He'd nearly gone to her place a dozen times in the past two months, whenever he'd been home. But always he'd hesitated.

"You sure about that, man?"

"Black hair, golden skin, body that could make a man

promise her anything so long as he got to explore it? Yeah, I'm pretty fucking sure. Woman like that stands out in a crowd. And she's definitely standing out tonight."

Wolf's gut twisted. Did he want to walk in there and see her? What would he do? What would he say? Probably best if he didn't, come to think of it.

"Yeah, well, why are you telling me?"

Gem snorted. "Why? Because you kissed her in front of everyone and then spent the night with her even though you pretended you didn't? Because you've been a grumpy bastard for the past two months? Because I haven't seen you with a woman since that mission—because I've watched you *turn down* free pussy like a gay man with no use for it?"

Wolf growled. "Since when are you my daddy, Gem?"

"Look, just thought you'd like to know she's here."

"Not really," he said, though it wasn't true and now he was dying to get into the ballroom and see her with his own eyes.

"Good thing, I guess."

"Why's that?"

"Why? Because she's at a table with Oscar Silva—and he's looking mighty interested in what he sees."

Wolf's guts turned to ice. Oscar Silva? He wasn't the kind of man a girl like Haylee should get involved with. Silva was rumored to be dirty, though nobody had any proof of it. Informants disappeared. Evidence was somehow dismissed for being fabricated. Silva was, by all appearances, completely blameless. And yet things happened near him, like he was the eye of the storm and everything swirled in a crazy dark mass around his orbit. He was rich, power-ful, and connected. And he owned a lot of property on the border with Mexico.

Shit. She was still digging, still trying to piece together how the drugs that killed her friend had gotten into the country. And if she'd set her sights on Silva, she was aiming mighty high indeed. Not that he knew it for sure. But if anybody was involved in the drug trade, it was Silva.

"Soon as this cake gets to the kitchen, I'm on my way."

"Thought so, hoss."

"Shut up, Gem."

Gem laughed. "Yeah, like that ever worked before. See you in a few—and try not to blow a gasket when you see her, okay? Girl is hot as fuck. Over and out, Wolfman."

The line went dead and Wolf dropped his phone into his suit jacket with a snarl. What the hell? Why couldn't he just have an uncomplicated life for a change? He'd avoided Haylee because his life was too crazy for her and she deserved better, but now he was about to walk into a room and lay eyes on her for the first time since he'd stood over her sleeping form and dropped a kiss on her forehead. He didn't know how that was going to make him feel, but he suspected it was going to be more painful than he was ready for.

Because he'd liked her. A lot. And not only that,

but he'd felt a certain kind of peace with her that night. Like being with her was somehow better than being with any other woman. Kissing her, licking her, sliding into her body and hearing her moans, feeling her pulsate around him as she came—he could remember it as if it was yesterday. He'd wanted more of her, and he'd intended to get it when he'd walked away that morning.

But then he'd gotten on the plane that took them out of El Salvador and he'd started thinking about what it would mean to see her back home. To actually show up on her doorstep. Would he take her on a date? Would they have sex? Would he want more of the same? And what happened when he had to leave her and head out on another mission? Or when she wanted more from him than no-strings sex?

He'd actually thought about it. Thought the whole thing out. He watched Saint and Hacker with their women and he imagined what it would be like if he had a woman. If Haylee was his woman. He took it all the way to a picket fence and a baby before his freak-out meter pegged.

And then he'd really thought about it and realized it wasn't going to happen. He couldn't afford to get distracted, and Haylee was a huge distraction. Not just because of the sex. It was more than that. She was smart and insightful and she wasn't ever going to be content with a man like him. There was too much he couldn't tell her, because of the job, and Haylee wasn't the type of woman to accept long absences and vague explanations.

Wolf clenched his teeth together and told himself he'd made the right decision. He finished escorting the cake to the kitchen and then walked to the ball-room and stood outside the service entrance for a second. Then he pushed the door open and prepared to come face to face with the woman he hadn't stopped thinking about since the moment their eyes had met in the Guatemalan jungle two months ago.

———

OSCAR SILVA WAS A POMPOUS ASS. A narcissistic, self-important, pompous ass. Haylee sat at his table and smiled, nodding as he talked. He skimmed his fingers along her arm from time to time, and she tried not to shudder with revulsion.

"And so I focus money on the problem," he said. "It is a very real problem, and I support Senator Watson in his desire to rid our country of this terrible nuisance."

"My best friend died," Haylee interjected. "From pills that were not what they seemed."

Oscar Silva's face contorted in a frown. "Oh, that is terrible, Miss Jamison. May I call you Haylee?" His thumb skimmed the inside of her wrist and his lips curved in a slick smile.

"Yes, of course," she said, tamping down on the disgust rising like bile in her throat.

"It is a real problem, Haylee. And yet it would not be if there were not a demand for it."

She should keep her mouth shut and just listen, but she couldn't. "Are you saying that people who take prescription drugs as directed, and then get addicted, are somehow to blame for that addiction?" She couldn't keep the hard edge out of her voice, no matter how she tried.

Oscar Silva's eyes sparked for a second. "Not at all, my dear. I'm simply saying that if there was not a demand, the cartels would not supply it. Until we curb the demand, we cannot expect to completely eradicate the supply."

Haylee's heart throbbed. "We can't? Even when we have borders and protocols? We can't stop illegal drugs from coming into this country and reaching the streets of cities like Washington, DC? Really, that is beyond our ability?"

Oscar Silva's gaze grew icy. Haylee told herself to stop, just stop, but her anger wasn't going to let her. She'd only meant to sit and listen, to simper and flatter and glean whatever information she could from him, but she wasn't capable of simpering.

He drew himself up coolly. "It's not so simple as you wish. Nothing ever is."

Haylee chastised herself and tried to be meek. She even managed to squeeze his hand for a second before letting it go again. "Of course you are right. I'm just so passionate about the cause that I sometimes forget myself."

He seemed to relax, his smile inching upward again. He leaned in and let his gaze drop to her chest. Linger. *Do not visibly recoil, Haylee. Do NOT.*

"Understandable, my dear." He threaded his fingers in hers and then lifted her hand and kissed it. "I must make the rounds, but perhaps we can escape the crowds in half an hour or so? Continue our discussion somewhere more private?"

Her stomach churned. "That sounds lovely, Mr. Silva."

"Oscar. Please."

"Oscar then."

He stood and bowed over her hand like a courtly knight of old. It was completely fake and utterly insulting, but Haylee smiled as if flattered beyond belief.

"I'll send someone for you, pretty lady. Until then, amuse yourself."

Amuse herself? Really? Was this a fucking historical romance and he was the duke? Haylee's smile ached. "I shall, dear Oscar."

Uh oh, that was over the top.

Except he didn't blink an eye. He kissed her hand again and strode away, into the crowd. Haylee let out the breath she didn't know she'd been holding. Then she picked up her drink and took a healthy swig. "Holy cow," she muttered. "What have I gotten myself into?"

She set the drink down and let her gaze roam the crowd. What was she supposed to do now? Accept

Silva's invitation to go somewhere more private, where he would no doubt make advances she was unwilling to accept, even in the name of research? Or disappear now, with no more information than she'd had before?

If she wanted to get to the bottom of this, she had to keep going, right? Despite her revulsion, she had to do it for Nicole.

Her gaze slid across the room—and then rocked to a stop when it landed on a man standing near the wall. His gaze was on her, and their eyes locked. Her heart skipped several beats. Wolf was in a suit, tall and broad and imposing, and he glared back at her with a heat she couldn't ignore. He was suddenly on the move, making his way toward her, and her belly turned inside out.

She couldn't move. She was frozen like a rabbit who'd sighted the big bad wolf. Inside, her brain laughed hysterically at the joke. Outside, she pasted on a fake smile and waited. He loomed tall and large in front of her. She lifted her drink and sipped as if she didn't have a care in the world though inside she quaked.

"Haylee Jamison," he said, a truckload of meaning contained in those two words. "How are you?"

She ran through a thousand scenarios in her head. None of them were the perfect combination of set down and cool response that she wanted them to be.

"Well, well. Dean. Didn't expect to see you again.

No, wait, I *did* expect to see you again. About six weeks ago or so."

His eyes popped for a second, and then he laughed. "Goddamn, Haylee. You don't waste any time getting to the point, do you?"

"No. Why prevaricate? You said you'd find me. I expected you to do so. You owe me money." Not that she cared about the money. In fact, the money was the farthest thing from her mind. She was more hurt that he'd ignored her. That he'd lied when he said he'd come for her once they were home again. He'd memorized her address—or pretended to—and then nothing.

"I know," he said softly. "Haven't forgotten that. I've been busy."

"Oh, really? Sorry to hear that." Ice couldn't melt in her mouth. She was cold and unattached and uncaring. And yet her heart hammered a million beats a second. Her pulse was a crazy thing. Her skin heated and cooled and heated again.

"I should have gotten in touch sooner."

"You could have mailed a check, you know." She didn't care about the damned money. So why was she harping on it? *Because it was easy. Concrete. A thing to focus on.*

"Yep, could have. Should have."

God, he looked good. From his blond hair to his gray-blue eyes, to the muscles beneath the suit jacket he wore. She contrasted her reaction to Oscar Silva with her reaction to Wolf. Why was it so different?

Why couldn't she fake it better with Silva? Why did Wolf make her breath shorten and her belly twist and, God help her, her nipples harden?

Haylee waved a hand dismissively. "Forget it, Dean. It's not important. I don't really want your money. I was just pointing out what a hypocrite you are."

Oooh, bitter much?

His gaze dropped over her body. Unlike with Silva, her skin tingled at the heated look he gave her. "You look amazing, Haylee."

"Thanks." She slid her finger along the rim of her glass, around and around, trying so hard to ignore him. It didn't really work.

"So tell me what you're doing here."

"Oh, you know. Attending a function. I have a date, actually." She lifted her chin and craned her head around the room, looking for Tony. He'd disappeared, of course.

"You mean Oscar Silva? You sure you want to date a man like that?"

Her gaze snapped to his. His eyes blazed with anger. Shocking.

"First of all, you have no right to tell me what to do. Second of all, it's none of your business who I go out with. You and I were a one-night stand, nothing more." She flicked her fingers at him. "Move along, Dean."

"Silva is dangerous, Haylee," he growled, leaning in close. "Don't bait that tiger. It's not worth the risk."

"Once more, your opinion isn't required. You had your chance. We spent a night together. You decided that was enough for you—and you know what, it was enough for me as well. I don't need to beg a man for his attention, no matter how much fun we might have had. It's over and done and I have nothing left to say to you." She got to her feet, pulse throbbing, and even though she was wearing heels, she still had to crane her neck back to look up at him. "If you will excuse me."

She took a step, intending to march away—and probably out the door and into the lobby where she'd call an Uber—but his fingers wrapped around her elbow and pressed just enough to halt her progress.

She spun on him and hissed, "Let me go."

"No."

———

WOLF HELD her arm firmly but not too tightly. Haylee was spitting mad. Not that he blamed her for it, but he couldn't let her put herself in danger by leaving with Oscar Silva.

"No? Since when do you get to tell me what to do?"

Wolf gripped her arm tighter as memories of the two of them in bed together assailed him. Even without that, she was making him crazy. He'd walked into the ballroom, his gaze instantly finding her. He hadn't even had to search for her. She'd simply been

there, her gorgeous body encased in a white dress that
clung to her curves, her black hair sleek and gorgeous
as it flowed down her back, her legs long and silky,
ending in a sky-high black shoe with a tiny strap that
wrapped around her ankle. He was obsessed with that
strap. Wanted to undo it with his teeth.

Ridiculous.

"Told you what to do in the jungle. You listened."

Her dark eyes snapped fire. "That was the jungle,
Neanderthal. We're back in civilization now, and you
are not the boss of me."

"I was," he said heatedly, his meaning unmistak-
able. He knew she got it because she swallowed
visibly.

"No. I did what you told me to do because you
were saving me." She purposely misunderstood him.

He snorted. "Not what I was talking about and
you know it."

Her cheeks went red beneath the creamy caramel
of her skin. "What do you want, Dean? I'm
busy here."

He propelled her away from the table she'd been
sitting at with Silva and toward the door he'd recently
come through. "I want to talk to you, Haylee. Just you
and me."

She didn't fight him as he guided her through the
crowd. When he reached the door, he scanned the
room until he saw Gem. Then he nodded once. Gem
nodded back. Wolf opened the door and Haylee hesitated only a moment before she walked through. He

let her go, then closed it behind him and turned to face her. She folded her arms beneath her breasts and glared.

So pretty.

"All right. I'm listening. What did you want to say so badly?"

What did he want to say? Everything. Nothing. "Stay away from Oscar Silva, Haylee. He's dangerous and you aren't equipped to handle him."

Her delicate nostrils flared. She was angry. "Do you let your girlfriends tell you how to conduct your job?"

He blinked. "I don't have any girlfriends."

She rolled her eyes. "But if you did. Would you let them dictate how you did your job?"

"No."

She snapped her fingers in his face. "Bingo, hotshot. You don't tell me how to do my job and I won't tell you how to do yours."

He wanted to kiss her. He didn't think that would go over very well. "I'm just trying to keep you safe. Silva is a criminal."

"Then why isn't he locked up?"

"Because he's rich and he's got people in his back pocket, that's why. You know the same rules don't apply to rich people that apply to us. The man donates millions to political candidates through PACs, probably has a judge or two in his back pocket, a few sheriffs. There are people who literally get away with murder in this country because they're rich enough to grease their paths—and they aren't the ones who get their hands dirty."

She frowned. "I've heard that he's connected to the Juarez Cartel. He knows about the pills—how they get in, where they go, where the material comes from in the first place."

A chill slid down his spine. "Haylee—what the fuck are you planning? To ask him about his involvement? To demand he stop funding drug runners? What can you possibly do to stop him?"

"I don't know," she said softly. "But I have to do *something.*"

Chapter Twelve

HAYLEE GAZED UP AT WOLF AND TRIED VERY HARD not to let her lip quiver. She was overwhelmed and pretending not to be. After two months of thinking about him and slowly realizing he wasn't ever coming around, it was a lot to be standing here in an elegant hallway in the Ritz, talking to him as if he was involved in her life. As if he cared about her.

He didn't. Or, strike that, he didn't care about her in any meaningful way. Of course he cared whether or not she was putting herself in danger, because that's what he did, but she could be anybody walking into the lion's den that was Oscar Silva's life and he'd be trying to stop her.

Except she really wasn't that stupid and she'd already decided she needed another way. She couldn't ask Silva any further questions. She damned sure couldn't be alone with him. She could poke around on the periphery of his orbit, but she wasn't getting pulled in any closer. The man had dead eyes—and that was something she couldn't pretend not to see.

Wolf frowned down at her. Hard. "Didn't you learn a goddamn thing in the jungle? Those people don't care, Haylee. They'd have killed you if they hadn't thought they could get someone to pay a ransom for your return. If he's working with them, he's the kind of guy who can have you eliminated. The only questions anybody'll be asking will be on a missing person's poster—*have you seen this woman?*"

"Look," she said, taking a step closer to him and then immediately regretting it. He was too close. His body too big and warm and hard. She could smell his scent, that combination of man and danger that had turned her on so much that night in El Salvador. The night she'd lain beneath him and felt the power of his body as it moved inside hers.

Stop thinking about it.

Haylee pressed on, poking a finger against his chest—and not at all surprised when the iron hard muscle didn't give way. "I'm not an idiot, Wolf—and I'm not getting involved with that man. Or asking him any questions. For your information, I was planning on finding my date"—okay, so Tony totally wasn't a date but she wasn't admitting that to Wolf—"and telling him I was leaving. Then I was going home to dig as deeply as I can into Oscar Silva's connections. I know people, and I've heard things. And I plan to find out how he's involved. *Without* putting myself in danger, believe it or not."

Wolf growled as he gripped her wrist and prevented her from moving away. And then, before she could stop him, he tugged her in close. Intimately close. Their bodies pressed together from breast to hip to thigh. A powerful shudder rolled through her as his heat seeped into her skin, her bones. He didn't move his hips, but she knew he was growing hard. Her body started to melt from the inside out, liquid heat flooding her, readying her for a night of hot sex with this man.

Sorry, body. Ain't happening.

"You think because you're walking away that you won't be in danger? If you dig too deeply, probe too much—if it reaches his ears—the effect is the same as if you went back in there and asked him point blank if he's funneling illegal drugs over the border. Be careful, Haylee."

Her breath grew shallow. She wanted to wrap herself around him. Purr. Get naked beneath him again. And judging by the thickness pressing into her abdomen, he wanted it too.

"You think I should let it go? That if I just wait, karma will catch up to these evil men and they'll pay for what they did to Nicole and those like her? Is that how *you* work, Wolf? Just let karma take care of it for you? Or do you charge in there and kill people before they can hurt anyone else?"

His nostrils flared. His gaze hardened. His jaw flexed. "Goddammit, Haylee. It's not the same thing."

Magnificent man. Beautiful man. Dangerous man.

"Literally, no. But it is the same. You don't let bad people get away with their crimes. That's all I want. I want the bad guys to pay."

Her phone rang, startling her. She jumped and scrambled for her evening bag. Wolf let her go and she fumbled the flap open and took out her phone. It was Tony. "Hi, Tony. What's up?"

"I couldn't find you. Did you leave?"

Haylee's heart throbbed as she gazed at Wolf. He was still frowning. Still looking delicious and unattainable and that made her belly ache with longing and even a soft fury for the past two wasted months. "No, I didn't leave. Are you done with the senator?"

"For the moment, yes."

"Tell me where to meet you." It hurt to say those words because she really wanted to leave the party. With the man standing in front of her, but it wasn't what he wanted. She didn't even have to ask him to know.

"How about by the stage?"

"Sounds good. I'll see you in a couple of minutes." She ended the call and slipped her phone back into her bag.

"Was that Silva?"

She shook her head. "No, that's my date. Tony is an attorney for Senator Watson. He was called away, which is how I ended up talking to Silva. But he's done now, and I need to go and join him."

"Guess this is goodbye then."

"Guess so."

"It was good to see you again."

Anger twisted inside her. "No it wasn't. It would have been good if you'd wanted to see me—but you didn't. We both know it, so don't lie to make me feel better."

His expression clouded. "Haylee, it's not you. It was never you. You're terrific."

"I *am* terrific," she said, because his words hurt and she was angry. She turned to go, then spun back to him one more time. "Forget the money, Wolf. Send it to your parents. Did they get custody yet?"

He shook his head. "Soon. We hope."

"I hope so too. And I hope your sister gets better. Some people beat it and I really do hope she's one of them."

"I know you do. Thank you." He took his phone from his pocket when she started to leave him again. "Give me your number," he said.

She gaped at him. "Why?"

"Because I'm going to text you, that's why. So you'll have my number if you need it."

"Why would I need it?"

"I don't know. But if you ever do… Just give it to me, Haylee."

She didn't know why she did it, but she recited her number. A few seconds later, she felt a ping as he sent her a text. He put his phone away. "There. If you need me, I'll answer."

Haylee nodded. Then she marched over to the door they'd come through and yanked it open with blurry eyes. She strode through without looking back, her heart pounding the entire way.

WOLF CUSSED himself out for a good five minutes while he stood outside the ballroom. He was also waiting for his dick to calm the fuck down. Being pressed against her like that, even for a few moments, was almost more than he could take. Why did she had to be so soft in all the right places? Why did she have to smell so damned good and make him want things he couldn't have right now?

With a last snarl to himself for being such a fucking idiot, he headed back inside the ballroom and took up station near the stage where the senator was supposed to give a speech in about ten minutes. Gem was there too, and he lifted a brow in question. Wolf shook his head. Gem shrugged.

The crowd parted and Haylee stood nearby, talking to a tall, athletically built man with dark hair and wire-rimmed glasses. He looked smart and studious. Definitely a lawyer. He was smiling down at her and Wolf swallowed the urge to go over and wrap his arm around Haylee's shoulders and claim her for his.

So fucking pretty. She made his sternum ache just looking at her. An odd reaction for him, sure. But he liked her and he wished he'd gone about this whole damned thing differently.

He had her number, but he wasn't going to use it. He didn't know why he'd done it, but he'd been acting on impulse. And now he had a way to contact her even though he wouldn't.

She looked up, almost as if she felt his gaze on her, and their eyes met. His gut tightened. Her date said something else and then she turned away, hooked her arm in his, and let him lead her to a table. Senator Watson came out and made his speech and people clapped and cheered as he hit upon points they liked. When he finished, he headed out into the crowd to press hands and talk to his donors. Oscar Silva sat at a different table from Haylee, but his gaze kept straying to her whenever there was a lull in the conversation. Finally, he bent toward one man and said something in his ear. The man leaned forward, looked at Haylee, and then nodded.

Wolf stood his ground as the man approached her and made gestures to Silva's table. The man with Haylee—Tony, she'd called him—frowned at her, but eventually they both got up and went over to join Silva and his followers.

Easy sidled up to Wolf. "Man, you look like you could bite a railroad spike in two. What's eating you?"

"Her," he said, jerking his chin toward Haylee.

"Oh damn. Yeah, saw her earlier. You talk to her yet?"

"Yeah, we talked."

"Dude, not for nothing, but you haven't been quite the same since you banged her."

Wolf's gut churned. "Don't say that."

"Why not? It's true. You've been a lot quieter than usual."

"I'm talking about saying I banged her. Don't say that. It's disrespectful."

Easy studied him. "Okay, if that's what you want."
"It is."

"Then you haven't been the same since you *spent time* with her. We've all noticed it."

"I've had a lot going on in my life. It's not her."

Easy held up his hands. "Whatever you say, man. Though you just said it was her, by the way."

He had said that by omission. *Fuck.* "Go away."
"Sure thing."

Easy strolled away and Wolf circled the crowd, doing the job he'd been hired to do, but always keeping an eye on Haylee. After about an hour, she got up with her date. Wolf stopped and watched Silva's table as Haylee said her goodbyes. She put her hand in Silva's. He kissed the back of it rather than shaking it, and Tony's jaw tightened. So did Wolf's. A few moments later and she was walking out of the ballroom with Tony on her heels. Wolf hated to see her go, but he was also damned thankful she wasn't leaving with Silva. This Tony guy was bad enough, but not because he was dangerous.

Wolf didn't start to breathe again until she'd been gone for about twenty minutes. Silva hadn't moved. He was still holding court, laughing and drinking and eyeing beautiful women like they were his for the taking. Many of them were, but at least Haylee wasn't. She'd left. Walked out with her date and Silva's attention had moved on.

Thank God. Except that she'd also walked out with another man, and Wolf couldn't stop thinking about that. About how Tony had held his fingers in the small of her back like a perfect gentleman, escorting her from the room. How her white dress clung to her curves as she walked and how Tony's gaze must have surely been on her ass. Wolf's had been. He knew what it was like to have his hands on that ass, knew how soft her skin was and how perfectly she fit beneath him.

Knew what she tasted like.

"Shit," he muttered. "Stop. Just fucking stop."

"Man, you know what they say when you talk to yourself." Gem was standing beside him, eyebrow arched, grinning like an idiot.

Irritation shot through him. "No, what do they say?"

"That you aren't getting laid enough."

Wolf frowned at his teammate. Then he snorted. "They do not fucking say that. Nobody says that."

Gem laughed. "No, but maybe they should."

"Yeah, fine. Whatever."

"So you want to head to Buddy's when this is over? See who you can take home for the night?"

Wolf thought about it. He really did. He even thought about Haylee walking out the door with Tony on her heels. "Naw, man. I'm good. Just gonna go home and chill."

Gem shrugged. "Whatever makes you happy."

"Thanks for the invite anyway."

"Sure thing."

Trouble was, Wolf didn't know what made him happy anymore.

———

HAYLEE WOKE around two a.m. She didn't know what had made her wake, but her heart raced and she lay there listening in the darkness for any noise. Had there been a thump? A sound that jerked her awake?

Or had she been thinking about Wolf and the way his heat burned into her when they were pressed together outside the Ritz ballroom? If she slid her hand between her legs, she could take care of the ache that hadn't gone away since the moment she'd felt the hardness between his legs pushing back against her.

Haylee threw the covers back with a growl and slipped her legs over the side. No way was she lying here alone and rubbing herself into orgasm just because she'd seen that blue-eyed devil again. She sat for a moment, then got up and ghosted through the house. Listening for noise. Hoping there was none but then also hoping she hadn't simply awakened because her body ached for Wolf's.

She stopped in the living room, listening to the

darkness. There was nothing—and then there was. A thump outside her door. She squeaked and ran on silent feet to look out the peephole. Nobody was there. No shadow, no person. Nothing. The porch was bright and empty. The leaves on the trees rustled, but nothing moved besides that. Her heart raced and her breath rattled as she took a step back, frowning.

That was when she looked down. A white slip of paper lay halfway beneath the bottom of the door. She snatched it up and went over to the kitchen where she flipped on the light over the stove and held the paper up.

A gift, it said. A gift?

She turned it over, but there was nothing else there. And then she spun back toward the door. She peered through the peephole again, but there was no-one. So she undid the locks, except for the chain, and dragged the door open.

And there, on the porch, lay a manila envelope. Pulse thudding, fingers shaking, Haylee slipped the chain free and snatched up the envelope before slamming the door and redoing all the locks. She hugged the envelope to her as she returned to her bedroom upstairs and flipped on the light. She had to squint at first, but her eyes soon grew accustomed to it since she slept with a night light anyway.

Haylee climbed cross-legged onto the bed and opened the envelope. A sheaf of papers slipped out. And three photos. She lifted the photos and peered at them.

Oscar Silva's face was clear. Beside him was Senator Watson. And a third man she didn't recognize. She turned the photo over.

Silva—Frank Watson—Donnie Setter

Donnie Setter?

The other two photos were Setter only, no sign of Watson or Silva. But her stomach twisted as she recognized the landscape in the first. It was the jungle camp where she'd been held with the other hostages. The building behind Setter was the building where she'd stayed for three days, all the while thinking she was going to die.

In the second photo, Setter was grinning broadly, a beautiful, half-nude Mexican—or Guatemalan—woman on his lap. They were inside a much more lavish building than any she'd seen in the camp. The furnishings were velvet and gold, the air thick with smoke. There were other women in the background.

A brothel? Probably. Haylee set the photos down and started to read the papers. It was a series of shipping manifests and plane reservations. The manifests were for goods like pottery and tiles and sinks and wood-carvings, the kinds of items that tourists imported from Mexico in droves. The plane reservations were for Donnie Setter—Donald James Setter III, to be precise. Haylee frowned. Who was Donald James Setter III?

She reached across the bed for her laptop, which was plugged in and sitting on the bedside table. She flipped it open and typed in Setter's name.

She wasn't disappointed. Donnie Setter lived in New Mexico. He owned an import/export business, and he sold goods in a store he called Olde World Mexico Imports. It wasn't a huge business, or even anything she thought might appeal to anyone outside of the Southwest. But Setter appeared in photos with celebrities, government officials, and various other people she didn't recognize but who seemed to be part of a moneyed set. There were yachts, race cars, and oceanside vistas in a place that could be Mexico or California.

Haylee frowned. Someone had left this on her doorstep for a reason. She picked up the photo of Oscar Silva, Frank Watson, and Donnie Setter again. What did it mean?

Haylee yawned and shook her head, warding off any tiredness before she stood and went to the kitchen. Time to fix a pot of coffee and start digging deeper. There was a connection between the three men, and she planned to find out what it was.

No matter how long it took, or how much sleep she lost.

Chapter Thirteen

WOLF WOKE EARLY AND HEADED INTO HOT HQ. HE couldn't sleep anyway so why toss and turn? He'd gone home after the event, watched TV for a couple of hours, and then fallen asleep with Haylee on his mind. He feared she was going to get herself in trouble. Big trouble. And he also feared that she was sleeping with the guy who'd left the fundraiser with her. The thought of that guy touching her, his hands roaming her body, his lips finding the sweet spot beneath her ear, was enough to put Wolf in a bad mood.

He'd grabbed his phone and stared at her number. Thought of all the things he might possibly say to her if he texted her. In the end, he didn't text her. He fell into a rough sleep, then woke too early and dressed in his workout clothes so he could hit the gym at HOT before showering and getting ready for the day.

He pushed himself in the gym, working up a

sweat, showered and dressed, and then checked the time. It was still early so he headed for the range. It was satisfying to squeeze off a few hundred rounds so early in the morning. The smell of explosives and the feel of hot brass as it pinged off his skin every once in a while was comforting. It was what he knew. What he could control.

He pressed the button to bring the target back, satisfaction seeping through him at the tight groupings on the paper. Not that he hadn't expected it. He was HOT. Hitting what he aimed at was pretty much a guarantee. If it wasn't, he'd find his ass hauled in to the colonel with a lot of explaining to do.

Then he'd find himself on standby, prevented from going on missions, until he corrected that shit. There was no room for error when your teammates depended on your accuracy for their lives.

Wolf stowed his weapons in his bag, tossed the target, and washed his hands in the sink right outside the door to the range in order to remove the lead and other chemicals. He walked on the sticky paper to get the residue off his boots, then strode out and tugged his hearing protection off his head and put that in the bag as well. A stop to drop everything in Echo Squad's arsenal and he was on his way to the squad ready room.

Saint was there. So was Gem. The rest of them weren't in yet. Saint looked up as he entered. "Hey, man. Gem was just telling me about the senator's function. Haylee Jamison was there?"

Fucking hell. There were no secrets with these guys. "Yeah, she was there." He walked over to the console at one end of the room and poured a cup of coffee. Then he turned back to his teammates. "She had a date, too. Some lawyer named Tony. Works for Watson."

Saint's brows lifted. "Huh, interesting."

Wolf sipped his coffee. "Is it? Why?"

Gem and Saint exchanged a look. Wolf wanted to growl. He didn't. Why the fuck did everybody think he was hung up on that woman? He wasn't. He'd liked her. She was gorgeous and smart. They'd had a hell of a night together. What was so unusual about that?

"No reason," Saint said. "Just thought maybe you'd had intentions in that direction."

"I did," he said truthfully. "But after everything she went through out there, I kinda thought maybe she needed a normal guy in her life."

"Seemed to me like the kind of woman who could handle it," Saint said. "Though I could be wrong."

"She's a reporter, Saint. That might not be the best combination with us, don't you think?"

"Oh, I expect Mendez would put the fear in her. The threat of being charged for endangering national security tends to work with most people we encounter."

"True. But she's got Tony now, so she didn't need me at all."

Saint narrowed his eyes for a second. "Yeah, why

would she bother with your grumpy ass when she could date a hotshot DC lawyer? She's probably better off."

Wolf didn't like the way his guts twisted. Still, he grinned as if he wasn't affected at all. "Exactly my thoughts. Except for the grumpy part. I'm not grumpy."

"Could have fooled me," Gem said, adding to the conversation for the first time since Wolf had arrived. He picked up a donut and chomped into it. They all worked out hard and expended so many calories in training that donuts didn't make a damned bit of difference. Nobody around here was getting a pot belly from a morning binge.

Wolf snatched a donut of his own and took a bite. Sugar exploded on his tongue. Kind of how it felt to kiss Haylee. *Fuck.*

"You guys think what you want. I'm not grumpy. Just thinking about shit, okay?"

Saint's expression changed then. Softened a little. "How are your parents? Any closer to success?"

Wolf felt the ache in his soul. He'd told his team what was going on with his family because they were more than friends. They were brothers. And brothers shared all the deep shit going on with them. Or they were supposed to anyway. Sky "Hacker" Kelley hadn't told them much about himself, as they'd learned when his ex-wife showed up and started working with them, but ever since she'd come back into his life he was more of an open book. And that book was a sappy romance these days. The longing looks and goofy smiles were ridiculous sometimes.

"Last I heard, their lawyer thought they had a chance. But there are no guarantees. They're flying out to California next week for the hearing."

"Man, I hope it goes well for them. Any word on your sister?"

"Still in rehab."

"I'm sorry. That sucks. I hope she gets better."

Wolf was used to hearing that sentiment, but deep down he didn't think Cheryl was ever getting better. She had so much incentive with two adorable kids, but if that couldn't make her walk the straight and narrow, he didn't know what could. Though maybe he was wrong. Maybe she'd make it and prove him wrong. He damn sure hoped so.

"Yeah, me too. Thanks." Wolf took another bite of the donut. "What do we know about Oscar Silva's operations?"

Saint lifted an eyebrow. "Probably not much. Why?"

"He called Haylee to his table last night. She's convinced he's responsible for the drugs coming from Mexico."

"Probably is. But that's not our department."

"No. But you remember the OxyContin street pills that caused those deaths a few months ago?"

"Yeah."

"Her roommate was one of the ones who died."

"Shit."

Wolf loved that he didn't have to spell it out. His fears. His worry. His teammates knew. Gem was frowning. Saint looked like he was thinking deeply about something.

"Yeah," Wolf said. "She blames Silva and she was at his table last night—after getting her ass kidnapped in Mexico because she was down there poking around. What are the chances he has no idea who she is?"

Saint's expression was hard. "Little to none, I'd say. Those guys stole passports and IDs, so they knew the names of everyone they had."

Wolf drew in a breath that was both tight with worry and easier because he knew his teammates understood. "Think we can watch her for a while? Without her knowing, I mean."

"I'll talk to Mendez and Ghost."

"I'd appreciate it."

"You got it, Wolf. Haylee Jamison was pretty fucking cool—whipped your ass at pool like nothing I'd ever seen."

Wolf snorted. "Man, I so wanted to get her to play Cage."

"That would be a great matchup," Gem said, laughing. "Even better if Cage has no idea she can play."

"He'd figure it out pretty quickly," Saint said.

"Yeah, but what fun it'd be in those few moments when he was confused because she could sink all the balls without missing," Gem replied.

"She misses," Wolf said. "But not often."

"Dude, you really should call her. Steal her away from that lawyer while you still can."

Wolf's insides turned to ice. "What makes you think she wants to be stolen? She looked happy with the guy."

Gem snorted. "No she fucking didn't. She kept staring at *you*. Hell if I know why, but she did. Which tells me she's willing to be stolen. Probably make you work at it, but you could do it."

Wolf finished the donut. Licked the sugar from his fingers. Tried not to think about how it reminded him of sex with Haylee. "You're dreaming. Even if you aren't, I'm not interested."

Gem's eyebrows lifted in surprise. "Oh dude. Wow. You are so fucking clueless right now. But whatever. You keep telling yourself you aren't interested. Watch her walk away with that lawyer. Try not to cry into your pillow because you let her go."

Wolf tilted his head. "What the fuck, Gem? Am I attracted to her? Hell yes I am. But that's all. I'm not going to cry into my pillow because she's with some guy. There are plenty of other women out there."

Gem stared at him. Then he shrugged. "Okay, man. Whatever you say."

Saint spoke before Wolf could protest. "All right, guys, let's worry about the things that matter. Wolf's love life—or lack of one—isn't important right now."

"Damn straight," Wolf said. "Let's worry about protecting her and not who she's sleeping with."

Gem shrugged. "Not a problem for me. In fact, if you aren't interested, maybe I'll go see her—"

"No," Wolf said coldly, every fiber of his being growing hot as lava and icy as liquid nitrogen all at once. It was all he could do not to take a step toward his teammate, not to intimidate with his size and determination.

Gem laughed as he held up his hands, palm out. "Think I made my point. But you go on believing you don't want her if it makes you feel better."

It didn't make him feel better. Because he knew it wasn't true.

Fucking Gem and his fucking experiment.

HAYLEE HADN'T SLEPT in hours. She hadn't showered either. She'd been pouring over the papers left on her doorstep and researching the people on the internet. She'd accessed articles, photos, and she'd dug deep into the library archives for anything she could find on Donnie Setter and Frank Watson.

It took hours, but she found the connection. They were cousins. Donnie Setter was the child of Frank Watson's aunt from her second marriage. Donnie was a bit younger than Frank, but they were definitely related. Donnie cultivated an image of someone who was casual and kind of dorky, but in reality he was smart and connected. Graduated from Yale. Inherited money from his father, and the import/export busi-

ness. It had prospered under Donnie, growing exponentially in the seven years since he'd taken it over.

And his cousin had entered the US Senate four
years ago. Frank Watson was a first term senator after
serving as his state's attorney general and then lieu-
tenant governor. He was ambitious and young enough
to have a long political career ahead if he played his
cards right.

There was absolutely nothing dirty about Frank
Watson. He was a straight shooter, the kind of guy
who was harsh on crime and enforced the laws. He
was hard on drug dealers too, which was a point in his
favor. But there was Donnie, going to the jungle and
taking photos with drug dealers. What the hell was
that about?

Donnie donated to his cousin's campaign, though
not a ton of money. He'd also donated to Frank's
opponent in the early days, but he'd finally firmed up
his support and infused cash into Frank's campaign as
it picked up speed.

The photo of Silva, Watson, and Donnie was
taken at a fundraiser in Arizona a couple of years ago
when Frank was starting to raise money for his reelec-
tion campaign.

Haylee shoved a hand through her hair and
yawned. Why had somebody given her this information but not given her more? Did they know anything
or had they just hoped she'd find something dirty? But
on whom? And why her?

She shook her head and closed the computer. Was

it enough that Frank Watson and Donnie Setter were cousins? And that Setter was visiting drug dealers in the Guatemalan jungle? It was damning, no doubt about it. Add in Oscar Silva and yeah, it was pretty interesting information.

It was not, however, a smoking gun.

Haylee stood and stretched. Then she went to the bathroom, turned on the shower, and waited for the water to heat. After a nice long shower, she got dressed in leggings and a loose shirt made of soft jersey and then went to find something to eat. The refrigerator contained milk, cream, and some lunch meat. The cabinets were no better, unless she wanted cereal. But after the past few hours, she wanted something more substantial. Plus she wanted to get out of the house and walk in the fresh air, clear her head a bit. Think about the connections. Maybe what she had was enough. Just write an article and see where it went.

But what would the focus be? Haylee grabbed her purse and keys and headed for the door. She locked it behind her, then went out into the parking lot where her car sat. A dark sedan came around the corner, rolling slowly past as she unlocked her car and slipped inside. She twisted the key, but nothing happened. Dead battery. *Shit.*

She didn't drive enough these days and her car had been sitting. Since it wasn't all that new, it had issues. She slapped the wheel and shoved the door open. She really needed to get rid of the damn thing and just Uber everywhere that she couldn't take the Metro. She headed for the street, calling an Uber as she walked and grumbling to herself about the stupid car. She'd have to call Triple A when she got back.

A car turned the corner and slowed as it approached. The same black sedan. Not her Uber, which was supposed to be a silver Honda. The sedan rolled up and slid to a stop. The window went down in the back. The man from last night, the one who'd come over and asked her to join Oscar Silva at his table, stared back at her.

"Hello, Miss Jamison. Can I offer you a lift?"

Her heart thumped. "Um, that's okay. I have an Uber coming."

His expression was all politeness, but his eyes were hard. "No, really. I insist. Mr. Silva would be angry with me if I did not personally see you safely to your destination."

"I, uh, I'm fine. Really."

"Miss Jamison. Get in the car. I will drive you where you were going. We will talk along the way. Would you like to call a friend first? Let someone know where you are? Here, take the license plate down. Take a photo of it, and of me. I don't mind."

Haylee frowned. Then she drew out her phone. "All right. If you don't mind."

"I don't."

She went around back and snapped a photo of the plate. Then she snapped one of him. "Your ID?"

she asked, because what good was a photo of him without his identification?

He withdrew his wallet and pulled out a license. *John Payne.* She snapped that too. Then she texted it all to Wolf, because he was the first person that came to mind even though she knew her phone would blow up soon after. But if something happened to her, Wolf was the one she wanted to know about it. Not her editor at the paper. Not Tony. Not any of her friends.

Wolf.

"I've texted this to my SEAL buddy," she said, even though Wolf wasn't a SEAL.

"Sounds reasonable to me. You getting in?"

Haylee hesitated for a long moment, gazing up and down the street both ways. Her Uber was still a few blocks away.

"You can cancel it, you know."

"Yes." She sent the text to cancel and then went around and got into the car. Maybe it was dumb, but she didn't think so. Payne had been forthcoming with his information and she'd texted it to Wolf. If the object was to harm her, she didn't think the man would approach her so openly.

"So where are you headed?" he asked, light green eyes fixing on her face.

"Saffron Indian," she said, making a split second decision to get Indian food in a place that was surrounded by other shops and restaurants.

"You get that?" Payne said to the driver in the front. The man was silent, nondescript. White, brown hair, height and eye color unknown. Unremarkable in any way.

"Yes, sir." The car began to move and Haylee sat back against the seat, her heart thrumming and her belly twisting. What was she doing here? Her phone dinged and she knew Wolf was responding. Probably wanting to know what the ever-loving fuck she was up to.

"So, Miss Jamison. You're a reporter."

It wasn't a question. "Yes."

"Reporters have to be so careful," he said, not looking at her. "So many things they get wrong. Very dangerous work."

"It can be. But I do my research," she told him.

"That's good. Very good."

"What were you doing at my house, Mr. Payne?" Because no way was he driving through her neighborhood on a whim.

"Coming to see you, of course."

"But you drove by me. And then my car didn't start."

"Didn't it?" he murmured. "Too bad."

She ignored his almost-amused tone. "Why are you here? What do you want?"

Payne sighed heavily. Then he turned to her, his light eyes boring hard into hers. "The SEAL you sent your information to—is he the one who rescued you in Guatemala?"

Haylee tried not to gasp. She almost succeeded.

Payne's mouth twisted in satisfaction. "This is why

I'm here, Miss Jamison. To warn you. Whatever you think you know about Mr. Silva—drop it and find something else to occupy your time."

"I don't know what you're talking about."

"Don't you? You went out of your way to speak with him last night. You put yourself in his path."

Haylee's stomach dropped. "I did not."

"Oh, you definitely did. You're curious. Your friend died, so tragic, but you've not accepted it. You're looking for someone to blame. Instead of blaming your friend for making a bad decision, for taking drugs she should not have taken, you wish to assign blame elsewhere. You think that if only you could find someone to pay for her death, the abuse would stop. That people would be saved. But Miss Jamison, that is a lie—people have free will, and they abuse drugs because they want to get high. You can't change that."

Haylee was hot. And cold. And furious. Her heart throbbed and her skin flamed. Her phone began to ring. She didn't answer it. "How dare you," she said, her voice low and hard and angry. "How dare you blame addicts for making bad choices when nobody ever made the choice to get addicted in the first place. Especially to prescription opioids. Those pills are supposed to be safe, not laced with fentanyl from China—"

"Safe?" he interjected. "They are powerful drugs, Miss Jameson. They aren't safe. They're meant to help those in pain, not provide recreational highs for casual users. Those are the people who get in trouble, the ones who buy them on the black market. Not those who have legitimate conditions."

She wanted to reach across the seat and slap him. Not a good plan, of course. Her phone kept ringing. It stopped when it went to voice, then started again as soon as Wolf hung up and tried to call her once more.

"I pray you never need pain pills, Mr. Payne. I pray you never need them and that the pain doesn't stop once the pills run out. Because then we'd see how strong you really are, wouldn't we?" She reached into her bag to silence her phone. "But why don't you take one of your boss's Mexican imports anyway, if you're so sure? Just go ahead and take one. See what happens once you do."

Payne turned away from her, looked out the window. Then he twisted to look at her again, a vague smile on his face. "Here we are, Miss Jamison. Saffron Indian. Enjoy your meal."

Haylee sucked in a breath. They were at the plaza, the restaurant was right there. She was alive. And nothing that had happened would cause even a blip on most people's radar. John Payne hadn't threatened her, not really. He was creepy and he made insinuations, but he hadn't outright threatened her with anything.

She gazed at him for a long moment, warring with herself, trying to find the right words. And then she jerked the handle and shoved the door open. He smiled at her as she climbed from the car.

"Do be careful, Miss Jamison," he said. "The city is so dangerous these days." He unclipped his seatbelt, then reached over and pulled the door closed. The car accelerated down the street, whipped around a corner, and disappeared.

Haylee's phone blared and she snatched it up, trembling. "Wolf?"

Chapter Fourteen

Wolf gripped his phone as Haylee said his name. "Haylee—what the hell? Are you okay?"

"Yes, I'm fine."

He could hear traffic in the background. "Where are you?"

"White Flint. He just dropped me off."

Wolf shoved a hand through his hair. "What the fuck? You got in the car with somebody that scared you? Sent me a couple of damned pictures? What did you think I could do to help you?"

"I was bluffing him, Dean. Making sure he wasn't going to strangle me and drop me in a ditch somewhere. Which he did not. It's fine. Really."

He didn't believe her. Her voice was trembling. "No. You don't text me that shit and then pretend it's fine. This John Payne—who the fuck is he?"

"He works for Silva. He invited me to Silva's table last night. And then he was in my parking lot—my car wouldn't start—and he offered me a ride. He took me where I wanted to go, but he's gone now."

He remembered the guy who'd gone to invite her to Silva's table. A lackey, he'd thought. Though maybe the guy was slightly more than that. An enforcer, probably. Wolf didn't like this shit. At all. "What did he say to you?"

She took a moment to answer. As if she were gathering her thoughts. "Not a whole lot. He might have suggested that I shouldn't dig into his boss's dealings. And that drug addicts are pretty much scum and get what they deserve."

"Motherfucker," Wolf growled. He was pissed as shit at his sister, but he didn't think she deserved all that had happened to her. Was she responsible for her choices? Sure. But addiction wasn't a black and white issue. She wasn't scum. She was somebody's daughter. Somebody's sister. Somebody's mother. She mattered.

"Yes, exactly."

He could hear the anger and conviction behind Haylee's words. "Tell me where you are. I'm coming to get you." Because no way was he letting Haylee be alone right now.

"Oh please," she said. Not at all what he'd expected out of her. He frowned. "You explained to me last night how you didn't have time for me, etcetera, but now you want to come and pick me up? Why now, Dean?"

"Some asshole stalked you at your home, vaguely threatened you, and left you somewhere without a ride—and you want to know why I want to pick you up? Are you kidding me?"

"You aren't obligated. You already helped me once. Consider our night together as payment. You don't owe me anything else."

She sounded so self-righteous. And, really, he was going to fucking strangle her. Fury flared deep inside, heating up his skin, frying his brain. She was lucky he'd been able to answer the phone anyway. If he'd been in the secure areas of HOT, he wouldn't have gotten her message for a couple of hours or more. "Haylee, tell me where the fuck you are right damn now. I'm coming to get you. We can argue about this once you're safe."

"I'm safe. He's gone."

"No, the asshole threatened you. You're safe when I say you're safe."

He didn't think she'd reply. But then she did. Huffy. "Fine. But I'm starved and I'm going into a restaurant to order something to eat. You won't get here in less than twenty minutes if you're coming from Laurel anyway."

"Text me the address. And don't leave the restaurant until I get there."

"So bossy. That's not attractive, you know."

He growled. "Too bad, babe. Just like back in the jungle, do what I tell you. I'll be there in a few minutes."

He heard the moment the traffic sounds faded

and he knew she'd gone inside. "Do you want me to order you something?"

Her tone was clipped and he knew she was annoyed at his autocratic ways. Too bad.

"No, I'm good. Get yours to go." He was already on his feet and moving. He stopped briefly to give Saint a heads up, covering the phone while he said, "Haylee's in trouble. Going to pick her up."

"Copy," Saint replied, not missing a beat. "Need backup?"

"I don't think so. She's at a restaurant in White Flint. Got a photo and ID of the guy who dropped her. Can you run a check?"

"Yeah. Text it to me."

Wolf sent the text and kept walking. "You still there?" he asked.

"I'm here. Just ordered. You sure you don't want anything?"

"I'm good."

She sighed. "I have to pee, and I'm not taking you in there with me. So I'm hanging up now, but I won't move until you get here. Promise."

"Share your location with me so I know if you leave."

"I said I wouldn't," she huffed.

"I know that, Haylee. I'm more or less thinking about if that guy comes back and tries to force you to leave with him. If I have your location, it'll help."

"Oh. Of course. I'll do it. The moment we hang up."

"Good. Be there as soon as possible."

"Don't get a ticket for me, Dean," she said wryly. "Because I'm not paying it for you."

He laughed. "Not getting a ticket. Just hang tight for a few."

"Got it. Now let me go before I pee my pants."

Wolf ended the call and fished out his keys. Then he clicked his truck open, jumped inside, and started it up before shoving into gear and flooring it out of the parking lot.

———

HAYLEE SAT at a table near the counter and waited for her food. When her order was ready, she sat back down and continued to wait for Wolf to arrive. Maybe she should have eaten here anyway. But it wasn't five minutes after she'd gotten her food that he arrived. She knew him the instant he breezed through the door, tall, blond, and sexy as sin. He was wearing military camouflage today and her heart tripped over itself like someone who'd just gone ice skating for the first time. Back and forth, around and around, flailing about—and then landing hard on a solid surface, feeling dazed.

She was definitely dazed. He'd been spectacular in his rented tuxedo last night, but the uniform was even more attractive. Wolf was made to wear a uniform. The female members of staff, as well as the lady patrons, seemed to agree with her because all eyes turned to follow him as he made his way toward her.

His handsome face was set in a scowl. She didn't miss the way he cased the room, or the way her heart tripped when he settled that gaze on her as he approached. She forced herself to get to her feet, though it took a moment for her brain and her limbs to connect. She held up the bag, smiling and trying to be casual with him. "You're so gonna regret not getting your own."

"Nah, I'll just swipe some of yours."

Haylee pretended to be taken aback. "Seriously? I asked if you wanted your own and now you think you're getting mine? No way, mister."

He swiped the bag from her hand. "Chicken tikka masala with rice and an order of naan, am I right?"

She blinked. "Yes. How did you know?"

"First of all, chicken tikka masala is the most ordered dish by Americans. And second, unless you're a secret linebacker for the Redskins, you'll eat approximately half of this and save the rest for another meal. But I'm not hungry, so you're good."

Haylee folded her arms over her chest and tossed her hair. She liked it when they teased each other. It gave her a little thrill, though maybe she should be annoyed instead. "Maybe I'm a secret Ninja or something. You ever think of that?"

He snorted. "No. You ready to go?"

"Yes. But you really didn't have to come get me. I could have Ubered home."

He put his hand against her back, his fingertips sizzling into her even though there was the fabric of her shirt between them. "After you texted me the plate, photo, and ID of a man you weren't certain meant you any harm? No fucking way, baby," he growled in her ear.

She loved the way his voice vibrated down her spine. And it annoyed her too. Why did she have to be so attuned to this man? Why couldn't she ignore his effect on her? His fingertips burned into her skin and her sex tingled with heat at the feel of his hot breath in her ear.

So unnecessary. Just like the memories of their night together. Her lying beneath him, legs spread wide to accommodate his big body, his hard cock pounding into her and taking her to a heaven she wanted to experience again.

They walked out of the restaurant and into the parking lot. Traffic buzzed up and down the street and cars moved through the lot. Wolf steered her toward a silver Chevy Silverado, unlocking the doors and starting the engine remotely before they reached the truck.

Once she was inside, her food at her feet on the floor, he went around and got in, then reversed out of the parking spot. The smell of the food made her belly growl. She opened the bag and pulled out a piece of naan bread. "I live at 1050 Brighton Way," she said as he headed for the exit.

"Not taking you home, Haylee."

"What? Why not?"

"Saint's running a check on John Payne. We'll see what he turns up before we go back to your place."

"How long will that take?"

"Not too long."

"Define not too long."

"Depends on how professional Payne is, I guess. He's not a petty criminal, most likely, so we'll have to dig. Couple of hours at least."

She frowned. "So where are we going in the meantime?"

"My place."

Her belly tightened. "That's not necessary, is it?"

"Yeah, it is. I'm taking you to my place where you can eat and relax—and tell me what you've gotten yourself into with Oscar Silva."

"I haven't gotten myself into anything with Silva! I didn't even talk to him alone last night. You were there. You saw it."

"Define alone."

She frowned. "Okay, so we were at a table alone *some* of the time. But we were never alone in the sense nobody was there to see us. We never disappeared into a hallway or anything. Not like I did with you."

He seemed to ignore that statement. "That doesn't mean anything. You clearly pissed off someone—which is also why you're going to tell me exactly what happened and everything Payne said to you."

She thrilled to the note of command in his voice

even while she chafed against it. She'd been on her own, doing her own thing, for a long time. Her and Nicole against the world. Two chicks in the city, making their way and having fun while they did it.

Until Nicole started taking pain pills.

Haylee wasn't inclined to let anyone else take control, but maybe it was time to let it happen. Just for a little bit. Wolf was a good guy and he had her best interests at heart. She knew that from before.

"I'll tell you everything you want to know." She tore off a hunk of bread with her teeth and chewed. Thank God for yummy Indian food to make it all right again. At least for a little bit. "But first you need to know that someone dropped off an envelope with photos and papers on my doorstep last night."

His eyes shot to her before going back to the road. His grip on the wheel tightened. Was that a tick in his jaw?

"Somebody dropped an envelope on your doorstep? What precisely were the photos and papers about?"

"I'm not entirely sure yet. But there was one of Silva, Frank Watson, and a man called Donnie Setter. Setter is Watson's cousin and he owns an import/export business in New Mexico."

"Where are the papers now?"

"In my apartment."

"Tell me you made copies."

"I did, actually. Well, I mean I took pictures of them all and loaded the pics to my cloud."

"I want you to send me the pictures."

Her heart thumped. She hadn't expected that. "Why do you want them?"

"Because my guys can check those out too. Don't you think it's pretty convenient that the papers arrived last night and Payne was here this afternoon?"

"You aren't suggesting he's the one who left them?"

"Not at all. But what if he knows that somebody did? Could be why he showed up today."

"And he could have showed up because I was talking to Silva last night."

"True. Do you have any idea who could have dropped them off? Did you see anything?"

"I didn't see anything, no. And I've been thinking about it since I found them and I really don't know who would have brought them to me. I've asked a lot of questions of a lot of different people, but most of the answers were unremarkable. Some people denied knowing Silva at all. Some acted scared out of their wits at the thought of saying anything even slightly negative. I've got one guy willing to talk a little—but even he doesn't say everything. So far, Silva can't be definitively connected to anything shady."

"People won't talk, but they'll leave anonymous deliveries. Interesting."

"And the papers aren't all that incriminating, quite honestly. Sketchy for sure, but nothing that would hold up in court—or even in the court of public opinion. Silva is made of rubber or something because everything bounces off him."

Wolf turned onto a side street. "Yeah, but even guys like that make mistakes. Just takes time to find what they are."

"I keep looking for one. Haven't found it yet."

"It'll happen," he said. "But it might not be you who discovers it."

She didn't like that thought. She wanted to be the one who brought Silva and his drug empire down. For Nicole. But she didn't say that.

A few moments later, Wolf pulled into a driveway. The house was small, a brick rancher, probably mid-century when that style was popular. The bushes in front had been cut rather severely so that they didn't obscure the windows. The yard was neat, but unre-markable.

Wolf cut the engine and turned to her. "Home sweet home."

"It's cute," she said. "Though not what I expect-ed." She'd thought he'd be in an apartment some-where. A studio, perhaps.

"What did you expect?"

"A bachelor pad in a highrise."

He laughed. "My dad is a farmer. I grew up in the country. High-rises are not for me. At least not to live in."

"You have other experiences with high-rises?"

"I've stormed a few. You haven't lived until you've

plunged forty floors on top of an elevator in the dark. Good times."

Haylee couldn't help but gape at him. "You aren't serious." Forty floors in the dark? Wow. She'd pee herself, and yet he acted like it was totally normal.

"Dead serious, babe." He pushed his door open. "Now come on. Let's get you inside so you can eat."

Chapter Fifteen

WOLF HADN'T EXPECTED TO HAVE HAYLEE HERE IN HIS house. If he had, he might have cleaned up a little better. He went into the living room and picked up empty cans and bags of chips. He wasn't exactly a slob, but he wasn't overly concerned with house-keeping either. He had a giant television on one wall, a recliner, a couch, and little else in the room. Haylee's brows lifted.

"You need to fire your interior decorator, Dean."

He snorted. She was cute. "I don't have one, smartass."

"No kidding."

He dropped the trash in the can, then went over to the table to clear it of mail, plastic bags, coupons, and receipts. "Sorry. You can sit here and eat. Need anything?"

"Do you have a bottle of water, maybe?"

"Water, beer, soda. You name it."

"Just water, thanks."

He went and got her a bottle while she perched delicately in one of the chairs and pulled food out of her bag. She glanced up as he approached. So pretty, this girl. Long wavy hair, creamy golden skin, and dark eyes that sparkled. She had delicate features—fine eyebrows, a small nose, a pointed chin—and he thought she was just about the hottest woman he'd ever met.

"Bring a fork if you want some," she said as she opened the container of chicken tikka masala. "Do you have any paper plates?"

"Yeah, right here." He grabbed a stack off the bar that formed the opening between the kitchen and the dining room and handed it to her. She took them with a soft thanks and then proceeded to dip out food with the utensils that had been in the bag. "Sure you don't want any?"

It smelled delicious. He didn't eat Indian food often, but when he did, chicken tikka masala was a favorite. Typical American. "Sure, I'll try it," he said, reaching for a fork from the bar.

"Knew it," she said with a smile.

"Only because you keep offering."

She dished some out onto a plate for him, gave him a piece of her bread, and started eating. He forked up a bite. The fire was immediate. "Holy shit," he murmured as she laughed. He grabbed her water and took a swig.

"Sorry. I like it spicy."

He swallowed the water, though his mouth was still on fire. "Yeah, you do." He took another bite anyway, more prepared this time. It still set his mouth on fire, but it was good and flavorful.

"How have you been, Dean?" she asked after they'd eaten a few mouthfuls.

He didn't get addressed by his name much, unless it was his parents calling him to talk, but he liked it when she said it. The thrill of hearing his name on her lips hadn't faded from Guatemala to here. "Good. You?"

"Good." She didn't look up from her food as she said, "I was disappointed when you didn't come see me."

Real regret lanced through him. "I wanted to."

"So why didn't you?"

He sighed as he chewed a piece of bread. "I told you last night… I was busy."

She frowned. "That's bullshit and you know it."

"No, I have a demanding job—or didn't you notice when I parachuted into Guatemala to rescue you?"

"I noticed. Thanks for that. Again," she said.

"You're welcome. But that's not why I brought it up. So you'd have to thank me, I mean."

"I know." She smiled. "But when I said that's bull-shit, what I meant was that if you'd really wanted to see me, you would have done so. But I get it, Dean. I really do. We slept together and you're a one-night stand kind of guy. You got your rocks off. There was no need to pursue it after that."

"That's not why," he grumbled. It sounded so clinical when she said it like that. He thought of that night with her. The way she tasted. The sound of her moans and sighs. The way she shuddered beneath him while he thrust inside her body. The way his toes curled as he came hard, pouring himself out deep inside her body. It was the same way with every girl he'd ever slept with—and yet it was entirely different with Haylee too. It was *more*. More than he'd expected. He wanted it again. Wanted to know if it was as good as he remembered, or if he'd built it all up in his head into something impossible.

"I wanted to see you." Jesus, why had he admitted that? It only made things worse. He'd wanted to see her, but he hadn't called her. He'd ignored her.

She tilted her head to the side, fork hanging limply in her right hand. "Then why didn't you?"

"Cheryl," he finally said.

"Your sister?"

The fact Haylee remembered his sister's name when he'd only mentioned her once made his throat tighten. "Yeah. All my combat pay goes home to my parents so I can help them get custody of Jack and Taylor. I don't have the, uh, money to take somebody out to dinners and movies and clubs."

It was embarrassing, but there it was. His choice to send it all home, but what else could he do? Family was family. They meant everything.

Her jaw dropped slightly. Then she reached out and wrapped her fingers around his hand. "Oh, Wolf, that's so cute—and totally misguided."

He frowned at her even though his attention was utterly focused on his hand. On where they touched. "What does that mean?"

"It means this is the twenty-first century. You don't have to *buy* a girl dinner or movies. You have streaming, right?"

"I have one service, not all of them."

"Okay, so movies at your fingertips." She jerked her head toward the television. "You have a big screen there, so I'm sure movies are fine on it. And a couch. Take-out isn't expensive—look at us now—and sex is always free. Or should be between people like us, I mean."

He couldn't help but gape at her. "You wouldn't think I was cheaping out if I invited you over for take-out and a movie on streaming? And then wanted sex?"

She shook that glorious hair of hers. "Wolf, honestly—sometimes men are so clueless. So long as you put your tongue between my legs the way you did back in El Salvador, I'd eat McDonald's for a month and watch reruns of *Family Guy*—which I hate, by the way—just to be with you."

His dick was throbbing. He was still reeling from the thought of putting his tongue between her legs, as she so plainly put it. He thought of it more like devouring her sweet pussy, but whatever. "You hate

Family Guy?"

Hell, he'd hate it too if that's what it took to get her naked, but he was trying to be silly. Not that he watched a lot of it, but it was funny when he did.

"God, yes. So stupid. Stewie is the only character whose name I can recall, but I've never liked it."

"Jeez, Haylee. That shit is fucking hilarious."

"To you."

Focus, asshole. "Okay, so you hate Peter Griffin. I can deal with that. I guess."

She laughed. "So we'd watch *Family Guy* and something appropriately sappy, like *Love, Actually,* and then we'd have wild monkey sex. Doesn't sound like a bad thing to me."

He was picturing the monkey sex. Him. Her. Naked, fucking like bunnies, sweat rolling down their bodies as they rose and fell together, her legs wide and wrapped around him, his hips pistoning into hers. He'd fuck her missionary. Then he'd fuck her from behind, palming her tits, before flipping over and letting her ride him to completion. Oh, yeah, this monkey sex sounded good to him.

"No," he croaked. "It doesn't."

She laughed again. "Jeez, Wolf, you look like you've seen a ghost or something."

"Not a ghost. Just imagining wild monkey sex."

She looked smug as she took another bite of her food. "Yes, but you didn't call me. So that's not happening, is it?"

"You're here now."

"Not for a date." She wagged a finger at him. "No more sex for you just for breathing, mister. If you want all this"—she waved a hand—"you gotta work for it."

God, she was cute. "Tease."

She laughed. He loved the sound. "Right. You had your chance. Now you gotta start again. Talk me into it. Romance me off my feet."

"I don't recall romancing you off your feet the last time. It was animal attraction. And those kisses you won playing pool."

"Beating your ass at pool, you mean." She tossed her hair over her shoulder. "Well, we're here now and things have changed. If you'd come and found me when you promised, I'm sure we'd have fallen into bed right away. In fact, I'd have dragged you inside and fucked your brains out if you'd shown up within a week. But you gave me too much time to think. To wonder if you were the best decision after all."

His heart throbbed and his dick leapt. Had he ever been anybody's best decision?

He shook himself out of his stupor. Yeah, stupor. Because he was hanging on her every word, imagining them in bed again, and he wasn't thinking as sharply as he should. He loved pussy as much as the next man, but he'd never been stupid over it. He was feeling stupid right now—over one woman's pussy, not pussy in general. He thought that even if ten Dallas Cowboys' cheerleaders stripped in front of him and wanted to bang him as a team, he'd still prefer Haylee. And that was some fucked up shit right there.

Wolf frowned. Hard. He had to get over this sickness, whatever it was. Not only that, but she'd had a date last night at the fundraiser. A man she'd left with. For all he knew, she'd had sex with him too. "Did you text me those files yet, Haylee?"

She looked as if she'd run full tilt into a brick wall. Took her a moment to reorient herself. But then she shut down, just as cool as you please. Part of him cried out at the shuttering of all that warmth. "No."

"Then do it, please. I want to share the information with my team."

She took out her phone, her skin flushing as she dropped her gaze to the screen. The only indication she was affected. "Fine. Sending now."

His phone pinged. "Thanks."

"I worked hard to figure out the connections," she said, all business now. "But all I found was that Donnie Setter is Senator Watson's cousin—and he's been to the camp where I was held. But that's not a crime. Or at least not one you can pin on Senator Watson—or Oscar Silva."

Wolf stiffened as a chill of anger slid through him, chasing all the heat and confusion away. "Seriously? You can tie one of the senator's relatives to that camp?"

"Yes. Setter has an import/export business. He gets a lot of stuff from Mexico, and he travels there quite a bit."

Wolf opened his messages and began to type out a missive to Saint. Watson had never aroused suspicion of any kind, but that didn't mean he couldn't be a party to shady things—even if it was just turning a blind eye to his cousin's business dealings. Because the fact that Setter had been to the Guatemalan camp was huge. Traveling and doing business was one thing. But the camp? Yeah, that was fucked up.

"Just because the cousin is involved in some shady shit doesn't mean the senator is," Haylee said. "Watson is notoriously hard on drugs. Nobody can say he's not. He's constantly trying to make it harder for people to cross the border."

"Yeah, but most of the drugs come through legal ports of entry, so trying to tighten the border wouldn't affect that. I mean it affects other stuff like marijuana, but not the hard drugs coming through. Might even be a clever stance to take for somebody involved in the drug trade."

Haylee shook her head. "That's much too cunning."

Wolf shrugged. "Money will do a lot to change someone's mind. But you're right, just because Setter is involved somehow doesn't mean Watson is. That's what we gotta find out."

He sent the message, with attachments, and then speared a piece of chicken with his fork. "Now we wait."

Haylee stared at him. "Don't think I didn't notice that you changed the subject, by the way."

"What subject?"

"Us. You and me and dating. But that's okay. I can take a hint."

His chest tightened. "I wasn't hinting."

"Regardless, if you want more, you have to romance me. We aren't in the jungle this time, and you don't win by default."

He hadn't intended to pursue this at all, and yet he was insulted. "Wait a minute—are you saying you slept with me because I rescued you? Not because you wanted to?"

She shook her head. "Not what I said at all. What I said was that you didn't have to work very hard before. I want more than just the expectation it's happening this time. Assuming you plan to pursue it, that is."

Did he? He wanted to. More than he expected. But he also knew his limits. And then there was the guy she'd been with last night. She still hadn't mentioned him.

"I'm not romantic, Haylee," he told her truthfully. "I'll treat you right, worship your body, and make you come so hard you see stars. But I won't play games with you."

Chapter Sixteen

HAYLEE'S BODY TINGLED INVOLUNTARILY FROM THE way he said he'd make her come so hard she saw stars. He could. She knew he could. He already had. More than once, actually.

"I didn't say anything about playing games, Wolf. But a girl likes to know she has some value. Now if you don't want to work for it, that's fine. At least I'll know where I stand with you."

She could see him thinking about his answer. He sighed. "Where you stand is that I want you a lot more than I should. Beyond that, I don't know what to say. I think you're the sexiest woman I know. I want to strip you naked and make you come, but I'm not gonna buy flowers or spout poetry or surprise you with a cake I baked myself."

Haylee couldn't help but giggle at that image. "Really? No cakes you bake yourself?"

He shifted in his chair. Was he reddening? She wasn't sure.

"Fuck no. I don't bake. Besides, it was a metaphor."

"For what?"

"Romance, Haylee. I'm not a romantic."

"Fine. But you can't say you won't spout poetry. You quoted Robert Frost to me the first night I met you."

He rubbed the back of his neck. "Yeah, guess I did. Doesn't mean I'm memorizing Shakespeare for you."

"You already have some memorized. You're an English teacher's kid."

"Fine, yeah, I do. Doesn't mean it's appropriate. Unless you want to hear about brief candles and blood that won't wash out."

She laughed. "*MacBeth*, of course."

"I can tell you to get to a nunnery."

"*Hamlet*."

"Or maybe you'd like to think about a muse of fire that would ascend the brightest heaven of invention?"

"*Henry V*. Oh, Wolf, you keep talking like that and my panties might just fly off."

He grinned. "Well if that's your idea of working at it, I can do it. I know all kinds of random Shakespeare."

"It's called poetry."

"Fine, poetry. I can spout it sometimes. If it gets me in your panties quicker."

She ought to be offended. Instead, she was amused. "It might. Don't know until you try."

"You're one of a kind, Haylee." He looked like he might say something else, but it never came.

She thought he was probably trying to figure out how to let her down easily. She didn't want to hear it. She'd already been bolder than she liked. She'd shown him her cards, namely the ones where she was still thinking about him and the night they'd shared. Before he could speak, she pushed her plate away and offered him the containers. "Want some more?"

"No thanks, I'm good."

Haylee closed up the containers and gathered the paper plates and plastic utensils. But when she stood, he gestured to her to sit back down. "I got it."

He reached for the trash and took it into the kitchen, dumping it into a can beneath the sink. She watched the muscles in his arms flex as he did so. She didn't ordinarily go for big guys with big muscles, but this one had her jumping inside like oil on a hot griddle. He closed the can, washed his hands in the sink, and swaggered back to where she sat at the table.

She rested her chin on her palm and smiled up at him. She was happily full now, and her lack of sleep was beginning to catch up with her. Maybe that's why she wasn't too guarded in what she was willing to say. And even though she knew she was saying things she probably shouldn't, she took it one step farther. "So does that mean you might want to date me?"

A furrow appeared between his eyes. She wanted to smooth it out with her fingertips. Instead, she reached for his hand because it was closer. He didn't stop her as she twisted her fingers into his for a second. Warmth flowed into her. She wanted to get up and wrap herself in his arms but that was probably carrying things a little too far. She let him go again and dropped her hand to the table.

He put a finger beneath her chin, tipping her head up as he bent down to her. She closed her eyes in anticipation of his kiss but nothing happened. She opened them again to find him a whisper away, staring into her eyes.

"I do want to date you, Haylee. But what about the other guy?"

"Other guy?"

"Your date last night?"

"Oh, you mean Tony." She smiled. "He's just a friend."

Wolf's expression was serious. "He didn't look at you like a friend."

Haylee frowned. "Really? I didn't notice. He was dating Nicole when she died—I mean I didn't know about it because she didn't tell me, but they were going out and keeping it secret. Because of his position with the senator and her past as an addict, though she was getting over that. He took it hard when she died. He's been a little… clingy, I guess. But he's not interested in me."

"I wouldn't be too sure about that if I were you."

Her heart thumped. "You're wrong, Wolf."

"Okay, if you say so."

"So answer the question," she prompted. "Do you want to date me or not? You started to say you did, but I sensed a but that had nothing to do with Tony."

He sighed. "Look, you have to know it's not gonna be smooth or easy if we start to date. I won't play games with you, but I can't promise that you won't think that's what I'm doing sometimes. All you have to do is ask me. If I can tell you what's going on, I will. But there'll be times when I can't. I need you to understand that if we go forward. Got it?"

She nodded. "Got it."

He surprised her with a kiss then, his mouth sinking down onto hers like it belonged there. Haylee moaned a little, her lips opening, his tongue slipping inside to stroke hers. It was every bit as good as she remembered. Fire streaked through her, from her nipples to her pussy to her fingers and toes. Sex had never felt as good as it had with him. Her body remembered.

Wanted.

He broke the kiss in spite of her whimper, then pressed his lips to her forehead and straightened. "Have to stop or I'll be trying to get you naked in about three more minutes."

"It'll take you that long to try?"

"Actually, that's about as long as I could stop myself."

"Maybe I don't mind."

He gaped at her. Then he laughed. "You told me I have to work at it this time. What happened?"

She shrugged, then she put her chin in her palm again and stared dreamily at him. "I forgot how good you kissed."

"You're cute. And sleepy."

"I'm not," she lied, sitting up straight and tall.

"Your eyelids keep drooping. How much sleep did you get last night?"

Haylee yawned in spite of herself. "After I found the package at my door, I didn't go back to sleep." She pressed the back of her hand to her mouth as another yawn hit her. "Damn, this is ridiculous. You have any coffee?"

"I do—but baby, why don't you lie down and take a nap instead? You just ate and you're tired. You can use my bed, or the couch if you prefer."

Haylee started to protest that she was fine, but the thought of going to sleep in his sheets was tempting. Besides, she was safe here with him. She trusted him. She wouldn't sleep as well at home, not after last night or after today when John Payne had been waiting for her. Totally creepy thing to do.

"Maybe you're right," she said. "Just a little nap."

"Bed or couch?"

She glanced at the couch. It looked comfortable enough, but she really wanted to lie on his bed.

With him, though maybe she shouldn't mention that.

"Bed. So you don't have to tiptoe around your living room while I sleep." Sounded like a good excuse. She hoped so anyway.

He held out his hand to her. "Come on then."

She put her fingers in his, expecting the sizzle of electricity but still surprised by it. He wrapped his hand around hers and pulled her up. Then he led her down a short hallway and into his bedroom. It was sparse, like the living room, with a full-sized bed that almost took up the whole room and a dresser with a TV on top. There was a small bedside table that held a lamp and a phone charger and a remote. There were no curtains, only blinds, and they were pulled closed so that only a little bit of light reached into the room.

The bed was made and he went over and dragged the covers back. "You okay in that or do you want a T-shirt to sleep in?"

"A T-shirt would be great," she said, only partly because she didn't want to wrinkle her clothing. No, the biggest reason was that one of his T-shirts would probably smell like him. Even freshly laundered, because his detergent was probably different from hers.

He went over to the dresser and pulled out a black shirt and handed it to her. "You want me to wake you or do you want to set an alarm?"

"You can wake me. Please. If I'm tired enough,

I'll ignore an alarm." She hugged his shirt to her chest and gave him a smile. "Thank you, Wolf. For coming to get me. For making me feel safe."

"You're welcome."

She hoped he might kiss her again but instead he backed away, toward the door. "I'll come get you in an hour. That sound good?"

"Yes. Thank you."

He closed the door behind him and Haylee let out the breath she didn't realize she'd been holding. He totally twisted her up inside. But in a good way. She liked it more than she should, considering how reluctant he was to commit to even going on a date.

He'll break your heart, Haylee.

That was her mother talking. Her mother had never remarried after her father left. She'd grown bitter, and she disliked men with a passion. Haylee had never yet taken a man home that her mother liked. Well, okay, she hadn't taken any men home since she'd grown up and left her mother's house. But the boys she'd taken home as a teenager hadn't impressed her mom at all.

Mom was always telling her how unreliable men were, how she needed to make her own way and not rely on one.

"I'm not relying on him, Mom," she muttered as she ripped her shirt over her head and slipped into his T-shirt. It fell to mid-thigh and she shimmied out of her leggings and lay her clothing across the bottom of the bed. Then she climbed beneath Wolf's sheets, feeling both strange and decadent at once. The sheets smelled like him. So delicious and masculine. It was like being enveloped in his arms in a way.

Haylee turned onto her side, sighed—and promptly fell asleep.

———

WOLF ALMOST GROANED as he pictured Haylee getting undressed in his room. How the hell he'd gone from never planning to call her to here she was in his house, getting naked in his room before slipping between his sheets, and oh by the way he'd also agreed to date her after making sure she didn't have a boyfriend—well, he had no fucking idea.

Except that she smelled good and looked good and he felt happier when she was around. He had no idea why that was. He was probably a little too influenced by Saint and Hacker these days. And all the other HOT operators with wives and girlfriends since it seemed like there'd been an explosion of love at HOT HQ lately. All of Alpha Squad was paired up. Most of the SEALs.

He'd sworn he wasn't going to be one of them, but here he was, thinking about the woman in his bed and wishing he was there with her. Not just so he could come, but so he could feel her body curled up beside him, her soft breath on his skin as she slept.

His phone rang and he snatched it up. It was Saint. "Yeah, man? Find anything?"

"Nothing much. John Payne is indeed the guy's name. He works for Oscar Silva. Also, he's an attorney. No criminal history at all. No arrests, no charges, nothing to worry about."

"Other than he just happened to be in Haylee's neighborhood when her car wouldn't start and then offered her a ride, in which he also let it slip that he knew she'd been rescued by us in the jungle."

"Shady as hell, no doubt. He shouldn't know about the rescue—but there *were* eleven people on that trip. Somebody could have talked. Probably did talk."

"Yeah, but what are the chances he knows one of those people? They were from south Alabama, for fuck's sake. He knows because Silva knows."

"Agreed. But he's clean, Wolf. Nothing on the guy."

Wolf didn't like it. "Shit. What about the other stuff? The files Haylee got?"

"Still researching that. She's right about Donnie Setter and Frank Watson. They're cousins, though you don't see them together much. They don't appear to talk regularly."

"Yet they were at a fundraiser together with Silva."

"Yep, and Setter is definitely in that camp where we found the hostages. But the photo is at least a year old. Could have been before they started pressing opioids out there."

"Do you really think that? Because I don't. Setter is in the import/export business. He imports Mexican pottery and stuff like that so he has a legit reason to be in Mexico—but they aren't fucking making pottery in that camp. Not only that, but those containers he imports would be a good way to smuggle in some drugs."

"Not saying I disagree at all. But so far there's nothing there."

Wolf's throat tightened. "Don't tell me you're giving up on finding anything."

"Of course not. If it's there, we'll get it. You know that. I've informed Ghost. He'll brief Mendez. If they tell me to back off, then I have to. But so long as they don't, we could use a project. Hacker and Bliss are aching to start deep diving into the shadowy corners of the internet."

"Thanks, man. Appreciate it."

"You like this woman, don't you?"

"I like all women, Saint."

Saint laughed. "Yeah, but you like this one better than the rest."

"I hardly know her."

"Doesn't matter. Sometimes you don't have to. I liked Brooke from the beginning and I couldn't quite explain it. Wasn't up to me, though."

"You are not pairing me up just so you can have somebody else join yours and Hacker's club. Haylee is a gorgeous, sweet woman—but we aren't getting married and having babies or anything like that."

"Whatever you say," Saint said, laughing.

"Fuck you," Wolf said mildly.

Saint laughed harder. "I'll remind you of that in a few months."

"Go ahead. Won't make a difference because I'll be the same old me as always."

"Famous last words man. All right, let me get back to this. We've got training at 0600 tomorrow."

"I'll be there."

Wolf set his phone on the table and frowned. If there was anything to be found on Setter and Silva—and Frank Watson—his team would find it. Saint could tell him all day long there was nothing criminal on any of those men, but Wolf didn't believe it. He didn't think Saint did either.

Chapter Seventeen

Haylee blinked awake to utter darkness. She lay for a long moment in soft sheets that smelled surprisingly masculine for a hotel. Stretching, she tried to trace the trajectory of her day.

And then it hit her where she was and what had happened. She popped up with a squeak and scrambled from the bed. There was a sliver of light coming from under the door. She hurried over and pulled the door open, then padded down the hall and out into the living room where Wolf lounged on his couch, big body slouching against the cushions like a decadent god's. He had one arm over the back, the remote in his hand as he flipped channels. The other hand was against his face. His elbow was propped on the arm of the couch as he leaned into his palm and stared lazily at the television.

Until she arrived, that is. He dropped his arm and sat up straighter. His gaze slid over her and she realized belatedly that she hadn't put her leggings on. She was standing in his house, clad in his T-shirt that reached to mid-thigh, and she suddenly felt very exposed and out of place.

"What time is it?" she asked. And then groaned inwardly because it was a stupid question. She had a phone—which she'd left in his bedroom—and she could have checked the time before blasting out here like a cannonball on a mission.

He glanced at his watch. "Nearly eight."

"Oh my God, you let me sleep for five hours. What happened to waking me in an hour?" She had a sleep hangover, but the truth was she could probably go back to sleep in an hour or two for another four or five hours. She'd been seriously sleep deprived lately.

"I tried. You told me to fuck off."

Haylee felt herself turning red. Yes, that sounded exactly like her. She was grouchy as hell when she didn't get enough sleep. Mornings were not her best time. Or, apparently, afternoons and evenings when she hadn't been sleeping well. "Sorry."

He shrugged. "It's okay."

"I've imposed enough," she stammered. "I should probably get home and let you have your house back."

His gaze was hot on her body. It lingered on her legs, the hem of the T-shirt, before sliding back up to her face. Oh, those eyes. She loved those eyes. So sexy.

"I can take you home if that's what you want."

She hesitated. Was that what she wanted? "I… yes, I should go."

No, it wasn't what she wanted. But she also didn't want to hang around like a lovesick teenager trying to be close to her crush. She had more self-respect than that.

Is that why you slept with him the first night? Self-respect?

She didn't like that voice. It was her mother's and it was judgmental as hell. A woman could sleep with a man if she wanted to. It was about making your own choices and taking pleasure if you wanted it, not about being slutty or easy. What the hell did that mean anyway? Slutty? Easy? Why didn't those terms apply to men?

"I can call an Uber," she added when he started to stand. "You've done enough for me today."

He stared at her. His brows drew low, his eyes flashing hot. "An Uber? No fucking way, Haylee. What kind of man would I be if I let you go home with a stranger on the same day some asshole scared you?"

She swallowed. "I might have overreacted—"

"No, you didn't." He stood, all six-foot-whatever of him towering over her. "A man made you uncomfortable, made veiled threats, stalked you to your house. You didn't overreact."

A thought suddenly occurred to her. "Did you find out anything? About what I sent you?"

His expression hardened. "No. Payne is clean. So are Silva, Watson, and Setter. There's nothing to indicate they've done anything wrong—at least nothing we've found yet."

Her heart skipped a beat. "Silva is running that operation out of Mexico. You know he is. And Setter is probably receiving the drugs in his shipments."

"Yes, I know. But Silva's smart and there's nothing to connect him. As for Setter, nothing's ever been discovered in his containers."

"What if Watson is protecting them? Is that possible?"

"Of course it's possible. But there's no proof."

Haylee's blood felt like ice in her veins. Anger flooded her. And determination. She wouldn't go down without a fight. She wouldn't quit. "I have to find the connection, Wolf. For Nicole." Her throat felt so damned tight it hurt.

He closed the distance between them and put his hands on her shoulders. Squeezed. "I know, honey. I know you want to stop them. You want somebody to pay for your friend's death."

It was only through sheer force of will that she didn't tremble. "I do. But more than that, I don't want anyone else to take a drug they think will help them cope, but it kills them instead."

"No, I agree. But you have to be smart about it or you won't get a thing on any of them."

"I know." He was right, but she felt helpless. Lost. *Dammit!*

"Look, why don't you stay here tonight. You can have the bed and I'll take the couch. I have to be at training early, but when I'm done, I'll take you back to your place and help you get your car started. It's already getting late, and I'd feel better if I could check out your place thoroughly in daylight."

She should say no, but she really didn't want to. She didn't look forward to riding a half hour home and then flinching at every little noise outside because she'd be too paranoid to close her eyes for the rest of the night.

"Okay," she said. "I'll stay for tonight. Thank you."

He skimmed his hands down her arms, then dropped them away. "You want something to eat? I make a mean sandwich."

Her belly growled as if on cue. "That sounds good. Thanks. I should, uh, probably go put on my clothes though."

He grinned, and her heart flipped. "You don't have to on my account. I like your legs."

"Thank you." She stood there awkwardly for a moment. Then she jerked her thumb over her shoulder. "Still, I'm going to…"

He was already turning away. "Go ahead. I'll start the sandwiches. Ham and cheese okay with you?"

"Yes."

"Great. There's an extra toothbrush in the bathroom," he said as he walked away. "Use anything of mine you want. Brushes, combs—don't worry about asking first."

"Thank you. You're a good guy, Dean. I'm sorry I sharked you that night we played pool."

He laughed as he dragged open the refrigerator. Shot her a beautiful smile that made her pulse skip even faster than before. "I'm not," he told her. "Not at all."

———

WOLF FIXED sandwiches while Haylee went to dress. He'd been serious when he'd told her she didn't have to, but he was also glad she was doing so. Her bare legs were giving him ideas. And though he was pretty sure he could seduce her into bed before the night was through, he felt like he shouldn't do it. He hadn't asked her to stay so he could fuck her. He'd asked her to stay because he didn't want to take her home and leave her there just yet.

He wanted to take his time checking her house when it was daylight, when he could see everything better and make sure it was secure. He didn't think she really wanted to go home alone tonight anyway. By tomorrow night, she'd probably have it all worked out in her head and wouldn't be as vulnerable to the fear someone was trying to break in. Not that he could say for certain she'd have felt that way tonight, but experience had taught him that most people not in his profession usually spent a lot of time worrying about the *what-ifs* and *almosts*. Someone had shoved a note under her door last night and today someone threatened her. It was only natural to sit in her house and flinch at every little sound from outside.

But now she didn't have to. The fact she'd agreed told him she'd needed to be elsewhere tonight. He slathered mustard and mayo on the bread, layered on ham and cheese, and then cut the sandwiches in half. He had pickles in the fridge so he grabbed a couple of spears, then he picked up a bag of chips and took everything back to the living room and set it on the coffee table.

Haylee came sashaying out of the back, black leggings covering her limbs. But she still wore his T-shirt, and he got a very masculine thrill out of seeing her in it. She'd combed her hair and it hung in a shiny curtain down her back. She smiled at him as she came over to sit beside him.

"Wow, this looks really good. You even toasted the bread."

"I'm not just a pretty face, Haylee."

She laughed. He loved the way she sounded in that moment, so happy and carefree. Just a few minutes ago she'd been angry and frustrated. He liked hearing her laugh without pain or fear. It was why he'd made the joke.

"Apparently not." She picked up the sandwich and took a bite. "Mmm, oh wow. So good." She chewed and swallowed and he tried not to feel sexually aroused at the appreciative sounds she made.

"It's not sex, honey. Though I can provide that too if you're feeling hungry for more."

Dammit, not what he'd intended to say. He didn't want her to feel any pressure or discomfort.

She laughed again. "First of all, a man who makes you a sandwich this delicious doesn't have to provide sex in order to impress you. And second, a man who makes you a delicious sandwich *and* gives you an orgasm is definitely marriage material. You might want to dial it down there, Dean. I might never leave if you aren't careful."

He couldn't help but snort a laugh. She amused the hell out of him when he least expected it. "You're funny."

"Sometimes." She sighed happily and leaned back on the couch with her paper plate. "What's on TV? Anything good?"

"Depends on what you think is good."

"How about HGTV? Or the Food Channel. Oooh, I know—the Hallmark Channel!"

He tried not to let his horror show. He must have failed because she laughed again. "I'm kidding, stud. What do you like? Isn't there a football game on? Formula One? Something appropriately manly?"

"There's football," he said warily. "But are you serious about that or just saying it to accommodate me?"

She chucked his arm with her free hand. "Okay, so I do like those channels, but I was pretty sure you wouldn't so I said it to get a reaction. I *am* serious about football. I *like* football. So please put on the game."

He wondered if it was a test or something, but then she arched an eyebrow and he thought *Fuck it.* If she didn't like it she could say so. He turned on the game and grabbed his plate.

They watched the game in silence for several minutes. And then Haylee let out a groan when the quarterback got sacked. "Seriously, dude? You couldn't let go of the damned ball? Just throw the stupid thing for pete's sake!"

Wolf eyed her with interest. She glared at him. "What?"

He shook his head. "Nothing."

"He had three open receivers out there. But this guy couldn't throw a rock over a cliff, much less a football into the arms of a waiting receiver."

Wolf laughed. "Wouldn't have guessed you were such a fan."

"Wouldn't have guessed I could play pool either."

"No, you got me there." Damn he liked her. A lot. She was more interesting than any woman he'd ever dated before. This is the point at which he'd usually be wondering if the sex was any good, but he already knew the answer to that too.

Her phone dinged and she jumped. She picked it up and peered at the screen. He tried to keep his eyes on the game and not watch her expression, but he couldn't help himself. She was frowning.

"Anything wrong?" he asked.

She looked up. Pasted on a smile. "Of course not." She dropped her gaze to her phone again. But she didn't type an answer. Instead, she set it face down and picked up a potato chip.

He waited a few moments, but she didn't say anything. Just frowned at the television and mechanically ate potato chips.

"Haylee."

She jerked her gaze to his. "Yes?"

"The message. What is it?"

Her frown grew harder. Then she blew out a breath. "It's Tony. He wants to talk."

Jealousy twisted inside him. He didn't understand it, but there it was. "Did he say what about?"

"No. He said last night was fun. And that he wanted to call me if I wasn't busy."

"You didn't answer him."

"Because I'm busy. If I answered, then how busy could I be?"

He couldn't fault her logic there. "You don't look happy about it."

She blew out a breath. "Because now you've got me wondering if he wants more than friendship."

"You honestly had no clue he might?"

She closed her eyes for a second. "Okay, yes, I suspected. But until you confirmed it, I thought it was just me being paranoid."

"How long did he date your friend?"

"A couple of months. He was pretty broken up by her death."

"And now he's interested in you."

She sighed. "You might be right." She picked up

her phone again, started to type. Then she pressed send and gave him a smile. "I told him I can't right now as I'm on a date."

Wolf's eyebrows lifted. "Good play, Haylee."

"Thanks." Her mouth twisted as she looked at the TV again. "Come on, dude! Did you put butter all over your hands before walking onto the field today?"

Wolf snorted a laugh. Then he lay back on the couch and enjoyed himself.

Chapter Eighteen

THE GAME LASTED ANOTHER HOUR AND THEN IT WAS over and Haylee was yawning again. She liked watching the game with Wolf. He was quieter about it than she was, but he still got pissed at bad plays and bad calls. They high fived each other on the good plays, and cheered when their receivers were running down the field with the ball.

"One of the guys at work has a brother in the NFL," he said during a commercial break when he'd muted the TV. "Storm Kelley."

Haylee felt her jaw drop. "Storm Kelley? He's kind of a big deal."

"Yeah, sure is. Best quarterback in the league this season."

"Think he'll get a Super Bowl win?"

"Hard to say. I think his team isn't good enough to propel him."

"Their defense sucks," she said.

"They need a good first round pick to turn it around."

"Agreed." She stifled a yawn with the back of her hand. He noticed.

"You should go to bed. I have to be at training early, so I'll be leaving around five."

"Wow, that's super early."

"Yep. But you don't have to get up. Sleep in and when I get back I'll take you home. There's eggs and cereal and coffee. Have what you like."

"That's sweet of you."

He shrugged. "If you say so."

"It was sweet of you to pick me up today. And to let me stay. I'm sorry if I've inconvenienced you at all."

"You didn't inconvenience me. I told you to call me if you needed me. I didn't give you my number to be nice."

"I appreciate that." It felt awkward all of a sudden. Why was it awkward? "You know, I could sleep here on the couch." She eyed it. "It's certainly big enough for me. If you'd like your bed back."

His gaze was hot. "I remember how we slept in El Salvador."

Her heart thumped. "I remember it too. But that's not all we did."

"No." He shook his head. "You take the bed, Haylee. I'm fine out here."

She didn't want to go. In fact, she wanted to curl up against him like she had that night in El Salvador.

She got to her feet reluctantly. "Thanks, Wolf. For the sandwich and the company—and everything, really."

"You're welcome. You need anything to be comfortable? Another blanket? A different pillow?"

She shook her head. "No, I'm fine." She started to walk backward, toward the hall, her gaze still tangled with his, her belly twisting with fiery need. "Goodnight, Wolf," she said, determined to make it to his bedroom without asking him to join her.

His gaze was on fire. "Goodnight, Haylee. Sleep tight."

"You too."

She turned and fled, her body throbbing with thwarted desire as she closed the bedroom door behind her and leaned against it, eyes closing as she concentrated on breathing in and out, in and out.

Jeez, she'd given him that whole speech about how it wasn't going to be so easy for him this time around, that she wanted him to work for it, yet here she was wishing she could jump him right damn now.

Haylee went over and climbed beneath his sheets. She ached to feel the way she had back in El Salvador. To experience that perfect melding of bodies, the heated build to orgasm, the explosion of pleasure that wrung her out and left her craving more.

But there was something else too. Something she had to acknowledge. If she did that, if they spent the night together again, it wasn't just sex to her. There were emotions involved, at least for her—and she didn't really want to find out that she was the only one.

She lay there and strained to hear the sounds coming from the living room. The television stayed on, but she heard him walking around. He started to talk and her breathing grew shallow as she tried to hear the words. He was on the phone with someone, but what was he talking about? Her?

For a brief moment, she wondered if he was talking to a woman. If everything he'd told her was a lie and he was actually involved with someone else and that's why he hadn't come to see her like he'd said he would. It was possible. Anything was possible.

She'd known men who lived double lives. Her father had done so before he'd left them and married the younger woman he'd been seeing. Haylee bit her bottom lip. That had been a hard time. Her mother cried a lot, and then she suddenly didn't. Her father tried to stay involved, and then he didn't. Haylee had been young and confused, but she remembered those feelings vividly.

And she damned sure wasn't going through them as an adult. Which meant it didn't matter if he was involved with someone else because right now he wasn't involved with *her*. And she wasn't going to cross that line in the sand unless she was positive he didn't have anyone else. Haylee Jamison was nobody's side piece.

She lay in the dark and fumed for a while. She didn't remember falling asleep, but she awoke with a start sometime later. The room was dark and there was no sound coming from the living room. Not even the television. She fumbled for her phone to see the time.

Two a.m. *Lord.*

She lay there, more awake than she wanted to be, and scrolled through her phone. She checked messages—there was a return text from Tony, a text from her editor about the profile of a new congress-woman she was supposed to be working on, and a message from her mother that said simply *Are you coming home for Thanksgiving?*

Considering Thanksgiving was still two months away, she hadn't actually decided. Thanksgiving with her mother was typically low-key. Mom ordered a smoked turkey from a local BBQ restaurant, and they made sides. She invited some of her colleagues who were single. Everyone brought a dish. It often turned into a literary salon of sorts. Haylee loved it, but she also missed her own friends. And football, which her mom didn't watch.

Haylee left all the messages unanswered for now. She'd reply at a more decent hour. Most people turned on their Do Not Disturb function at night, but Haylee was pretty sure her mother did not. If she woke Mom with a text, she'd want a phone call. Haylee wasn't about to call her mother while she was sleeping in a man's bed. Not that Mom would know, but Haylee would.

She sighed and put the phone down. She needed

to pee. She pushed the covers back and got out of bed. The bathroom was in the hall so she opened the door very quietly and listened. There was no sound from the living room. She padded to the bathroom, closed the door, and did her business. Then she returned to the bedroom and considered calling an Uber. She could sneak out and head home and Wolf wouldn't be any wiser. Kind of the way he'd snuck out on her in El Salvador.

Something told her it wouldn't be that easy, though. She decided to test the theory by trekking to the kitchen for something to drink. The living room was dark as she tiptoed in. Wolf was a hulking figure on the couch. He lay on his back, face up, not moving.

She was almost to the kitchen when his voice rumbled into the night. "You okay, Haylee?"

She jumped. "Yes. Just looking for something to drink."

He stood with the grace of a cat rising from a nap. Then he was striding toward her as if he hadn't just been sleeping. How the hell did he do that?

"There's water," he said. "Or Gatorade."

"Water's good."

He moved past her, opened the fridge, and pulled out a bottle of water that he handed to her. She clutched it. "Thanks."

"You sure you're okay?" he asked after a few moments in which she didn't move.

She started. "Yes, fine. Why?"

"You seem nervous."

Did she? "I'm not. Sorry. Just thinking."

"You sleep good?"

"Yes." She sighed. "But I'm afraid I'm awake now. My sleep's been all screwed up."

"That's okay. I'm awake too."

She gave him a lopsided grin. "So now what?"

"Coffee?"

"Sounds good."

He went over and pressed a button on the coffee pot. She was impressed that he'd had it ready to go. It started to brew and she leaned against the counter, watching him move with a grace that always surprised her considering how big and masculine he was.

"It's two in the morning," she said unnecessarily. "How are you so awake?"

He shot her a look. "How are you?"

"My sleep schedule is whacked," she said. "It's part of the job, really. I mean I have appointments and do interviews and stuff during regular hours, but I also work on my own schedule. So long as the work gets done, they don't mind. What's your excuse?"

"The job," he told her. She must have frowned because he lifted an eyebrow. "No, really. You think parachuting into places like Guatemala happens on a nine to five schedule?"

She had a very strong vision of him—grease painted face, stark gray-blue eyes—ripping her attacker away and then asking her, very seriously, if she was okay. A wave of emotion flooded her. She didn't care to examine it. "I didn't think about it. Guess not."

"Nope. I get on a pretty regular schedule when we're home, but we've only been back about a week. It takes time."

She wanted to know more about him. Everything. And wasn't that just a little bit dangerous? "So how often do you, uh, do that kind of thing?"

"All the time, Haylee. It's the job."

A pang of something stabbed into her. Worry? "It's dangerous."

"Yes." He busied himself with getting cups out of the cabinets. "Cream? Sugar?"

"Cream."

He went to the refrigerator and pulled out the cream. Then he faced her. She was still reeling over the revelation what he did was dangerous. As if she didn't already know it. Seriously, who was she kidding? Of course she knew. She'd fucking *been* there.

"This is part of the reason I didn't come see you," he said quietly. "It's a lot to take in. One night stands? Easy. A relationship? Not so easy. I've been in Special Ops for seven years now—and I've never yet found a woman who could handle it. You said you wanted to date me—but do you really? Can you handle this, or would you rather chalk us up to a one-night stand and move on?"

SHE LOOKED like a deer caught in the headlights. Maybe he was pushing her too far too fast, but dammit, he'd lain on that uncomfortable fucking couch, tossing and turning and thinking hard about this. She wanted to date, but what the fuck was the end game? He liked her—a lot—but if she couldn't handle his life, then why start? She had to understand what it meant. Had to.

Or the whole damn thing was doomed.

The coffee maker beeped and he turned to get the pot. Poured it into two cups. Handed her a cup with a spoon so she could stir in cream. Lifted his and sipped while she splashed in the cream. Then she stirred and suddenly frowned as she watched him drink.

"Why do you have cream if you don't use it?"

"I use it in tea."

She tipped her head to the side in adorable confusion. "Really? You drink cream in tea but not coffee?"

He shrugged. "I don't drink tea often, but my mom always fixed it with cream. It's like going home again, you know?"

Her lashes dipped as she lifted her cup and drank. "Yes. I understand that. My mom's grilled cheese sandwiches are like that for me. She butters the inside of the bread, and she puts a slice of cheddar and mozzarella in there. It melts in your mouth."

"Sounds good."

"It's delicious. I'll make you one someday." She frowned suddenly, as if she hadn't meant to say that.

Maybe she thought she was being too forward. Or maybe the whole thing was just awkward.

"I'd like that," he said.

She lifted her gaze. "Would you?"

He didn't look away. "Yes." He wanted to kiss her. Wanted to take her coffee, set it down, and plunder her mouth. And he nearly did. But what if that wasn't the right move? What if it was too bold? Not that being bold typically bothered him. Experience told him that being bold usually worked out quite well. Women liked it when he took charge. But what if that was the women he usually slept with and not a woman like Haylee? She was strong, independent. She might not like him taking charge.

She hadn't seemed to mind in El Salvador, but that was a different situation. She'd almost advocated her power to him so she could let go without feeling guilty. Now? Now she was confident and vibrant and in charge of what she wanted. And he wasn't going to cross that without more concrete signals.

She smiled tentatively. "Then I guess we'll have to make it happen."

"Yeah, guess so."

She didn't say anything for a long moment. Then she fixed him with her dark gaze. "You said you wouldn't play games with me—so I just want to say, if you've got another woman out there, if you're the kind of guy who likes to have a few women on the hook, well, maybe just let me know that now, okay? I'd rather not get involved in that kind of thing."

His brow furrowed. "What makes you think I'd do that?"

She wouldn't look at him. "I heard you on the phone earlier. After I went to the bedroom. It occurred to me that I have no real idea who you are deep down… or what you'd do in pursuit of a goal."

He didn't blame her. Not really. And yet her distrust pinched somewhere deep inside. Not to mention the numbness of what he had to deal with in his personal life. But if he was going to share it with anyone, it would be her. Haylee understood. "I was talking to my mom. The custody hearing has been moved again. Taylor and Jack are still in state custody. Cheryl is still in a facility. She's making progress, but the state won't let her have the kids anytime soon."

"I'm so sorry, Dean."

He shrugged. "They're searching for the father right now. A waste of time since he won't want them either—though who knows, if they come with a check for their care, he might pull himself together long enough to convince child services he's fucking perfect for the job."

She reached out and put her hand on top of his where he'd rested it on the counter. Squeezed. He waited a moment, but she didn't let go. So he turned his hand into hers and squeezed back. Haylee got it. Really got it. He hated that she did, and he appreciated it too. "I'm sorry. I shouldn't have hit you with that right now. I shouldn't have doubted you."

He squeezed her hand again. Then he set his

coffee down, slid his fingers against the soft skin of her cheek. He didn't miss her intake of breath, or the way a small flame flickered to life deep inside him. "I'm not mad, Haylee. We don't really know each other, do we? It's understandable that you'd have doubts. But believe me when I tell you that I don't usually spend this much time with a woman I'm not, uh, you know…" he trailed off, unwilling to say that most of the time he spent with the opposite sex was spent in bed.

She smiled at him, and his heart hitched. What the hell?

"It's okay. I get it. You're saying most of the time you're with a woman, it's in bed."

"Uh, yeah. Sorry."

She didn't draw back her hand, and he didn't let it go. He liked holding her hand. Her skin was soft, and there was a certain kind of electricity that flowed into him as he did so. She made him want things he'd never thought possible. Companionship. Understanding. Belonging.

He had no idea why she affected him that way, but it was undeniable that she did.

He let her go and picked up his coffee again. She put both hands on her cup and drew it to her lips, lashes dropping as she took a drink. How could drinking coffee be sensual?

"How much longer does the lawyer think it will be?" she asked.

"She doesn't know. It's a never-ending cycle of

money and hearings and nothing getting done. My parents are coming to the end of their rope. Add in the current market for farmers, and life is really hard right now. Mom's retirement only goes so far to keep things afloat."

"Oh, Dean."

"It's okay," he said, drawing in a breath. "They've weathered bad markets before. I think they'll be okay. I hope they will."

Even if he was killed in the line of duty, his Serviceman's Group Life Insurance would only be a drop in the bucket of what they needed to keep the farm afloat and fight for the kids too. He didn't like to think about it, but sometimes he did. If the next mission meant he didn't come home, would the money help? It would, but only for a season.

"You look like you were thinking of something else there," she said quietly.

"It's nothing."

"Is it?"

He firmed his resolve. "Yeah, nothing."

"Okay," she said.

That one word hurt more than it should. Not because it was the wrong word to say, but because it showed that she respected him enough not to push. Why would that hurt? He didn't know. He reached for her hand again, lifted it to his lips and kissed it.

She set her coffee down and ran her free hand through his hair. His scalp tingled, the pleasurable sensation shooting down his spine. Into his balls.

Everything within him urged him to kiss her. Yet his brain held him back. Why was he so uncertain with this woman? Why did she make him feel like he had no clue what he was doing?

"This is crazy," she whispered, echoing what was in his head.

"Yes."

"I want—" She broke off. Swallowed. Shook her head.

"What?" He wanted to hear her say it. So badly he thought he might die if she didn't.

"I don't, um…" She drew in a breath, huffed it out. "You," she said simply, seeming to give up on any denials. "I want you."

"It's mutual, Haylee," he said, his voice rough. Like the quiet joy that surged inside him at her words. "But I don't want to do anything that's going to make you regret it tomorrow. I don't want you to think all I want from you is sex."

She laughed. It was a small, uncertain sound. "I appreciate that, Wolf. But what else is there? We haven't tried to do anything else together, have we?"

He frowned. "Not true. We've talked. I've told you things I've never told anyone else. Not even my team. I mean they know about Cheryl and the kids, but they don't know how much it bothers me. Or how much I'm willing to sacrifice to fix it."

"Oh, Wolf. You can't fix it. You know that, right?"

He hated the pain in his gut. "Yeah, I know. But I have to try."

"I know, honey," she said softly. "If I could fix it for you, I would. But I can't. Nobody can."

"You understand better than anyone I've met. I'm glad for that—and sorry too. I'm sorry you lost your friend."

Her smile was sad. "I know. But nothing can change that. Hopefully, your sister will have a better chance. I really hope she does. Maybe she can recover and learn to live a normal life."

"I hope so," he said. "But honestly, Haylee— " He swallowed. He'd never said this to anyone else. "Honestly, I don't think it's possible. The temptation will always be there. Cheryl will always be an addict. One slip and she's done."

"All you can do is make sure she gets the help she needs. And have Narcan on hand if possible."

"I want her to get out of there and go back to Iowa. The farm is peaceful. Winter's coming and it'll be colder than shit, but Mom and Dad would give her everything she needed. The kids would play in the snow the way we did growing up. And Christmas? They'd be so happy. Mom really goes all out—cookies, hot chocolate, fresh cedar trees and pine garlands. Homemade ornaments, movies—and Dad has a Santa outfit. He used to put his work boots on and stomp around in the snow on Christmas Eve after we'd gone to bed just so we could see Santa's footprints. And sometimes it'd snow after he'd done it and he'd have to go do it again."

He caught himself before he kept on talking.

What the fuck was he doing, rattling on about child-hood Christmases anyway?

Haylee smiled. "It sounds amazing. How long did it take you to stop believing in Santa Claus anyway?"

He snorted. "A bit longer than it should have. I held on until about eleven, I think. The kids at school would tease me, but I had those footprints, you see."

"Were you mad when you finally learned the truth?"

He remembered his mom sitting him down. Explaining. "Nope. My mom had a way of making me think I was being initiated into a secret club of adults who knew the sacred truth."

"She sounds pretty terrific."

"She is. So's Dad. That's why it's so hard to sit by and be unable to do a damned thing about this. What I do—well, I fix things. I make things right again. And I can't make this right, no matter how much money I throw at it."

Haylee set her cup down and straightened. Then she stepped into his space and his breath hitched in. She didn't meet his gaze for the longest moment. She put her hand on his forearm, traced it up his biceps to his shoulder, her eyes following her progress. Then she lifted her gaze to his and what he saw there made his gut clench. Her eyes were dark, shiny, and filled with emotion.

"I'm beginning to think we aren't conventional in any sense," she said. "That a few weeks of chaste dating and getting to know each other isn't going to work for us."

He turned his cheek into her palm as she skimmed her fingers along his jaw. "Then what will?"

"This," she whispered. And then she stood on tiptoe and pressed her lips to his.

Chapter Nineteen

It was useless to deny it. She was crazy over this man, a man she'd only met a few weeks ago and slept with for one night. But what was the point in taking it slow and getting to know each other? How much more could she know about him beyond the fact he was deeply emotional about his family? He loved his parents, his sister, his niece and nephew. He wanted what was best for them and it tore him up inside that he couldn't get it.

And then there was the way he'd treated her. He'd saved her from a sexual assault before he even knew her name. Then he'd spent hours getting her to safety, protecting her, talking with her. As if that wasn't enough, he'd worshipped her body and gave her the best sex of her life in a thoughtful, tender, sexy way.

No, he hadn't gotten in touch with her after that night like he'd said he would. But when she'd needed him today, he'd been there. He'd come to get her after

John Payne threatened her, and he'd been working to find answers.

So she'd made a decision based on gut feelings. And she knew it was right. Knew it down to her soul. It was this: she wasn't taking it slow, no matter what she'd said earlier.

What a stupid idea anyway.

That's right, girlfriend. Take what you want. Grab happiness with both hands, for however long it lasts. That's what I'd do if I could.

Nicole's voice in her head was sweet and sad at the same time. Not that it was *really* Nicole. But it's what Nicole would say if she were here. If Nicole had another chance, would she waste time taking it slowly?

Hell no.

Wolf was still for a second, and then his arms came around her body, his big hands crushing her to him as he opened his mouth and took what she offered. She felt him hardening against her and she knew where this was going. Where she wanted it to go.

He was here and she was here and nothing was holding her back now. Life was too short. He ached for his sister and she ached for Nicole, and by God they both understood how important life and happiness—and just *living*—were.

Wolf grabbed her ass, lifted her as she wrapped her legs around his hips. It put his hardness right where she wanted it and she gasped as he flexed and sent sparks flying behind her eyes. She reached for the hem of his shirt, shoved her hands beneath it until she could touch hot, naked skin. She spread her hands over his pecs, gloried in all that hard, smooth muscle as it flexed and jumped beneath her fingers.

He set her on the counter, leaned into her, kissing her as if he were starved for her. And maybe he was, because she was starved for him. He tasted like coffee and determination, and liquid heat flooded her, making her molten, ready to go up in flames.

She dropped her hands to the waistband of the athletic shorts he wore, intending to dive beneath and find the good stuff. But he gripped her wrists gently, tore his mouth from hers.

"Wait," he said, his gaze searching hers as her eyes popped open to meet his.

"What?"

A line appeared on his forehead. "Why? Earlier, you wanted to go slow—what's this about, Haylee? Because I don't want to do anything you'll end up regretting later."

"Do you want to go slow, Wolf?"

He frowned. "Is this a pop quiz? Because I want what you want. I want what's going make you happy."

Her heart skipped around in her chest. "Why?"

He looked surprised. "Why? Because I don't want you to feel any doubts."

Oh, he was adorable. "Yes, but *why?* Why don't you want me to feel doubts or regrets?"

"Because I don't want to fuck this up. I want to

see you again, and I can wait for sex if it means we get to know each other better."

She ran her hands up his chest, behind his neck, into his hair. She felt remarkably free to do so. It was kinda crazy, really. He didn't move. His eyes speared intensely into hers.

"I know all I need to know about you, Wolf. I mean I want to know more, but I know enough to tell me that being with you like this is exactly what I want. What do you want to know about me?"

He hesitated. "What's your favorite color?"

She laughed in confusion. "Color? I don't know. It changes, but I think I like pink more than the rest. I definitely like pink nail polish on my toes. Pink roses are lovely. And a pink sky at dawn or dusk—love that, though maybe it's more salmon sometimes…" She shook her head and laughed again. "You didn't really want to know all that."

"Yes. I did."

Her heart fluttered.

"I want to know what you like and what you don't," he said. "I want to know the little things and the big things. Gotta start somewhere, right?"

"You want to know what else I like?"

"Yeah, hit me with it."

"I like the way you kiss me. Not too much tongue, nor too little. Just enough. I like that you seem to know what to do with it. You'd be surprised how many guys don't have a clue. But not you. You *know*."

He grinned. "I can do a lot with this tongue."

"I know you can."

"You know, I'm thinking about giving you a demonstration. But it's gonna be shorter than I'd like since I have to be to work in about three hours."

Her belly tightened. Her pussy ached. She *needed*. "Three hours? Isn't that enough time?"

"No, but looks like we'll have to work with what we've got." He grinned then and she smiled back. He was too adorable. And sexy as hell. Confidently sexy. She knew he could deliver on everything he'd promised.

"So no more talking about colors and stuff like that?"

"Not right now. So long as you're sure you're ready for this step."

She took his hand in hers, pulled it between her legs and placed it over her center. "You feel that heat?"

His eyes sparked. His expression filled with such promise that she nearly moaned. "Fuck yeah, I feel it."

"That's for you, Wolf. I'm hot and wet and ready. For you. You make me crazy."

He gripped her hips and tugged her forward, lifting her up. "Honey, the feeling is mutual. I'm crazy to get in there again. Nothing feels as good as you do."

———

HE LOVED women and sex and all the pleasurable feelings that went with getting naked with a willing woman. But there was something about Haylee that was more exciting—more profound—than anything he'd ever experienced. He desperately wanted to be inside her body again. And he desperately wanted to make her feel the most intense pleasure she'd ever known.

He picked her up and she wrapped her legs around him. She smelled so good. Like flowers and sunshine and other sweet stuff. He put his nose to her skin, inhaled. Then he licked her neck while she held on to him and gasped.

"Bed or couch?" he asked, soul deep hunger rolling through him in a wave.

"Don't care," she gasped. "Counter, floor, table. Fuck me, Wolf. I don't care where."

Jesus. He put a hand to the back of her head, fused his mouth to hers. They kissed hungrily, deeply. He walked them toward the bedroom—or he thought he did—but he only made it as far as the couch. He tumbled her backward, falling with her, coming down on top of her on the soft cushions. Their mouths didn't cease taking from each other, sucking and kissing and licking, until the heat was so intense he lifted himself off her and tugged at her shirt. It came off easily. She wasn't wearing a bra, and he groaned as he dropped down to suck her nipples. She arched into him, and his urgency increased exponentially. He dragged her leggings down, her panties, and then she was spread beneath him, pretty legs falling open, enticing him into heaven.

He lifted his eyes to hers even as his fingers fell to her wet seam. Slipped against her clit while she gasped, her eyes rolling back in her head.

"Wolf," she gasped.

"Yeah, baby. Come for me."

"Not without you," she moaned.

"Just the first time," he soothed. "I want to see it." He dropped down between her legs, pushed them wider, and licked his way around her juicy center. Her moans were an aphrodisiac. He kept his eyes on her face, watching as she started to come apart beneath his tongue. He licked her hard and soft, fast and slow, until she stiffened and cried out, her entire body shaking apart beneath him.

He licked her harder then, faster, driving her over the edge of her own personal cliff, his heart racing as he did so. Loving her cries. Her taste. Wanting more of her than he had a right to want.

She collapsed with a sigh, and his blood pounded in his temples. His cock was harder than stone. He wanted to possess her. Right damn now. Thrust in her body and make her fly apart again.

"Haylee," he growled, and she looked up at him, her eyes wide and pretty. Something twisted in his belly. Emotion threatened to flood him, but he shut it off at the source. Or shut most of it off, anyway. "You're fucking beautiful."

She smiled. "So are you."

Goddamn it.

"I have to go get a condom. Be right back."

"Okay. But, Wolf," she began. He stared at her, waiting. "I'm on the pill. And I've, uh, not been with anybody but you in a very long time. I'm healthy. In case you are," she finished softly.

He swallowed. Were they really going there? "Before you, I was with different women often. Since you? Nobody. But I never go without protection. Never. Which means I haven't been bare inside a woman since I was a teenager—and I get tested regularly."

"It's up to you," she said, running her fingers through his hair, over his jaw. "But I trust you."

His heart flipped. She trusted him. And he damned sure knew he trusted her. He couldn't say why, not with one hundred percent certainty, but he knew that he did. Haylee was special.

He lifted himself off her and tore his shirt up and off. She reached for his waistband, pushed his shorts down his hips until his cock sprang free. He held himself above her on his fists, staring down at her pretty body—pointy nipples, firm breasts, caramel skin, narrow waist, generous hips, and a glistening pussy that begged him to slip inside. He grasped his cock, dipped it into her wetness, and rubbed it up and down her slit before sinking into her.

"Fuck," he said as his dick glided into her body. Her passage was tight, hot, and so wet it was perfect. He could live like this. Just buried inside her, feeling his heart beating in his veins, the fire dancing over his skin, the dark urge to thrust until he exploded barely contained within him.

"I hope so," she said, and he had to stop moving and just think. Think hard about not coming within six seconds and ending everything right now.

"Haylee," he groaned. And then he kissed her. Fused his mouth to hers and started to move, slowly to begin with, then faster and faster. Until the two of them were rising and falling together, hearts beating hard, breath sawing in and out, pleasure building like steam in a pressure cooker.

Sweat beaded on his forehead, his chest. He wrapped his hands in hers and pushed them high above their heads, shifting until he could fuck her at another angle.

"Wolf," she moaned, tearing her mouth from his. "Oh, please. Please."

"Haylee—damn, you feel good," he moaned in her ear before he nipped the skin of her neck. She gasped, and he kissed the hurt he'd made. "Sorry, baby. Sorry."

"No," she said. "I like it."

He slipped a hand between them, into the slick heat of her. Her breath caught as he rubbed her clit. She exploded with no warning, gasping, her body quivering with the force of her orgasm.

He wanted to finish right then, but he also wanted it to last. He pulled out of her body, flipped her over while she still panted and moaned, and slammed into her from behind. Her back arched, her hair splaying over the smooth expanse of her skin. Her ass was perfect, heart shaped. She made him absolutely fucking crazy.

Wolf wrapped his hands around her hips and held her still as he pumped into her. Slowly at first. So slowly it fucking hurt.

"I love watching my cock disappear inside you," he bit out. "The way you take me—it's beautiful."

She reached between them, cupping his balls, rolling them together, and he lost it. Just fucking lost it. Three damn pumps and he was done, shooting into her body like she was his first lover and he had no control.

Which he didn't. Not right now. He jerked hard, his cock emptying inside her, a groan tearing from him as he came harder than he'd ever come in his life. Long seconds passed until he slipped from her body.

"Stay there," he told her, standing and going into the bathroom to grab a towel. He returned with it and gave it to her so she could clean up. Once she was done, he took it and tossed it on the floor, then he gathered her against him and settled on the couch, their naked bodies pressed together, her arms around his neck as she lay on her side in front of him.

"That was amazing," he told her, kissing her softly. She kissed him back, and his heart lurched just a little bit.

"I could get used to this," she said.

"Me too."

Chapter Twenty

"HEY, BABY, I GOTTA GO," WOLF SAID, WAKING HER from a pleasant dream in which he'd been going down on her again. Or was it a dream?

She blinked up at him. She was lying in his bed, where they'd ended up after another hot session in the shower just a little while earlier. Her body was sated, her mind at rest. Happiness suffused her.

Wolf bent down and kissed her on the forehead. She protested, reaching for him, but he laughed and dodged her grip.

"As much as I want to stay with you, if I don't go to work, there'll be hell to pay."

"Call in sick," she said, only half serious.

"Can't, baby. That's not what we do in the military."

She sighed and stretched. "No, I know it. Go save the world, Wolf."

He bent and kissed her again, this time on the

mouth. She moaned a little bit, her body sizzling to life with his mouth on hers. He straightened. "Don't go anywhere, Haylee. Stay here and I'll be back as soon as I can. Might be afternoon though. Probably will be."

"I have work to do."

"You can use my computer. There's a guest login. It's secure and you can surf wherever you need to go. I'm not worried about viruses or anything."

"Thank you."

"Now go back to sleep. Eat whatever you want when you wake. Watch TV, work on the computer. But don't leave until I can go with you, okay?"

She gazed up at him standing there in the dim light, clad in camouflage, looking so calm and competent. And commanding. Definitely commanding. She shouldn't like that about him, but she did.

"Okay. But why are you so worried about me calling an Uber and going home?"

"Not worried, babe. I'd just like to check your place myself. Make sure it's secure for you. I'll feel better about you being there if I can do that."

She wanted to melt. "Then I'll wait here for you to get back."

He gave her a grin. "Call me if something happens."

"I will." She listened as the door closed and his truck started. Then she lay there in the semi-darkness, surrounded by his scent in the sheets, her naked body sensitive to every soft scrape of the fabric against her skin.

I hope you know what you're doing.

Her voice, not Nicole's. "I hope so too," she murmured before she turned over and fell asleep again. When next she woke, light streamed in beneath the curtains. She reached for her phone, which Wolf had plugged into his charger for her, to check the time. Nine o'clock. Wow, she'd slept longer than she usually did.

She got up and tugged on Wolf's T-shirt and her leggings. Then she sauntered into his kitchen and dragged open the fridge. There was yogurt, so she grabbed one of those. When she was searching for a spoon, she spotted a sticky note on the coffee pot.

It's ready to go. Just press the button.

Oh, could it get any better? Haylee turned the machine on and peeled open the yogurt. When she was finished, she dropped the empty container in the trash and poured a cup of coffee. Then she stood and looked out the kitchen window. There was a house across the street with a child in the yard and a young woman on her phone watching the kid. She sat on a porch step, cigarette in her mouth, and occasionally barked something at the child. But the child looked happy and the women eventually ended the call, stubbed out the cigarette, and went over to investigate whatever it was the child wanted to show her. Just a normal day in suburbia.

Haylee turned and spied Wolf's computer on the

kitchen table. There was another sticky note waiting for her. This one said *Guest login is guest. All lowercase. Set it up for you this morning.*

Awww. Her heart squeezed. He'd set it up specifically for her. She lifted the lid and logged on. She checked her email first. There was all the usual spam, a message from her editor, and something from Tony. She opened Tony's email first.

HEY, Haylee. Sorry to disturb you during your date. I didn't realize you were seeing anyone. Call me when you get this. I think I've found something you could use.

HAYLEE FROWNED. Something she could use? What did that mean. She picked up her phone and dialed Tony. He answered on the second ring.

"Haylee, hi." He sounded like he was walking outside somewhere.

"Hi, Tony. Got your message. What's up?"

"You back home yet?" he asked.

She frowned. Back home? How did he know she wasn't there? "Not at the moment. Just running some errands."

"When do you plan to be back?"

Haylee hesitated. "In a bit. Not quite sure yet."

"Guess it's serious with this guy, huh?"

She started to deny it. And then she decided, what the fuck, it really wasn't any of his business anyway so he didn't deserve delicacy. "It's complicated."

Because it was.

"Is it the guy you disappeared with at the fundraiser?"

Haylee gritted her teeth. "His name is Dean. Yes, he's the one. And like I said, it's complicated."

"I had no idea you were involved with anyone." He sounded a bit self-righteous. Haylee bristled.

"I really don't want to talk about this, Tony. What do you have for me?"

"I'd rather not discuss it over the phone. That's why I was asking if you were home. I have something you should hear. For the story."

Her heart skipped. "Okay. What time is good for you?"

"I've got a brief to attend this morning, and then some meetings after. How about this afternoon? One o'clock?"

Haylee chewed her lip. She hoped like hell Wolf was back by then. "Yeah, sounds good." She didn't want to go without Wolf, but she would if she had to.

"Your place at one, then. See you there."

"See you."

Haylee frowned at her email for several moments. Then she texted Wolf.

"DUDE, your shots were a little off today," Saint said as they left the range.

Wolf grumbled. He'd shot well, but not as well as he usually did. He'd been distracted. Thinking about Haylee and how he wanted to be lying in bed with her instead of standing in a bay at six in the fucking morning and aiming at targets.

"Won't happen again."

"No, probably won't. You've just got to get your head in the game. Stop thinking about fucking your girl."

Wolf stiffened. "Saint," he began.

"Speaking from experience, man. Don't get offended."

"Fine."

"In fact, your shots were competent and on point. Just not as accurate as usual. You missed a couple you wouldn't normally miss. Distraction."

"Yeah." He hated that he'd missed any. It happened to all of them. But not one of them liked it when it did.

Saint stopped before they reached the locker rooms where they'd wash up and change. "We're headed out again soon. A week, maybe. You need to get your situation with Haylee figured out."

Fuck. "Any idea where?"

Saint shook his head. "No. Maybe South America. Maybe the Middle East. I don't know, but I know our ops tempo is increasing and Echo is going again soon."

Wolf gritted his teeth. "I'll be ready."

"I know. Just thought you'd like the heads up."

"I'd like it better if there was some dirt on Silva we could use."

"I know. I'm trying, but he's not officially our problem."

"He's everybody's problem, Saint."

"Not disagreeing with you. But he's not specifically *our* charge. We pulled the hostages from Guatemala. That was our job. It's up to the DEA to nail Silva, though if Hacker and Bliss find anything we can use to help it along, I'm all for it. I trust Viking's wife to get it done with or without us, though."

Dane "Viking" Erikson was the SEAL team commander and his wife was a DEA agent who'd been involved in a joint effort with HOT to take down a drug submarine stolen by terrorists a while back. Wolf had met Ivy Erikson a couple of times and he fully believed her capable of eliminating drug lords without an ounce of remorse. But he had a personal interest in this drug lord. He hadn't liked the way Silva looked at Haylee, or the way his henchman felt free to threaten her so boldly and openly.

"What about John Payne?"

Saint blew out a breath. "He's clean so far."

"If he approaches Haylee again, I'm going to pay him a visit."

"Dude, you can't do anything of the sort," Saint groaned. Wolf started to protest, but Saint stopped him. "That's the official position," he added. "But if Payne threatens her again, I'll help you pay him a visit. So will the rest of us. I've already asked and they've said yes. So count on it."

Warmth flooded him. Jesus he loved these guys. "Appreciate it."

"Hopefully it won't come to that. I'd hate to explain to Ghost—or, worse, Mendez—why Echo paid a personal visit to Silva's right hand man. Just be patient, Wolf. Setter has a new shipment arriving in a couple of days. It'll be thoroughly inspected. Maybe we'll get lucky."

"I fucking hope so." He wanted these assholes taken care of before Haylee poked them again. Because it was only a matter of time before she did.

His phone pinged and he pulled it out of his pocket. The message was from Haylee.

Tony wants to meet me at 1. My place. He says he has something to share with me.

Wolf growled as he started to type. *Baby, you can't go without me. Don't even think about it.*

I'm thinking about it, Wolf. It might be important.

Goddammit. *No. It's not safe. Wait for me and I'll go with you.*

When?

After work. 4. Maybe 5.

I don't know if I can stall him that long. He seemed a little anxious.

Wolf closed his eyes. *Fine, make it 3. I'll pick you up. Text him—but don't tell him I'll be with you.*

Okay.

I mean it, Haylee. Don't tell him.

You don't trust him, do you?

No. But I don't trust anybody.

…

He waited for the dots to resolve, wondering what she was typing. It seemed to take an awfully long time. And then it happened, and he blinked at the words.

I think I could love you, Wolf. If that scares you, then I guess it's something I needed to know. Before this goes any further.

He sucked in a breath. And then he typed.

It doesn't scare me.

No, it didn't scare him. Stunned him. Thrilled him. But fear? Nope, not an ounce of it.

Good. I'm not there yet, so don't worry. But it won't take long. You are the perfect man. Badass as hell, thoughtful—you made the coffee for me!—fix a mean sandwich…

He waited for the rest of it, but nothing came. He quickly typed *That's all?*

She sent over the laughing-so-hard-I'm-crying emoji. *What do you want me to say, Dean? That you give me the best orgasms of my life?*

What guy didn't want to know he could do that for a woman?

That would be a start.

Then yes, you do. I already love your [eggplant emoji]. *And what you can do with it.*

He was going to get a hard on right here if he let

himself dwell on that. *I'd like to do a few more things with it later when I see you again.*

Oh, I sure hope so.

Gotta go now, babe. You won't be able to reach me for a couple of hours. Don't go back home, no matter what Tony says he has. Promise me.

I promise, Wolf.

Wolf reluctantly turned his phone off and deposited it in his locker in the HOT gym. He had to head into the secure areas for a while so he'd be out of touch. He hoped like hell Haylee did as she'd promised. If she didn't, he wasn't sure this thing they had would survive.

Chapter Twenty-One

Haylee stalled Tony until three, then got onto the computer and started trying to track down more information on Silva and the Juarez Cartel. She spent two hours searching, but came up with nothing. She slapped the lid of the computer closed and huffed a sigh of frustration. If she didn't get this figured out, nothing would change and more people could die. But they'd die anyway, really, because stopping a single cartel wasn't going to stop the flow of drugs. It was like sticking your finger into a dam to plug a leak. If she disrupted Silva and the Juarezes, others would take their place.

But that didn't mean it wasn't worth doing. The more people who knew about the illicit drugs, and the dangers of buying Oxy off the street, the better. What she was really trying to do was save the person who thought turning to dealers was better than trying to get doctors to keep writing prescriptions—a thing that got harder the longer you took the pills. Maybe the idea someone could suffer the same fate as Nicole might make them think twice. If even one person was saved because of something they learned from Nicole's story, then it was worthwhile.

It was right before two when Haylee heard a vehicle pull into the drive. She went over to the window. Wolf got out of his truck and strode to the door. Mercy, she loved watching him move. He was power and grace, a combination of lethality and sexiness that set up a thrumming in her core.

She heard the key in the lock and had a moment of panic. What should she do? Stand at the door and throw her arms around him when he came inside? Or sit on the couch and try to look dignified? Or maybe she should go to the fridge and pretend she was getting a drink.

She did none of those things. She stood at the window, her heart hammering, and waited for the door to swing open. When it did, he searched the room, his gaze landing on her almost immediately. A grin broke out on his face, and the tap dancing inside her got a whole lot faster.

"Hey," he said, closing the door behind him and swiping the cap from his head.

"Hey yourself," she replied, feet glued to the floor for some inexplicable reason.

He strolled toward her, dropping the cap on the coffee table, his eyes filled with wicked intent. "You're still here."

She tipped her head back to gaze up at him. "Of course I am."

"Wasn't sure you'd stay," he told her, frowning a little bit as he said it.

"I said I would."

"Would you if Tony'd insisted on one o'clock?"

She pursed her lips. All she could do was answer him honestly. "I'm not sure. You know how much I want to get this story."

He curled his fingers around the back of her neck, tugged her with the barest pressure toward him. Of course she didn't need much encouraging. She took the step, her palms going to his chest.

"Thanks for being honest," he said. And then he dipped his head and kissed her. Haylee's insides melted. Liquid heat pooled between her legs. Her pussy throbbed. She stepped into him again, bringing their bodies together. He groaned as she came in contact with his cock. He was hard and ready.

Mercy.

He broke the kiss by stepping backward. "As much as I want to be inside you right now, I think we'd better get over to your place."

"We have a few minutes."

He shook his head. "No, not really. I want to get there before Tony does. Check things out. Be prepared."

She was stupid right now. Horny and stupid. She couldn't think. Thank God he could. "Prepared for what?"

"Anything. These aren't nice people you're dealing with, Haylee."

The fog of desire started to fade as she took the hint. He was talking about violence. "Tony isn't part of that. He's a good guy."

"Maybe so, but I don't know him and therefore don't trust him."

She understood. "Okay. I'm ready when you are."

"Gotta change out of the uniform," he told her, fingers already working the buttons of his camouflage shirt.

Her mouth started to water. "You might want to do that behind a closed door," she told him as she watched his fingers make the trip downward. Thank God he had a T-shirt underneath.

"Why?"

She looked up, met his gaze. His eyes sparked with humor. He knew what he did to her, damn him. "Because we can't be late and I'm weak when you start stripping."

He laughed as he started walking backward, away from her. "I'll be done in a few seconds."

Haylee put a hand to her heart after he'd disappeared down the hallway. "Easy, girl," she muttered. Wolf was turning her into a sex maniac.

True to his word, he was back quickly, wearing a dark blue henley and a pair of faded jeans with scuffed boots. Too sexy for words.

"Let's get moving," he said, leading the way to his truck. He opened her door, waited for her to climb inside, then went around and got in beside her. It was twenty minutes to her place, longer in traffic, but it was a good time of day and they weren't held up anywhere. When he turned onto her street, he slowed.

"I'm going to drive by first. Tell me if anything looks strange."

He made a slow roll past the townhouse she'd shared with Nicole, past her car that still sat where she'd left it, while she scrutinized her front walk and the door and windows.

"Looks normal."

"Good." He turned onto the next street and pulled into a parking place. "We're going in the back door instead of the front. In case anyone is watching."

Haylee dug out her keys and stepped from his truck. He locked it with the press of a button, dropped his keys in his pocket, and came around to take her hand in his. Excitement zipped through her.

Now wasn't the time, but she couldn't help it. Touching Wolf made her nerves sing. She led them to the back gate of the townhouse and then up and onto the rear porch. Wolf took the key from her hand and inserted it into the lock. He swung the door inward, reaching beneath his shirt at his back as he did so. When he brought out a pistol, she had to bite back a gasp.

"Stay inside the door while I clear the house, okay? If you hear anything unusual, get outside." He reached into his pocket and fished out his truck keys.

"Go to my truck and get to the police station. And before you ask, I'll be fine. Just do what I tell you."

She took the keys, nodding because her throat was suddenly too tight to speak. She stood in place while he slipped into her kitchen, through the door to the living room, and disappeared. Haylee waited, straining to hear any sounds, but the only thing she heard was the occasional creak of the floors as he moved. He was back within minutes. The pistol was gone, tucked away again.

"You're clear. But you need a security system in here. The locks are laughable, and the windows could be breached by a determined toddler."

Haylee made a face even though her heart pounded in her ears. "Really? A toddler?"

He shrugged. "Hey, you'd be surprised what a toddler can do. Leave them alone for a minute and you never know what'll happen."

"And how do you know this?"

"Church youth group. Let one toddler out of your sight, let that kid climb up into the baptismal font and decide to take an impromptu bath, and you'll never forget it. Or live it down."

She'd thought he was just making it up to ease the tension. Apparently not. "Oh wow. That could have been bad."

He nodded. "Yep, I was lucky the kid didn't drown himself. But I never got tasked with watching the toddlers again, which was a good thing."

Haylee moved away from the back door and he went over to lock it behind her.

"All doors locked, Haylee. Always."

"I usually do. But I have to admit you're scaring me just a little bit."

He put his hands on her upper arms, squeezed reassuringly. "This is what I do. I'm always going to be a bit intense about personal safety. Not trying to scare you."

"I know. And I appreciate it."

He looked up, taking in the kitchen and the small sitting room it opened onto as if really seeing it for the first time. It was decorated warmly, she thought. She and Nicole had loved to make their space homey and comfortable. There were things missing now, things her parents had taken when they'd come for Nicole's belongings. But it was still pretty. She liked pretty.

"I like it," he said, and warmth filled her. "Looks inviting."

"Thank you."

"Huh, maybe I do need to fire my interior decorator," he teased. "Maybe yours is available?"

"She might be," Haylee said. "For a price."

"What kind of price?"

She liked this silly back and forth with him. It made sparks fly in her belly in a way that surprised her. "The kind you can pay with your body."

He laughed. Ran a hand over his chest. "That's why I work out." He shook himself a moment later. "Okay, we need to get serious, babe. You've got ten minutes until he shows, so where do you intend to talk to him?"

"Living room."

"Great. Let's go." They headed for the living room at the front of the house. He studied the room and she knew he was cataloging everything about it. Not because he liked it, but because he wanted to know how to fight and how to escape if it became necessary.

"So what's the plan?" she asked.

He swung his gaze to hers. "I'm sitting over there," he said, nodding toward the chair beside the opening that led to the kitchen.

"You can't stay in the same room when he arrives," she said in a rush. "He might not talk if he knows you're here."

Wolf frowned. "Do you really think he has something, or is he just trying to get close to you?"

Haylee felt the first stirrings of doubt. "Honestly, I don't know. He sounded pretty serious, and I have to believe he's not wasting my time when he knows how important this is to me. Tony and I have been friends for months now. He knows what it means to me to get justice for Nicole."

"If he cared for Nicole like you say—and if he cares for you—then he should tell you what he came to say whether I'm here or not."

Her belly twisted. "You say that, but not everybody thinks like you do. You're intimidating, Wolf. And if he sees you, then he might just decide he can tell me later—and then I'm back at square one. No, I don't know that Tony has anything worthwhile—or why he just couldn't tell me over the phone. But I'm a reporter, and I know that people can get weird about stuff when talking to reporters. Tony knows me as a Hill correspondent, but he also knows I want to do something more important—which means I could be somewhat dangerous to his career, I guess? I don't know, but I can't risk him getting nervous because you're here."

He blew out a breath. "Fine. I'll stay in the kitchen. But if he threatens you at all, I'm not sitting there quietly. You feel me?"

Haylee shivered at the intensity of his words. It was exciting to be the focus of all that determination. To know that the intimidating man with the big muscles and hard stare was so utterly dialed in on her safety. "I do," she said. "And I'm grateful."

He nodded, his frown not easing. "I'll be in there. Listening. Anything makes you uncomfortable, you say something."

"I will, Wolf. Promise."

Her phone blared just then, sending her nerves shooting skyward. Haylee scrambled for her bag. "Hey, Tony," she said, her heart still hammering in her chest. Wolf was watching her intently.

"Haylee," Tony replied. The connection sounded tinny. "Run… don't… tried… Nicole shouldn't have…"

"What? Tony, you're breaking up. What did you say?"

"Check… email… sent… Bye, Haylee."

"Tony? What's going on? Tony!" The line went dead and she jerked the phone from her ear to hit the redial button. It went straight to voicemail.

"What's happening?" Wolf asked.

She snapped her gaze to him. "I don't know. It was Tony, but he sounded… scared, maybe? The signal wasn't good and he kept breaking up. I don't like this, Wolf. It's all wrong."

His face was hard. He jerked his phone from his pocket and dialed a number. "Stand by," he told her. "Saint, need to track someone's cell phone." He gestured to her and she handed him her phone. He pulled up her last call and read off Tony's number. "No, I don't know what's going on, but Tony Davis just called Haylee and she said he sounded scared. He's supposed to be meeting with her at her place, but I somehow don't think he's coming… Yeah, thanks. I'll be here."

Wolf ended the call. "I've got my guys tracking him. We'll see where he is."

"He's not coming though, is he? I mean he could be, but I don't think so. I couldn't make out what he said, but one of the things was *Nicole shouldn't have*. Shouldn't have what? I have no idea."

"There's no way to know. You just have to wait and hope he calls back. Or knocks on the door."

"But he's not going to. You know it as well as I do."

He nodded. Her expression must have fallen because he came over and drew her into his arms. She put her arms around his waist, closing her eyes as she pressed her face to his chest and breathed him in. He was comforting. His presence was comforting.

"I'm sorry," he said. "Something's spooked him, probably. Doesn't mean you won't get the information. Just not right now."

"I hate this shit," she said, her throat tight. "The cloak and dagger stuff. The secrecy and jockeying."

He stroked her hair. "I know. I hate it for you. But it's what happens when you're down in the muck with criminals."

She pushed away and gazed up at him. "I hope Tony's not one of them. I really hope he's not."

"He might not be. But he knows more than he's been telling you."

She wanted to protest, but Wolf's phone rang. He stepped away and took the call. "Hey, Saint. Whatchu got? … Seriously? … Okay, yeah, thanks."

"What?" she asked when he hung up.

His brows were drawn low. "Last known location was in Virginia. Headed west."

Shock coursed through her. "But that doesn't make any sense."

He grasped her shoulders. "What else did he say?"

"I don't… I didn't understand most of it. Something about running. And email. I think he said to check email?" She shook her head. "I don't know."

"Check it. See if he sent you anything."

She nodded shakily. Brought up her phone and hit the email app. There was nothing new. Her heart fell. And then, in an instant, there was. An email from Tony hit her inbox. With an attachment.

IF YOU'RE GETTING THIS, then something has happened and I wasn't able to show you personally. Take them down, Haylee. Take them all down.

HAYLEE'S FINGER hovered over the download when another sound penetrated her ears. Car doors slamming outside. And then Wolf changed before her eyes. Went from the sexy, growly, flirty badass she knew to an utterly lethal machine. His drew his weapon, stalked to the window and peered outside. Then he turned and strode to her, grabbing her arm and propelling her back to the kitchen and the rear door.

"What is it? What's going on?" she asked even as she hurried to do his bidding.

"Company," he said. "And I'm pretty sure they aren't here for a social call."

Chapter Twenty-Two

WOLF CURSED UNDER HIS BREATH EVEN WHILE HE made plans and hustled Haylee toward the back door. He didn't know who the men outside were, but he was pretty sure they weren't here for any legitimate reason. DEA, FBI—those guys had a look that Wolf recognized. These men had a look too, and it was one Wolf usually saw from people who were up to no good. Considering that Tony Davis was supposed to be arriving for a meeting right now, Wolf would bet these guys knew something about that and were here, if not to intercept Tony, then to do something about Haylee.

There were two men, one white and one Latino, their weapons outlined beneath the fabric of their shirts at their waistbands. They weren't even trying to hide that they were armed. Never a good sign, especially in a state like Maryland with strict concealed carry laws. It was possible they were legit, but Wolf wasn't taking that chance.

Now he just had to hope they weren't smart enough to put anyone at the back of the house. He stopped at the door, peering outside. Haylee's doorbell rang. She turned her head to look back. Wolf scanned the rear yard and the fence, the alley beyond. There was nothing there, but that didn't mean they weren't blockading either end of the alley. Depended on how thorough their plan was and how much trouble they expected from their target.

Wolf glanced down at Haylee. She looked determined, brave. His heart kicked with an emotion he didn't recognize, but he knew he admired her. So damned much. "Here's what we're going to do, Haylee. We're going out the backdoor. Me first, you behind. Follow my lead and do exactly as I tell you, okay?"

"Yes, of course. But why can't we stay here? Call the police?"

"Not enough time. Those men aren't going to wait outside for long, and we can't take the chance that the police won't get here in time."

As if on cue, the men started pounding on the door. Haylee's eyes widened. Pretty soon, they'd graduate to breaking in. Her front door was recessed in an entry nook and hidden from view, except for head on. Bad in general but good for them right now because it meant these guys weren't going around back when they had cover to break in at the front.

"We're heading for my truck, then we're getting inside and getting the hell out of here."

"Okay, lead the way."

Wolf pressed a quick kiss to her lips, then opened the door and pulled Haylee behind him as they made their way across the yard and out the gate. A quick check of the alley showed no one there. Wolf put a hand beneath his shirt, wrapping it around his pistol grip as they hurried toward where he'd parked the truck. They reached it without incident and he fired it up, laying his pistol on the console between them. Haylee's eyes met his. Her mouth was a flat line. He couldn't tell if she was scared or angry or numb.

"Just in case," he said.

"Do you really think they were here for me?"

"I don't know for sure, but it's not a chance I want to take." He reversed the truck, then shoved it into gear and shot for the main road. A quick check of the rearview showed nobody behind him.

Haylee was on her phone, no doubt downloading whatever Tony had sent her. Then she started to play a video. "Oh wow," she breathed.

He couldn't take his eyes from the road and the mirrors. "What is it?" He heard people talking in Spanish but he didn't understand it.

"It's a video showing the Juarez Cartel manufac-turing opioids. There's a sweep of the pill pressing operation and oh—"

"What's wrong?"

"It's Oscar Silva. *In* the facility, Wolf—and oh my

God, there's John Payne and Donnie Setter too. They're all there. There's no doubt it's them, no doubt what's going on." She pressed a hand to her chest. "This is it—this is what I needed. The missing piece tying those men to the operation."

He could hear the emotion in her voice. "What about Watson?"

"He's not in it—but what if Tony knows something about that? Or maybe Watson isn't involved at all. But his cousin sure is. Damn, I wish I could talk to Tony right now. I want to know where he got this."

Wolf didn't know, but he didn't like the implications. "He's an attorney on Watson's staff and he sent you this video—I'm guessing Watson is involved somehow."

"Maybe so. But this is enough to stop Silva—and that's the most important part to me."

"Do you think Tony is the one who sent the papers too?"

She blew out a breath. "I think it had to be. But why didn't he just give them to me? He wants justice for Nicole as much as I do. We've talked about it often enough."

"I think you have your answer in the fact he's running right now. Somebody figured out he was passing information—and he's afraid."

"And I'm afraid for him."

He glanced at her when she didn't say anything else. "But not for yourself? You're involved too. Those guys weren't selling time shares, you know."

A slow smile lit her face. "Nope, I'm not. Because I have you."

————

SHE SHOULD BE SCARED. Abstractly, she was just a little bit. But mostly she knew she had Wolf on her side, and that counted for a lot. If she'd been alone right now, God knows what would have happened to her. But she wasn't alone. Wolf was there, and he knew what to do. He trusted his instincts and he got them the hell out of her house before those men could do anything.

Wolf pressed a button on his steering wheel. A voice told him to say a command. "Dial Saint."

"Dialing Saint," the voice said.

A second later a man picked up. "What's up?"

"Two men breaking into Haylee's house." He gave a description that was shockingly complete considering how little time they'd had to get away. "Can you get the cops on it?"

"Got it. You okay?"

"We're good. Heading back to my place. I'll be in touch."

"Copy that. Stay safe."

"Roger."

"You didn't give him my address," Haylee said after he'd ended the call.

He glanced at her. "Didn't need to. He already knows."

"Do you guys know everything?"

He almost laughed. "No, but we know what we need to."

"Including what those guys looked like with only a glance."

He shrugged. "Hazard of the profession. You pay attention to everything."

Haylee clutched her phone, the video fresh in her mind. "I can't figure out how Tony got this. And if he was the one who put the documents under my door, why didn't he just give them to me? I mean we were at the fundraiser together that night. Why all the cloak and dagger stuff?"

"He's a lawyer. Maybe he was scared about being connected to the evidence. Or maybe he's just an asshole."

Haylee hated the way her insides churned. "Or maybe it wasn't him at all. Maybe somebody else left the documents."

"It's possible. I don't think it's likely now that you've seen the video, but it's possible."

"I wish I could talk to him."

"I wish we both could," he grumbled.

Wolf didn't take the most logical route back to his place. He spent more than forty-five minutes taking back roads and side streets, criss crossing his path until he finally turned into his driveway.

They went inside and Haylee felt a moment's defeat that she hadn't even gotten any fresh clothes or her computer from her place. And then she wondered if those men had broken in trashed the place before the police arrived.

"Send me the video," Wolf said as he locked the door behind them. "I'll send it to my team and see what they can find."

Haylee hesitated. Wolf waited, one eyebrow lifting when she didn't move to do as he asked. "I'm sorry," she said, still clutching her phone. "It's just that I've waited so long to get some kind of evidence and I'm afraid to share it."

Wolf came over and took her free hand. Led her over to the couch and sat, tugging her onto his lap as he did so. She went willingly. Happily. He lifted his hand, brushed her hair behind her ear. "I get that you're worried about it, but you need to let me and my team do everything we can to keep you safe. Analyzing the video will give us access to information that's not readily apparent on the recording. There might be more there."

"I know." She lifted her phone, opened a text, and forwarded the video to Wolf. Then she let out a breath. "There."

He put a hand behind her neck, pulled her in close. "Thanks, baby," he said before he kissed her.

One touch of his lips and her body went up in flame. Desire ached deep inside her. She wanted him so much, and she didn't quite understand how she felt this much for him this quickly. He mattered to her. So damned much.

Right now, her life felt as if it was spiraling out of

control. As if the things she'd thought were real somehow weren't. But this was real. Wolf was real.

She felt him growing hard beneath her and she shifted against him, wanting more. He groaned, squeezing her tight for a moment. And then he let her go. "Much as I want to, there's work to do first," he said as he picked up his phone. "I need to send this to the guys."

She nuzzled his neck, then dropped down to her knees on the floor in front of him and went for the buttons on his jeans while he typed. "You work, I'll play."

He didn't stop her from opening his jeans, or from reaching inside and wrapping her hand around his hot flesh. "Haylee." Her name was half groan, half rebuke. His fingers stilled on the keypad. "Gotta work."

"Shush. Help me get these off. I want to make you feel good." This was the only thing she could believe in right now. Her and Wolf and the passion between them.

He put a finger beneath her chin. "You already do."

The look in his eyes made her heart flip. She told herself not to read too much into his words, but she couldn't help herself. It hit her that she wanted more than sex with him. She wanted to spend time with him, talking, watching TV, smiling at each other over a breakfast table.

"Up," she ordered to mask the emotion threatening to overwhelm her. He obeyed, lifting his hips just enough so she could tug his jeans down. His cock sprang free and she grasped it with both hands. "I've missed you," she said reverently, her eyes fixed on it. "So much."

Wolf laughed. "He missed you too."

"Stay out of this, Dean. Finish your text, or whatever it is you're doing. This gorgeous beast and I need to be together." She licked the length of him, from the tip to his balls, as he groaned and laughed at the same time. The phone dropped to the couch and she knew he'd finished his text. He was hers now. His fingers speared into her hair, holding her lightly but firmly as he thrust his hips forward and let her do what she wanted.

What she wanted was a lot. Licking, sucking, exploring. Feeling every twitch and throb of him. Learning his taste and texture. Feeling him swell in her mouth as he got close, and then doubling down when he tried to pull her away. Making him explode was her goal. And then he did, stiffening beneath her, his dick swelling bigger than ever, his balls tightening before he spilled everything he had. "Fucking hell," he groaned as she drank him down.

When she let him go and smiled up at him triumphantly, the look on his face made her heart skip. He seemed conflicted, but she had no time to study him because he reached for her, dragged her up, and kissed her hard.

"Goddamn, that was a turn on," he told her.

"There's plenty more where that came from," she said, running the backs of her fingers along his cheek, her heart throbbing with emotion. Was it love? If felt like it could be. She'd told him she could fall for him—but it was too late. She already had. She'd never known a man as decent as this one. As strong and honorable and protective. Wolf was exactly the kind of man she wanted in her life. Love was a risk, but maybe it was a risk worth taking.

Except for the part where she didn't know if he felt the same. How did you ask a guy that?

He turned her and dropped her down on the couch, reaching for the waistband of her pants. "Your turn, Haylee. I'm going to lick you until you scream."

"I like the sound of that," she murmured. He freed her from the fabric and she spread her legs without prompting. Wolf sank to his knees and kept his promise…

WOLF HAD JUST SHOWERED and dressed again when his phone rang. It was Hacker. "Hey, man. Find anything on that video?"

Hacker whistled. "Dude, that thing is all kinds of legit. Somebody was wearing a body cam. Whoever it is doesn't speak much at all, and nobody addresses him by name during the footage Davis sent. But I can't believe those guys would have talked about the things they'd talked about if they'd known the camera was there."

Wolf's gut tightened. "Such as?"

"The operation. Numbers. How many pills they could press, how they were getting them into the US —Setter's containers—how much Setter's cut would be. And Watson—holy fuck, he's involved, though he'll be able to deny it since he isn't actually there. But Setter *was* there and he didn't have any trouble discussing his cousin's participation in the scheme. Watson is hard on drugs for his state, but so long as the pills were going somewhere else, he didn't seem to care. Or so Setter claims. Like I said, Watson has plausible deniability about the whole thing. Probably won't be able to pin it on him without some hardcore evidence, though the optics are certainly bad."

Wolf was trying to process it all. A sitting senator guilty of taking drug money—and his attorney was on the run. What were the chances they'd get Watson? Depended on Tony Davis, probably. "Any luck tracking Davis?"

"Not since he went silent. He turned his phone off, or the battery died. Or somebody intercepted him and the phone is still in his last known location. It could be any of the three. Haylee's place was clear. Those guys broke in and started to ransack the place but they didn't leave any recording or listening devices behind. They didn't get too far before the cops showed up and they had to run. Saint sent Easy and

Gem over to secure the doors and plant cameras in case they return."

"They check out her car?"

"Couldn't find a key and couldn't break into it because the neighbors are nervous after this afternoon. Gem said there was an old lady who came out on her lawn and stared at them until they left."

Wolf chuckled. He could just imagine Gem and Easy being stared down by an old woman determined to stop more criminals from plaguing the neighborhood. "Yeah, fine. I'll get her keys and check it out later."

Her car wasn't a priority at the moment. Not with this new information about the cartel's drug pipeline. Wolf looked up as Haylee sauntered out of the bathroom. She wasn't wearing a stitch of clothing and she smiled at him as she passed. His dick started to harden. He watched her ass swaying as she walked and imagined himself biting those pretty cheeks.

Damn.

"Need you to come in, Wolf. Saint's calling a meeting. Ghost and Mendez are being briefed right now."

He'd expected that. "I'll be there. But I've got Haylee with me. I can't leave her here alone with this shit going down."

"Bring her with you. We'll get somebody to keep her company in the visitor's area."

Haylee strolled out of his bedroom wearing one of his T-shirts. It went to her knees. Sexy as fuck. He wanted to lift it up and put his head beneath it. Lick her pussy again until she sobbed with pleasure.

"I can do that. But she's going to need clothing."

Hacker snorted. Haylee snapped her gaze to his, a question in her eyes. "Of course she does. What did you do, rip everything off her?"

"No, asswipe. She left her house yesterday for a meal, not an overnight trip. And today when I took her back, we had to get out fast when those guys showed up. There wasn't any time to pack a bag."

"We'll get her something."

"Thanks. We'll be there soon. Have to swing by and pickup dinner first."

"We're ordering Chinese if that works for you."

"I'll ask Haylee. But we'll be there."

"See you soon."

"Yep."

"Hey, Wolf?"

"Yeah?"

"Welcome to the club."

His gut tightened. "What club?"

Hacker laughed. "The club where you can't stop thinking about one special lady. The club where you'd chew your own arm off if it meant you could save her from harm. The club where you're a goner over her."

Wolf tightened his grip on the phone. "Didn't say any of that, did I?"

Hacker's laugh grew louder. "Didn't have to, man. See you in a few."

The line went dead. Wolf fixed his gaze on

Haylee. She frowned adorably. All he wanted to do was wrap her in his arms and protect her. Was he a goner over her? Probably. Sure felt like it.

"What's up?" she asked.

"First of all, your place is fine. The cops scared those guys off before they could do any damage and a couple of my guys went and secured the doors. Second, we've got to go to HQ."

She frowned. "That's nice of them. Thank you. But… *we* have to go?"

"Yes. Both of us. It's not safe for you to go home or stay here, Haylee. And I'd be just a little distracted if you stayed and I couldn't look out for you. So we're both going. There'll be food and clothes, and a comfortable place to sit while I work."

She cocked a hip. "Wait—we won't be together?"

"No. I have to go to the secure area—that's where you need a security clearance to enter—but we have a really nice visitor's section. You'll be comfortable there."

"I need to work, Wolf. Will I have access to the internet?"

"You will—but honey, I think I'm going to have to ask you not to make anything public just yet."

Her frown grew harder. "I wasn't planning on it— it'll take longer than a couple of hours. But Wolf, this is *my* story, remember? Y'all aren't taking it away from me."

"No, nobody's taking it away from you. But there's more at stake here than just a story." He knew he'd said something wrong when her face grew red.

"Just a story? It's more than *just* a story, Wolf! People died. And nobody has answered for that yet—"

He closed the distance between them and wrapped his arms around her, tugging her against him where he could hold her close. Her body trembled with outrage. "I know, Haylee. I swear with everything in me that I'm going to make sure they do. You follow me?"

Her arms went around him. "Yes," she said, her voice small.

He tipped her chin back, gazed into her eyes. Dark eyes, so soulful and full of pain. And something more that he couldn't identify. "I promise you'll get your say. But if we have a chance to put a stop to the operation, are you going to begrudge us that?"

"No, of course not."

"Then let's go and see what's up, okay? I don't know that we'll do anything about it, but if there's a chance, then I'm not saying no. I hope you understand that."

"I do." She sighed. "I just want them stopped, Wolf. I don't really care how. I want them stopped, and I want people to know who Nicole was, that she lived and suffered and didn't deserve what happened to her. Nobody deserves that."

His heart squeezed. "No, I know."

She cupped his jaw. "I know you do. I want to do

this for Nicole—and for Cheryl and everyone like them who gets dragged beneath the surface of something far bigger than they are. It's not just them either —it's the kids, the parents, the siblings and the friends who suffer too. I want people to know and understand, not write them off as drug addicts who deserve whatever they got themselves into."

She was amazing. So filled with compassion and dedication. He admired her for it. He thought of Cheryl. Had he fought hard enough for her? Or was he content just sending home money and letting his parents deal with everything? He didn't know what more he could do, but maybe he needed to get more involved than he was. Fly out to California and visit Cheryl in rehab. See how she was doing with his own eyes. Talk to her.

"Then we'll make sure it happens that way." He set her away from him and swatted her ass. "Better put on some clothes, baby, or you'll start a riot at HQ."

Chapter Twenty-Three

HAYLEE DIDN'T KNOW WHAT TO EXPECT AT WOLF'S HQ, but a plush area with couches and workstations where she could sit and wait was not it. She'd probably watched one too many military dramas on television—not to mention the fact she'd been a part of one herself in Guatemala and El Salvador—so she'd expected something less like the lobby of an upscale hotel and more like an industrial building with concrete floors and hard couches. She was profoundly grateful she'd been wrong.

Getting inside this place hadn't been easy. It had required fingerprints and paperwork and a slow progression through a highly secured entryway. Since this wasn't the SCIF, as Wolf had described the area where he was going, she hated to think about the amount of security required to access that since this area had been bad enough. Probably needed a blood sacrifice and a burnt offering for that one.

Haylee had a computer with limited internet access. Wolf had told her she couldn't send anything out, but she could access her files in the cloud. That was all she needed since she wanted to work on shaping her story. Except that she couldn't think right now. She kept rereading the same paragraph and getting nowhere. It was frustrating. And probably due to not knowing what was going on in Wolf's meeting.

She was wearing the same leggings and shirt she'd worn yesterday, but Wolf had promised there'd be clothing for her. He'd had to leave before it'd materialized, however. He'd given her a quick kiss and a promise he'd be back as soon as he could. The two men with him, Hacker and Saint, had smirked at each other behind Wolf's back. Or she'd sworn they had anyway. Hard to be sure when Wolf commanded all her attention when he kissed her. It might have been quick, but it was thorough and hot, that's for sure.

The door opened and a small blond-haired woman walked in. Haylee wouldn't have thought the woman was here to see her except that she made a straight line for Haylee and smiled broadly as she approached.

"Hi, you must be Haylee," she said as she came up and dropped an Old Navy shopping bag onto the table.

"Yes, hi."

The woman held out her hand, her bubbly smile never leaving her face. "I'm Brooke Sullivan. I'm Cade's fiancé."

"Cade?" The name was familiar but Haylee couldn't put a face to it just yet.

Brooke waved as if dismissing the thought. "The men call him Saint. I never know who knows which name and I have to say I find the whole thing confusing sometimes—but I think they like it that way, quite honestly."

Haylee grinned. "You're probably right. Yes, I know who Saint is. Tall, dark, and handsome. The guy in charge of Wolf's team."

"That's him."

"Congratulations on your engagement."

"Thank you." Brooke beamed with happiness. Haylee envied that.

The door opened again and another woman strode in. This one was dark-haired. "Hey, y'all," she said. "How's it going?"

"Bliss!" Brooke cried as she hurried over to hug the other woman. "You've been working so hard lately I feel like I haven't seen you in ages. How are you, girlfriend?"

Bliss smiled. "I was at your house two weeks ago, Brooke. But yes, I've been working a lot since then. And I'm doing great! How about you?"

"You know. Planning a wedding. Taking care of my man. Running a business. In other words, living the dream." Brooke turned back to Haylee. "This is Haylee Jamison. She's Wolf's lady."

Haylee's belly flipped at that description. Was she Wolf's lady? She wanted to be.

Bliss put out her hand and Haylee took it. "Bliss Bennett. Sky—or Hacker, as you may have heard him called—is my fiancé."

"Oh my goodness," Brooke said suddenly. "I'm losing my mind." She lifted the shopping bag and held it out. "I picked you up some things, Haylee. I hope they fit. Cade gave me your measurements so blame him if they don't."

Haylee started to wonder where on earth Cade had gotten her measurements, but then she thought back to El Salvador and the questions she'd answered there. Clearly, even though she'd given her answers to a nurse, these guys had access to them.

Haylee took the bag. "Thank you so much. I had to leave home quickly, or I'd have grabbed some things. I can pay you back, of course."

"I'm not worried. I feel like we're going to get to know each other pretty well over the next few weeks or so. Welcome to HOT, Haylee."

"HOT?"

Bliss and Brooke exchanged a look. "You're here, so you're going to be briefed," Bliss said. "But basically we're a counterterrorism group with missions spanning the globe. We do covert ops, like the rescue where you met Wolf. If something bad is going on in the world, we're there to put out the fire and mop up the bad guys."

Haylee's gaze bounced between them. "You said we. You're both part of this HOT?"

Brooke laughed. "Not me. I bake cupcakes. But Bliss works here."

"I'm an information technology specialist," Bliss said.

"A computer hacker," Brooke added.

Bliss grinned. "Something like that."

"What is HOT?" Haylee asked. "I've never heard of it. I mean we were briefed after the rescue, but no one mentioned HOT."

"It's an acronym for the Hostile Operations Team. Like Delta Force and Navy SEALs—you've heard of those, right?"

"Definitely."

Bliss nodded. "We're Special Ops. Our missions are dangerous and secret. And though you and Brooke aren't officially part of the mission, you *are* part of the mission. There's a briefing for spouses— you'll get it soon enough."

Haylee shook her head even while her heart throbbed. "I'm not a spouse. I'm not even a girlfriend."

Brooke laughed. "Oh honey, trust me, you're a girlfriend. I've known Wolf for several months now, and one thing I can tell you is that I've never seen him with the same woman twice. Heck, I've never actually seen him with any woman. I mean I've seen him flirt with them at bars and restaurants, but he's never brought anyone to a team gathering, much less to HQ."

"I don't think he had a choice, actually. He's helping me out with a problem."

"A problem you could call the police for?"

"I, uh… Yes, I suppose I could."

"But he wouldn't let you, right? Told you he'd protect you?"

"Yes."

Brooke and Bliss exchanged a look. "You're a girl-friend. Accept it, Haylee. Wolf has claimed you for his own."

"He's just being nice. I wouldn't say there's any claiming going on." But the thought of him claiming her made her all gooey inside.

Brooke arched an eyebrow as her gaze dropped to Haylee's neck and back up again. She could feel the mark Wolf had left last night. The bite mark that had made her wild with pleasure as her body exploded beneath his.

"Whatever you say, honey," Brooke said. "Now why don't you head over to the bathroom and see if those clothes fit? If they don't, I'll run out again."

Haylee clutched the bag as her gaze bounced between the two women. They were watching her expectantly. Their expressions were welcoming though, not at all challenging or waspish. She decided to just go with it. Maybe they were right and she was Wolf's girlfriend. She hoped so. Or maybe they were wrong and he was just helping her out. Just because her heart was engaged didn't mean his was. She started for the bathroom when Bliss called out. Haylee turned.

"These men are stubborn as hell. They're so used to being strong and needing no one, but they fall, Haylee. They fall and sometimes they need a kick in the pants to understand it's happening. So don't let Wolf get away with keeping you guessing. Fight for him. Make him admit what's going on."

Haylee could only stare. Her heart beat with hope and happiness, but ingrained lessons from childhood were there to keep that hope from flaring bright. Sometimes, you loved people and they didn't love you back. "I'll try," she said. She had to force the words past the tightness in throat, but once she did she felt the hope swelling within.

Bliss looked fierce. "Good. And if the going gets tough, you've got us to fall back on. We've been there and we know what it's like. But trust me, the fight is worth it in the end."

———

"ORDINARILY, we can't move on something like this," Alex "Ghost" Bishop said to the assembled members of Echo Squad and the SEAL Team that had come to join them a few minutes ago. They were in the ready room, the video Tony Davis had sent to Haylee playing on the big screen at one end. It'd been over an hour since Wolf arrived, and they'd been working and discussing plans since. "This is DEA territory. They've been following the Juarez Cartel for months now and, with these details, they're ready to take them down. They've requested our help with the process. Echo and the SEALs are going in to help takedown the manufacturing facility. The shipments to Setter will be intercepted at the port and thoroughly searched."

Satisfaction flared in Wolf's chest. And apprehension too. He'd have to leave Haylee behind. Could he convince her to stay at his place? Or would she want to go home?

"What about Oscar Silva, sir?" Wolf asked. "This is the evidence to finally tie him to the operation. The only thing that connects him to the cartel."

"Yes, it is," Ghost said, his expression serious. "The FBI will be waiting to arrest him as soon as we storm the facility. If we arrest him first, the cartel could be tipped off that something is coming. And if we wait, then there's a chance someone will warn him when the premises are under attack. It has to happen simultaneously."

"Watson's going to lawyer up as soon as this goes down," Saint said.

"Unfortunately, yes," Ghost replied. "All we've got on him is his cousin's claim he's involved. Which he's going to deny."

"Fucker," somebody said.

Ghost looked at his watch. "Go time is now, gentlemen. You'll join the DEA team at Andrews and go over the plan en route. Any questions?"

"No, sir," the men said in unison.

Except for Wolf. "Yes," he broke in. Ghost looked up. Every gaze in the place turned to Wolf. He suddenly knew what it must feel like to be under a microscope. "Haylee Jamison. She could be in danger if she goes back home. Will she have protection?"

"We can arrange something," Ghost said. "All right, people. Dismissed. And good luck out there."

Chairs scraped as everyone stood and headed for the equipment room where they'd grab their packs. Everything was ready, because they'd known they were headed out again soon even if they hadn't known precisely where. Wolf's heart throbbed and a strange kind of panic began to swell inside him. He stopped in the hall. Saint stopped with him.

"What's up, Wolf?"

"Haylee. I need to tell her."

"Ghost will take care of her. She'll know you've gone."

He started to turn in the direction of the visitor's area, but Saint grabbed his arm, his grip tight. "No time, Wolf. We have to go. This will be over in a few hours and you'll be back here with all the time in the world to tell her how you feel."

Wolf blinked. *Tell her how you feel?* Was that what he'd meant when he said he needed to tell her? He'd thought he meant he needed to tell her he was leaving on a mission. But what if he'd meant more than that? Was it so obvious to his teammates but not to him? What did he feel anyway?

Love, his heart whispered. *You love her.*

I barely know her.
You know her well enough.

And he did. His heart knew hers. They'd recognized each other two months ago in the Guatemalan jungle. He'd been the one fighting against the inevitable, not his heart. His heart knew the moment he first saw her that she was the one. *The one.*

Jesus H. Christ. So this was what it felt like to need someone so much you could barely breathe.

His throat was suddenly, painfully tight. "How do you do it?" he asked. Saint's brows drew down and Wolf hurried to clarify. "Leave Brooke every time. How?"

Saint blew out a breath and shook his head. "I just do. Because it's the job. She understands this is the life she chose when she said yes to me. Thank God she did, because she's the reason I wake up every day. Do I hate the look in her eyes when I tell her we're headed downrange soon? Yeah, I do. Do I hate it when we get the go order and there's no time to make love to her one more time? Fuck yeah, I do. But I keep her in my heart and I know—I fucking *know*— that I'm going to hold her again soon."

That was so much more than Wolf had expected. And yet his racing heartbeat eased a bit and the panic subsided beneath the surface. He had a job to do—a job that would give Haylee what she most wanted in the end. Justice for her friend. The Juarez Cartel was about to have a come-to-Jesus-meeting with the best of the best. And they weren't going to survive it.

Wolf gritted his teeth. Then he nodded. "All right then. Let's do this thing and get back home safe so we can make love to our women."

Saint's grin was huge. "Goddamn, Wolf. You're really in love with her."

"Seems as if I am." He rubbed the back of his neck. "Don't know how it happened."

Saint snorted. "Dude, love is the stealthiest operator of all. Sneaks up silently and then slams you in the gut with the force of a rocket engine hurtling into space. You can't escape it."

Wolf sucked in a deep breath as they started to walk toward the equipment room again. Euphoria bubbled in his veins. He wanted to shout it to the world. "Who would want to escape a feeling like this?"

Chapter Twenty-Four

HAYLEE WAS SITTING WITH BROOKE IN THE VISITOR'S area—Bliss had left them about twenty minutes prior when she got a call about some work she needed to do —when two men came strolling in. They were both tall, both wearing military uniforms, both handsome. One was older than the other, with a full head of gray hair threaded through with black. The other had dark hair with a little gray at the temples.

"Ladies," the older one said as they strode up.

"Hello, colonel," Brooke replied with a sunny smile. "I assume if you're here, then my fiancé is on his way somewhere."

"You'd be correct about that, Miss Sullivan." He turned and held out his hand to Haylee. "Hello, Miss Jamison. I'm Colonel Mendez. This is Colonel Bishop."

Haylee took his hand for a brief shake. Her skin tingled from the contact, though not in the same way it did when she and Wolf touched. Still, this man was stunningly attractive. It was like meeting a movie star and being awestruck even though you had a handsome man of your own at home. "Hello," she said to them both, shaking Colonel Bishop's hand too.

"Thank you for your help regarding the Juarez Cartel. That video you provided means we're solving an issue that's far overdue."

Her gaze moved between them. Neither face gave anything away. Smooth and in control, these two. "I can't take credit for it. A friend sent it to me."

"Tony Davis."

"Yes. Have you found where he went?"

"Not yet. But if he turns his phone on, we'll find him. Miss Jamison, I need to ask you not to return home for the next couple of days. Your safety can't be guaranteed if you do."

Haylee swallowed. "I've been staying with Wolf."

"Yes. And you can return to his house if you want to do so. Or you can stay with a friend."

It hit her then that wherever Saint had gone, Wolf was with him. She didn't know why she hadn't figured that out from the first. Brooke had known right away. But this was all so new to her and she hadn't even thought about it.

"You can stay with me," Brooke said. "Cade and I have a house. I also have a really big German Shepard named Max who is guaranteed to make you feel safe."

Haylee turned to the other woman. Brooke was

such a pretty thing, petite and blond, so much like Nicole in a way. But not Nicole. "Oh, I couldn't impose."

"You aren't imposing. Besides, we were supposed to go to Grace's tonight for dinner and she's already planned for us being there. She'll make too much food as usual, and then she'll insist I take home leftovers. If you're there, she won't have as much to give away."

Haylee considered it. If she went back to Wolf's place, she'd be alone and she wouldn't have anyone to keep her informed about Wolf's whereabouts. If she stayed with his team leader's fiancé, she might learn how to deal with his absence from someone who was accustomed to it herself. "If you're sure it's not an imposition."

"It's not. We have a guest room."

"Okay, then thank you."

"I need to remind you, Miss Jamison," Colonel Mendez said, "Not to contact anyone about your whereabouts. You're new to us and how we work, but it's best you don't mention today either. Not this place, not the video, nothing."

She remembered the debrief she and the dental group had gotten after they'd flown back from El Salvador. It had been stressed not to discuss their ordeal then either.

"I understand. But colonel, I *am* a journalist. I intend to write about my friend's death and the things I've pieced together in the months since."

"That's your right, of course. But consider very

carefully anything you mean to say that involves this organization or anyone in it. What we do is dangerous, Miss Jamison. You don't want to compromise national security—or anyone's safety—by being too specific."

He meant them all, but of course she thought instantly of Wolf. No, she wouldn't do anything that could expose him or bring him harm. He'd been willing to take a bullet for her in the jungle. She'd do the same for him if she had to. "I wouldn't do that."

"Good. In a few days, when the dust has settled, you'll want to come back for a proper briefing. There are things you need to know if you're going to be in a relationship with one of my soldiers."

Haylee didn't bother to state there was no relationship with Wolf. Not yet anyway. She wanted there to be one, of course. Maybe Bliss was right and it did come down to fighting for what you wanted. If that was true, then she'd fight.

"Thank you. I look forward to it."

"Miss Sullivan. Miss Jamison," Mendez said, nodding at them both before he and the other man turned and strode out the door.

"Wow," Haylee said after they were gone.

Brooke laughed. "Wow is right. That man is a legend around here. I don't know as much about Ghost, but I suspect he's just as interesting. Those two are the heart and soul of this place. Saint would follow them anywhere. I suspect everyone here would do the same."

Panic was a tight ball in her chest. It threatened to lose structural integrity and flood her body with fear any second. "I don't know what to expect, Brooke. How long will Wolf be gone? How do I keep from being scared the whole time? How do I function while he's heading into danger?"

Brooke squeezed her hand. "Honey, that's why you have to come to Grace's with me tonight. Several of the HOT girls will be there—that's the women who are engaged or married to the men of HOT, plus a couple of women who work for HOT. We'll tell you everything you need to know."

————

THE RAID on the drug facility was a ball-busting experience. Echo and the SEALs dropped in from the sky with a DEA FAST team and stormed the base where the workers were busy pressing pills for ship-ment to the US. Wolf couldn't help but think of Haylee when he stood in the middle of the facility, sweat running down his face, gunpowder filling his nostrils, and swept his gaze over the piles of drugs and paraphernalia it took to make and package them.

"Motherfuckers," he growled as Gem strolled up, rifle cradled in his arms.

"Yeah, you got that right."

The workers were flat on the floor, hands behind their heads as they were zip-tied and flipped over onto their backs again. The place stank of sweat and unwashed bodies as well as chemicals and spent ammunition.

"Why the fuck do people do this to other people?" Wolf asked of no one in particular.

"Because they're scumbags," Gem said. "Because it's easy to dehumanize the people you won't see get hooked on this shit or die because of it. Because they *can*."

"Yeah." There was nothing else he could say. Haylee's best friend had died because of the shit from this place. It could just as easily have been Cheryl who got the wrong pills. She'd bought them off the street before. He knew she had. She was lucky she hadn't suffered the same fate as Nicole.

Wolf shuddered.

"Fentanyl," Easy said as he joined them. "Fucking Chinese shit. Bags of it back there."

Wolf was glad Haylee couldn't see this place. She knew abstractly what was going on, but until you saw it and smelled it you just couldn't understand how terrible it really was. And he wasn't telling her.

They spent time marching the cartel workers out of the buildings and rounding them all up in one area. And then they got to do the best part of the operation. They torched the buildings and let it all burn to the ground. Millions of dollars worth of drugs incinerated. Silva and the Juarez Cartel were finished. Others would eventually take their place, but for now it was done.

Halle-fucking-lujah.

THEY'D BEEN GONE for four days. Wolf sat in the bus taking them back to HOT HQ and yawned. His team was spread out, the SEALs too, all their equipment piled into empty seats. Some of them leaned on their duffels, catching a few z's, while others stared out the window at the passing lights. Nobody had their phones because those were in their lockers at HQ. That meant that nobody was calling loved ones just yet though most were thinking about it.

Today was the first time he was jonesing to call a woman and hear her voice. Usually, once the mission was over and he was on his way home again, he wasn't even thinking about who he planned to call. Oh, he'd usually call his parents at some point just to check in and see how they were, but they never knew when he was gone so there was no urgency to contact them the moment he returned.

He'd watched some of the other guys with that wild look, toes tapping, fingers drumming, while they waited the interminable minutes until they could get their hands on their phones again. And then, almost as soon as they did, they made those calls. Tucked into corners, behind desks, in hallways. Wherever they could get a little bit of privacy, he'd heard their low voices speaking to someone on the other end. He'd watched the tension leave their shoulders and the breath fill their lungs and he'd known they were relieved somehow.

He'd never understood that feeling until now. Right now, he wanted to hear Haylee's voice so badly. He wanted to stab his fingers into her hair and feel her lips beneath his. Then he wanted to strip her naked and give her so much pleasure she'd never think about another man ever again. And then, finally, he wanted to feel that crazy high feeling he felt whenever he joined his body with hers.

He didn't even know where she was, and that drove him just a little bit nuts. But Ghost had sworn she'd have protection, and he believed the deputy commander. HOT took care of their own, even when they didn't actually work for the organization. And Haylee was theirs now even if she didn't know it. More specifically, she was his. And he intended to let her know it just as soon as possible.

They made it back to HQ, turned in their equipment, and headed for the shower. Then they attended a debriefing session, followed by a quick briefing where they learned that Oscar Silva, Donnie Setter and John Payne had all been picked up. Setter's containers contained drugs that were hidden deep and masked with coffee, but they'd been found this time.

Frank Watson was denying involvement through his spokespeople, as predicted, and Tony Davis hadn't yet been located. His phone had not powered on again.

Finally, the teams got to their lockers and the cell phones they'd stowed there. Wolf's hand closed around his phone. His fingers were actually trembling. He lifted it to make the call—and the damned thing was dead. Son of a bitch. He tracked down the cable and went to plug it in when Saint came sauntering over. Dude was smiling.

"Haylee's with Brooke at our house. She's fine. You want to go get her?"

Did he want to go get her? What kind of question was that? "Hell yeah, when are we leaving?"

"Right now good enough for you?"

"It'll do," he said, shouldering his back pack.

Saint laughed. "Then let's get moving."

They went out to the parking lot and fired up their vehicles. Wolf waited for Saint to pull out and then followed him down the empty streets until they arrived at his house. The lights were on inside, which meant that Brooke was waiting. Had she wakened Haylee? Wolf's guts twisted with apprehension as he put a booted foot on the ground and then another. He slammed the door behind him and went to meet Saint in front of his truck.

"You ready for this?" Saint asked.

"What's there to be ready for? I'm picking up Haylee."

"You're picking up the woman you love, man. And you haven't told her yet."

Shit. "Yeah, thanks for that, asshole. If you're trying to make me crap my pants, you're nearly there."

LYNN RAYE HARRIS

Saint laughed. "It's easy. Just tell her how you feel."

Easy. As if you were saying the weather was nice or asking for a cheeseburger at a drive thru. *Easy.*

"Was it easy when you told Brooke?"

It was still dark out but Wolf thought his teammate turned a little red. "I told her in a text."

Wolf blinked. "A text?" Why the fuck hadn't he thought of that? Oh yeah, his damned phone was dead.

"We did a lot of our relationship through text in the beginning. It's just the way it was."

"So you texted that you loved her and you didn't have to worry she might laugh in your face or tell you it was fun but she didn't feel the same way? Yeah, not quite the same thing."

"Don't be a baby, man. Go in there and kiss the hell out of her. If there's fire, tell her. If there's not, then don't. Your choice."

Before Wolf could tell Saint to shove it up his ass, the front door opened and Brooke ran out followed by her giant German Shepard.

"Cade," she cried as she launched herself at him. He caught her, laughing, the dog barking like a fool, spinning her around and kissing her even while he reached out and ruffled Max's head. Wolf was so mesmerized by the sight of his teammate's homecoming that he didn't notice the small figure silhouetted in the doorway.

And then he did and his heart stopped beating, his

tongue stopped working, and his feet froze to the ground.

————

HAYLEE'S EYES WERE WATERING. She was still tired, having fallen asleep only a couple of hours ago, but when Brooke came knocking on her bedroom door, telling her the men were back and on their way home, she'd bolted awake. She'd brushed her teeth, combed her hair with trembling hands, and donned a tank top and button down shirt with leggings that Brooke had gotten her at Old Navy. She'd thought about meeting him in the T-shirt she'd been sleeping in, but that would leave her too exposed.

Brooke was wearing her cute pajamas and nothing else. Cade was big and gorgeous in his camouflage, squeezing Brooke to him and spinning her around. Haylee's eyes went to Wolf, who stood there so still he could have been a statue. He'd been watching Cade and Brooke and now he was looking at her.

He too wore camouflage. He was also big and gorgeous and solid-looking. But was he solid or was she dreaming?

Without conscious thought, she stumbled out the door and down the steps toward him. He still hadn't moved. He grew blurry and she swiped at her eyes, realizing that she was tearing up at the sight of him. She stopped, her chest aching with every breath. Stared. He stared back.

"Dean?" she asked, her voice sounding very small to her own ears.

He opened his arms and, suddenly freed from the bounds of gravity, she barreled into them, slamming her body against his. Wrapping her arms around him. And then she was shaking and crying and telling herself to get a damned grip.

But Wolf held her tightly, his hands coming up to cup her skull. Gently massaging her scalp. His mouth dropped to her temple.

"Haylee," he whispered. "Baby, don't cry."

She squeezed him harder. "I'm not crying."

His chest shook as he laughed. "You are. But you don't have to."

She shoved away from him and tilted her head back to gaze up at him. "I was worried about you. I didn't even get to say goodbye!"

He rubbed his thumb across her bottom lip. "I know, baby. That's what it's like sometimes. Can you handle that?"

Her heart cracked a little bit. But happiness filled the gaps. He was here. He was well. She could handle anything so long as those things were true.

"Yes."

He tugged her toward him again, dropped his mouth to hers. Their kiss was hard and desperate and sexy as hell. Her pussy was instantly wet. His dick was granite. Fire flared in her limbs, her core. She needed him so badly. His hands splayed against her back, held her tightly to him.

"Haylee," he groaned. "Haylee."

"Wolf—please, I need you. So much."

"Yes, God yes." He shuddered and pushed her away from him suddenly. "Not here. We need to get out of here."

"Yes."

"Get your things. We're going."

Haylee ran inside, gathered up the little bit she had, and ran back. She passed Brooke and Cade on the way. Brooke smiled as Haylee careened to a stop, not sure what to say. "Go, Haylee. We'll talk soon."

"Yes, soon." Then she hugged Brooke tight and laughed before running out the door and into Wolf's arms.

They got into his truck and she grabbed his hand, holding it tight while he drove the twenty minutes to his place. "I missed you," she said. An understatement.

"I missed you too, baby."

"Did you… Did you get the cartel?"

"We got them. All of them, Haylee. Silva won't send anyone to threaten you again."

She squeezed his hand. "I knew you would." She sucked in a trembling breath. "I was so worried."

He shrugged as he glanced at her. "It was a routine op. Nothing to fear."

But his hand tightened on hers and she wasn't sure she believed him. Not after talking to the women of HOT. Brooke, Grace—who was the president of the United States's daughter—Bliss, Cristina, Ella—

who was a real life princess—Quinn, Evie, Georgie, Emily, Sophie, and Annabelle. There were a few women missing, she'd been told, but she knew she'd meet them all eventually. They'd accepted her as one of their own and filled her in on what it was like being in love with a Special Operator. If she'd known those things to begin with, maybe she'd have stopped herself from falling.

Yeah, right. That was Nicole. Haylee almost laughed. Okay, fine, like she had any control over who she fell for. She wanted to tell him, and yet she didn't know how to say it. All she could think of was her mother, and the bitterness that permeated her life. Love hadn't worked out for Lillian Bright. Not at all.

They reached Wolf's house. He pulled into the drive and they both got out of the truck. He came around to her side, frowning. "I would have gotten the door for you."

"It's okay."

He took her bag and they headed inside. He closed the door behind them, set her bag on the counter, and turned to her. They stared at each other, suddenly awkward.

"What?" she finally asked after long moments of tense silence.

"I missed you," he said, his voice scraping down her spine in the most delicious way.

"I missed you too."

"I'm not used to this kind of thing."

"What kind of thing?"

He spread his hands. Shrugged. "Need, Haylee. I'm not used to needing someone. Wanting them beyond reason. Thinking about them all the time. Going crazy because I can't be with them."

Her heart was hammering. "You thought about me?"

"All the fucking time."

She sucked in a breath. Clenched her fists at her sides. "Why are we standing here staring at each other and trying to find words? We should be naked. Fucking."

"Making love," he corrected.

"Don't you have to be in love to make love?" She sounded breathless. Her heart beat so hard she was going to have to sit down soon.

"Yes," he said, closing the distance between them. "You do."

Chapter Twenty-Five

Light was streaming between the blinds when Wolf woke. He rolled his head on the pillow and reached for his phone. Nine a.m. Much later than he usually slept. Haylee lay against him, her body tucked into his side. She had an arm over his torso and a leg over his thighs. They were both naked.

His body ached with pain from the mission, but the pleasure from last night was even stronger. Better. She sighed and moved against him, and his dick began to throb. He pushed away from her reluctantly and went to the bathroom to piss and brush his teeth. He wanted to fix coffee for them, and breakfast. He'd bring her eggs and toast in bed.

He returned to the bedroom to drag on a pair of athletic shorts. Haylee was curled into a ball in his bed. He left her to go to the kitchen and start the coffee. Then he stared out the window at the trees swaying gently in the breeze. So this was love. This feeling of contentment and desperation. When you were happy with someone and wanted to possess them at the same time.

"Hey."

He turned at the sound of her voice. Haylee sauntered toward him, wearing his T-shirt and nothing else, and his gut twisted. So beautiful. So damned amazing.

"Hey," he said.

She came over and leaned against the counter. Smiled up at him. "I'm so glad you're back."

"Me too."

She reached for him, trailed her fingers along his skin. He shivered like a lovesick teenager. "Last night… It was amazing."

"Yeah."

"So what is this Wolf? You were so intense last night, and now…"

"Now?"

She shrugged. "I'm not sure. I thought maybe…" She didn't finish the sentence.

He was in over his head. Treading water. *Tell her how you feel.* Damned Saint. So smug and sure. The bastard had told Brooke by text.

The coffee pot beeped and he let out a breath. Turned to pour. Cream for her, nothing for him. His phone was in his pocket so he took it out and quickly typed. Then he hit send before he could think twice. A distant ding sounded from his bedroom. Haylee lifted her cup in both hands and seemed not at all inclined to check messages. Then it dinged again and she sighed.

"Guess I should see who that is in case it's important."

"Probably so."

She took her cup with her as she headed for the bedroom. He waited, heart throbbing. His phone dinged.

I love you, too.

Wolf felt as if his spine was made of hot wax. He melted, propping himself against the counter, his breath erratic as hell. Haylee walked back out of the bedroom, phone in one hand and coffee in the other. She smiled.

"I thought we solved that last night," she said.

"I wasn't sure."

"We made love. You said so yourself."

"I know. But maybe feelings were running high. Who knows what daylight brings."

She came and stood beside him, hip-bumped him at the counter. "I spent four days in hell, Wolf. Four days in which I realized you're my world and I never want another day to go by where you don't know it. But I also didn't know if you felt the same, which made the whole thing that much more scary."

He set his coffee down and turned to her. Pulled her against him. "I feel the same. You've captivated me, Haylee. From the beginning. I was yours the minute I saw you."

"You mean the minute that asshole dragged me outside and tried to rape me?"

His stomach bottomed out. But he wouldn't lie. "Yeah, that minute. Does that bother you?"

"No. Because you didn't let it happen."

"*You* didn't let it happen, honey. You kicked that jackass in the balls. I merely took advantage of what you'd already done."

"For which I am profoundly grateful." She smoothed her palms over his chest. "If you've spent any time at all thinking that I was horrified by what you did—I wasn't, Dean. You aren't the same as that man. You were my hero. You *are* my hero. I love you so much. I'm scared of what you do and proud of it too."

"You have no idea how happy I am to hear you say that. Being part of HOT is a tough job, but it's the best job. You want justice for Nicole, and I understand that. Fighting for justice and what's right *is* my job. I need to fight for Cheryl, too. I've been thinking about it, and I need to do more. I want to go see her, and I'd like you to go with me."

She cupped his face and gazed into his eyes. "I'm with you every step of the way, Dean. But you also need to know that you can only do so much. Addicts have to want to change. They need the support to make the change, but it's ultimately up to them. If she slides into the hole again, it's not your fault. I had to realize that with Nicole. I wanted to save her, tried so hard, but the demon was hers to fight. She failed and it hurts me every day, but I don't blame her for it. The demon was bigger than she was. It doesn't have to be that way for Cheryl though, and having us in her corner might be enough."

"And it might not be." It was hard to acknowledge the truth of that, but he had to.

"Right. But that's not because of anything you do or don't do."

He let his hands slide down to her ass. It gave him a thrill unlike any other to touch her so freely. To know she was his. "I like having you here with me. Think you can maybe bring some clothes over and stay for a while?"

Her hands roamed down to his ass, squeezed. "I've been planning to downsize now that it's just me in that big townhouse. I could find a place closer to here, stay with you while I'm looking."

He wanted her to stay with him all the time, but he also understood it was awfully quick to be planning to live together. "That sounds good to me. But if you never find a place you want to live in, you can just keep living here. Or maybe we'll find a place together, one where you can hire that fancy decorator of yours."

She laughed. "Oh, I think I can get her to give me some advice for this place. But yes, maybe we'll find a place we both like. It's an option."

It was time to get serious. "All the options are open, Haylee. The truth is I want to be with you. I want to wake up and go to sleep with you, and I want to know you're here when I come home. But if you need to keep the idea of your own space alive, then I'm for that too. Just know that I want you in my bed every night. Can't imagine not having you next to me."

Her eyes grew shiny with tears. "That's so sweet."

"Sweet?" he growled. "Not sweet. Selfish. I need you in my arms. Beneath me, on top of me, beside me. I need to feel your pussy wrapped around my cock and your tongue against mine. I need it to feel complete."

"Wow," she said, blinking up at him. "That's probably the most romantic thing anyone has ever said to me."

He bent and hooked an arm behind her knees, sweeping her up and into his arms while she laughed. "Hang on, baby. The romance is about to get even better."

"Oh, I can hardly wait…"

———

HAYLEE HAD NEVER BEEN SO happy in her life. With Wolf, she was comfortable. She felt like she belonged. Like they belonged together. For the first time, she was eager to leave the townhouse she'd shared with Nicole behind. She'd been hanging on for months, even though it was too big for just her, but now after a couple of days with Wolf, she knew she was ready to give notice and move out.

"You ready?" Wolf asked as he emerged from the bedroom, looking so handsome in his jeans and long-sleeved henley. The weather was starting to get a little cooler now. It was the first part of October and she still hadn't answered her mother's query about Thanksgiving. She didn't quite know how to answer. Was it too soon to bring it up to Wolf? Would he want to go to his parents' instead? Would he be on a mission? She had no idea, so she shoved it under the metaphorical carpet and didn't deal with it.

"Ready."

They were headed over to her place to pack up her clothes and shoes. She planned to take an inventory of her furniture and figure out what to do with that as well.

Wolf opened the passenger door for her and she climbed into his truck. It took them about twenty minutes to reach her place. Wolf pulled into one of the guest spots and her heart thumped as she remembered the last time they'd been here. His guys had secured her doors after that. She hadn't gotten to thank them personally, but she would the next time she saw them.

"Gonna need your car keys, babe. If it's the battery, I'll jump it for you."

She dug them from her purse and handed them over. "It feels so weird to be here now. I guess it really is time to move on."

"It's safe, if you're thinking about that. Nobody's tried to enter the house again. We put up cameras."

"I was thinking about it a little, but I was also thinking how much things have changed for me in the past few days. Not just you, but there's an end to Nicole's story now. I just have to write it."

She wasn't the one breaking the story about Oscar Silva and the cartel, but she could still write about Nicole's life, her addiction, and her death from the tainted pills. The story was still important, and Haylee was going to make sure she did it justice. Even if nobody wanted to publish it.

"You'll do a great job, Haylee."

"You don't actually know that," she said softly.

"Yeah, I do. Because you're the kind of person who throws your whole heart into things. You'll do it right because you can't do it any other way."

God, she loved this man. How had she gotten so lucky?

"Stop," he said.

She blinked. "Stop what?"

"Thinking that I'm just being nice."

"Okay," she whispered.

He kissed her hard. "There's more of that when we get back home."

"Then I guess we'd better get moving."

They got out of the car and went inside. Nothing was out of place, though of course Wolf went totally badass on her and swept through with a weapon like he had the first time they'd entered.

"What about the cameras?" she asked when he

returned and slipped the gun into its holster beneath his shirt.

"They're working just fine. I wanted to impress you."

"I'm impressed."

He grinned. "Get your shit, babe. I'll go and have a look at the car."

"Okay." She watched him walk away from her, his ass filling out those jeans in a way that made her mouth water. When he was gone, she got her suitcase out of the hall closet and took it into her bedroom to begin packing her things.

It was going to be a process to get completely out, but she was ready for it. Surprisingly ready. "I miss you, Nicole," she said as she tugged open her drawers. "But Wolf is a good guy and I'm so happy with him. I wish you could have met him. You'd like him. And I know he'd like you."

Her phone rang and she picked it up without looking at it, distracted by her task and figuring it was Wolf calling her from the parking lot. "Hello," she said, tucking the phone between her shoulder and ear as she tugged out another drawer.

"Haylee. Thank God you're okay."

Haylee nearly dropped the phone. "Tony? Where have you been? I've been worried about you!"

"Have you really?" He sounded a little bitter, though maybe he was just tired.

"Of course I have. You disappeared days ago, and I've heard nothing from you since that weird phone call. I thought maybe somebody had hurt you!"

"No, nobody hurt me," he said. "I had to get out of town while I could."

She sank onto the bed and put her forehead in her hand. "Why didn't you tell me what was going on? You could have just given me everything. You didn't have to go to such lengths. I'm assuming the papers on my porch was you, too. Was it?"

She was mad over how he'd gone about it, but she didn't want to let him know that. He sounded stressed enough without her adding to it. But dammit, if he'd just been forthcoming with everything, maybe they could have done something about the cartel and the drugs sooner. All those months she'd been searching. How long had he known?

"Yes, it was me. I didn't want to endanger you, Haylee. You needed plausible deniability if anybody asked where you got the information."

Haylee sighed. Maybe he *had* only recently found the information, but what he really meant was that he hadn't wanted to be implicated. "Silva and the cartel can't hurt you now. You're safe."

He snorted disdainfully. "No, I'm really not. Who do you think prosecutors will want to testify against them?"

She wasn't sure what Tony knew about the organization and she wasn't going to ask. It was too late for that. "Maybe you can go into witness protection. Or maybe it's not necessary at all. I don't know, Tony. But you need to come back. Talk to the FBI. Assess the situation."

"I want you to go with me."

Her heart throbbed. She didn't want to go to the FBI with him, but what could she say? Maybe Wolf could go too. "Okay. If that will make you feel better."

"I think it would. Yes."

She heard footsteps on the stairs. Wolf was coming up. She'd have to explain this to him. He was on the landing now, his dark form throwing a shadow across the space. Then he stepped into the room and Haylee's stomach dove to the floor. Tony pocketed his phone. Alarm bells jangled in her head but she didn't know why. Tony wasn't the bad guy. The bad guys were in jail.

He shrugged, his frame looking more gaunt than it had the last time she'd seen him. "I used the key you keep in the plant at the back door. Sorry I couldn't tell you I was coming up."

She stood. "Tony. You scared me."

"I didn't mean to." His gaze fell to her suitcase. "Are you ready?"

"Ready?"

"To come with me."

She stared. "I, uh, no. I meant I'd go with you to the FBI, not go *with* you. To where, Tony? Why?"

"Away," he said. "Where we can start over."

Haylee's heart thudded. "You aren't making any

sense. We can't just leave and start over. It doesn't work that way."

"Why not? I think we can do anything we want to do. I fucked up with Nicole, but I won't do that with you. I know better now."

Her skin prickled. "Fucked up? What do you mean?"

There were dark circles under his eyes. "I didn't know the pills would kill her. I swear I didn't."

Haylee's blood ran cold. "Tony—you gave Nicole the pills she ODed on? Why would you do that? She was an addict."

He ran a hand over his face. His gaze was bloodshot. His eyes were hollow. "I didn't know. She didn't tell me."

"That wouldn't have mattered! Street pills are inherently dangerous—you had to know that much."

He shook his head back and forth, almost as if hadn't heard her. "I didn't want the senator to have her. He wasn't treating her right. Hiding their relationship. Using me as their cover. He said he'd marry her, but he had no intention of divorcing his wife. I tried to tell her. She wouldn't listen."

Haylee reeled. Nicole and Frank Watson? But it made a strange kind of sense. Nicole had never really talked about Tony, which Haylee had always found a little bit odd once she'd learned about him. But Nicole had talked about the senator a lot, though she'd never said she was dating him. Having an affair with him. Was she? Or was Tony making it all up?

"Why are you telling me this now?" Her heart hurt at what he was saying. At all the connections in her head that were suddenly snapping into place. Nicole had been a little withdrawn in the days before she died. Frank Watson and his wife had announced to the world that she was pregnant around that time. *Oh Jesus.*

"I was the one who was going to pick up the pieces. She was in pain and I gave her something for it. I would have taken care of her, Haylee. But she took too many. She must have taken too many."

Fury scalded her. "Those pills were tainted, Tony! They were cut with fentanyl—that's what killed her. You should have *never* given them to her! How could you do that?"

"I didn't know."

Tears flooded her eyes. "That's no excuse." She brought her phone up, intending to call Wolf and tell him to get in here.

But Tony was on her in a flash, snatching the phone from her hand. "No," he said savagely. "You aren't calling *him*. He doesn't get to have you. You're mine."

"No, I'm not. I can't be."

He pulled his hand from his pocket—and pointed a pistol at her heart. "You're mine—or you're nobody's."

Chapter Twenty-Six

WOLF POPPED OPEN THE HOOD OF HAYLEE'S HONDA Accord and swore. The battery was disconnected, the cables removed from the posts. His blood ran cold at the sight. No doubt Silva's men had done it so John Payne could show up and offer her that ride. Mother-fuckers.

Wolf went to his truck and grabbed his tools so he could reconnect the battery. He'd have to clean the posts too since they were somewhat corroded. The car had definitely seen better days. Haylee said she didn't drive it often and he could believe that. He'd get it running again and then see how much work it needed. He didn't want her driving around in a death trap. She meant too much to him.

He cleaned the posts and tightened the cables, then went and turned the key. The car didn't start so he pulled his truck up and connected jumper cables.

Then he took out his phone and sent her a text while he gave the battery a few minutes to charge. Just because. *How's it going in there, babe? Need any help?*

She didn't answer right away. He didn't expect her to. But a tingling sensation started buzzing inside him at her lack of a reply. He told himself it was ridiculous, that she was packing—or maybe she was in the bathroom and forgot to take the phone with her—and that he was being overprotective. He glanced in either direction. The neighborhood looked perfectly normal. Cars drove by and people went about their business. Nothing strange about that.

Besides, Silva and his men were in jail. Why would anyone come after Haylee now? She'd had nothing to do with their arrests. It wasn't like she was the only witness to a crime and needed to be eliminated. It was just that he still had the jungle on his mind, the smell of the drug manufacturing camp and the satisfaction when it went up in smoke. It was still fresh, and it made him think of all that could be lost so easily.

He waited a couple more minutes, and then he texted again. *Haylee?*

She was going to text him back any second, roll her eyes at him for being overprotective. He waited for the three dots that indicated she was typing. Nothing happened. He lifted his gaze to the windows of her townhouse. The blinds were closed so he wouldn't be able to see movement anyway. He told himself not to do it, that he was being crazy, but he turned on the tracking for her phone. Just to see where she was.

A white BMW turned the corner up ahead as the program searched for her signal. The car accelerated away and his gaze landed on the license plate out of habit. It was a Virginia plate.

A second later, the tracking program pinpointed Haylee's phone. It was moving away from him. Ice formed in his veins, turned his guts to stone. How in the hell?

The BMW. She was in the BMW.

Wolf launched into action.

———

"WHERE ARE YOU TAKING ME?" Haylee asked. She was trying to be calm, trying to keep Tony talking. Maybe if she talked enough, he'd realize he couldn't get away with this.

But why couldn't he? He had one hand on the wheel and the other held the gun pointed at her. He hadn't restrained her in any way, but he hadn't lowered the gun either. She didn't think he'd shoot, but the truth was she didn't really know. She didn't know him as well as she'd thought.

She'd thought he was decent, kind. Stable. He wasn't any of those things. He was neurotic and maybe a bit crazy. Or deluded. He was definitely deluded.

"You'll find out when we get there." He waved the

gun around and she shrank into her seat. "It's going to be fine. I'll take care of you. I'll give you everything I would have given to Nicole. You'll see."

She forced herself to stay calm. "I want you to let me go, Tony. That's all I want from you."

"I can't do that. I loved Nicole, but she didn't love me. I won't make that mistake again. I've spent too much time with you to let anyone else have you. You weren't supposed to be dating anyone, Haylee." He snorted. "A military guy, no less. I'm a lawyer! I can give you things. A lifestyle. I was willing to be patient, but you had to go and ruin it all."

Haylee bit the inside of her lip. He was talking like a crazy person. How had he managed to hide his obsession for so long? She'd known though, hadn't she, that he'd been a bit obsessed with Nicole? Of course she had. She'd ignored the signs because she'd loved having someone to talk to about her friend. Someone who missed Nicole's smile, her laughter. Someone who claimed to love her. It had been a comfort to have him at first, and then later he'd been so supportive while Haylee worked and researched and tried to write a story about illicit street drugs.

Her heart hammered as he accelerated toward the main street. She wanted out, but there was no way she could escape. She glanced in the mirror—and saw a truck behind them. Was it Wolf? The truck wasn't close enough, but it looked like his. A silver truck barreling toward them. She prayed it was him.

Tony had pocketed her phone. She'd heard the

dings from messages, but she didn't know if it was Wolf sending them. Why would he when he'd been outside and could have just walked inside to talk to her? But maybe he had, and maybe he knew.

Please, Wolf. Please help me.

The truck was coming fast. Tony looked up into the rearview and swore. Then he stomped the gas and she was knocked against the seat as the car sped toward the stop sign ahead. He still had the gun on her, his eyes fixed on the road ahead, his face red with anger.

"Tony, for God's sake, stop!" she cried out when he approached the intersection at high speed.

Cars zoomed at them from the cross street. Haylee screamed as he braked hard and whipped the steering wheel, skidding through the intersection as cars honked and swerved around them. There was a moment—a single moment—when their forward momentum stalled as the tires squealed to gain purchase. Tony grabbed the wheel with both hands— and Haylee took her chance.

She threw the door opened and jumped, landing on the embankment with enough force to knock the breath out of her. Pain exploded in her body—and the metallic taste of blood flooded her mouth as metal and glass shattered in her ears.

"Haylee! Jesus Christ," a voice cried. Then a pair of big hands were on her, gently prodding her. "Baby, talk to me. Tell me you're okay."

"Wolf," she whispered. "Love you."

It hurt to breathe. Hurt to move.

"Don't fucking move," he ordered. "Let me check you for injuries."

"I'm… Fine. Just hit kind of hard." The breath had been knocked out of her and she'd bit her tongue —that's where the blood was from. She was pretty sure that was it anyway.

She didn't really know if she was fine, though. But she needed him to believe she was. She started to shift but he put a hand on her, held her firmly but gently.

"Move and I'll spank your ass as soon as you've recovered."

She cracked an eye open. "Promises, promises."

"Does your back hurt? Neck? Abdomen? Any severe pain?"

"Yes… No. I didn't hit my head, but I landed on my side and I bit my tongue."

"Don't fucking move. Help is on the way."

She gripped his arm. "Don't leave me."

His gaze lifted for a second. Then his expression hardened. "I won't."

"Tony? What happened? I heard a crash…"

"He's hurt pretty bad, Haylee. T-boned by a trash truck right after you jumped out of the car—Jesus, why did you do that? Though I'm thankful you did. I hate to think…"

"Had to get away. I couldn't let him take me."

He lay down beside her and smoothed his hand through her hair. Everything hurt, but his touch was soothing. "That's my Haylee. Always taking care of business."

"Your Haylee," she whispered. "Always."

Chapter Twenty-Seven

Haylee was in and out of pain. She thought she might have been in the hospital, but then she woke up in the dark and she was certain she was in Wolf's bed. She tried to get up and go find him, but the pain was too much and she lay there exhausted. Sleep claimed her soon after.

When she woke again, it was dark out and she knew for certain she was in Wolf's bed. She knew it because she could smell his scent on the pillows. If she was here, then she wasn't dead. Or in danger of dying. That was a relief.

She dragged herself upright and yawned. She was stiff and sore, but the pain wasn't blinding. It was a dull roar now. She couldn't find the lamp in the darkness so she felt for her phone before she remembered that Tony had it last. Had Wolf gotten it back?

There was a low hum of noise from the living room. Wolf was probably watching television. She called out to him, her voice rusty with disuse. A moment later the hum stopped and the door opened. Wolf was silhouetted in the opening for the briefest of moments before he was at her side, dropping down on the bed and kissing her forehead.

"How are you, baby?"

"Sore. How are you?"

"I'll feel better when you do." He twined his fingers with hers.

"What happened after the accident? Was I in the hospital?"

"You were there for a few hours. No internal injuries. Your muscles seized up from the impact, so they sent you home with relaxers to ease the pain. You've been sleeping it off for about twenty-four hours now."

"Muscle relaxers always knock me out."

"No kidding." He kissed her forehead again. "You scared me."

"I scared me, too… What happened to Tony?"

"Maybe we should talk about that later."

She squeezed his hand. "No, now."

He sighed. "Okay. He didn't make it, Haylee. The collision impacted the driver's side of the car. He died at the scene."

Her voice caught. "Oh God."

"I'm sorry."

"Me too." She'd been trying to come to terms with everything that Tony had said and done, but she'd also thought of him as a friend for a few months. It was hard to flip a switch in her brain and disconnect him entirely.

"What happened, Haylee? Can you tell me?"

She swallowed. "He was angry about you, Wolf. That I was with you. And he said things about Nicole…" She swallowed. She'd been trying so hard to process it.

"You can tell me, baby."

She squeezed his hand. "I know. They were never dating, Wolf. Nicole wasn't with Tony. She was with Senator Watson. Tony acted as cover for them—and he somehow got the idea that he was in love with her. That it was his job to save her."

If he was surprised, he didn't show it. "I'm sorry, Haylee."

"I am too. I had no idea, though it makes sense in retrospect." It hurt to think about her friend in anything but the best light, yet she'd known that Nicole had destructive tendencies. Addictive tendencies. "She could be a thrill-seeker. She liked the finer things, and she often talked about the senator. Her group was lobbying his office and she went there often. I just thought it was part of the excitement of the job. Maybe I was naïve, but she talked about the senator the way she should have talked about Tony if they were the ones dating."

She pulled in a breath and rushed on. Maybe if she got it all out, it might stop hurting so much. "Tony gave her the drugs. He says he didn't know she was an addict. She was upset and in pain and he gave them to her to help ease it. He wanted to be the one who picked up the pieces of her broken heart. Stupid asshole."

Wolf turned until he could lean against the headboard. Then he dragged her gently into his arms and held her. She was surprised to discover her face was wet. She swiped the tears and tried to hold them in.

"Cry if you need to, Haylee. It's okay."

She let her tears fall freely. Wolf handed her a tissue.

"I think maybe Tony started to crack after Nicole died. He convinced himself he was in love with her, that she wouldn't have died if she'd gone out with him instead of the senator. And then he turned that obsession onto me. When you came onto the scene, he thought it was Nicole and Senator Watson all over again." She wiped the tears from her cheeks. "I think he thought he was saving me from you."

"He pulled a gun on you, Haylee. Any man who truly cared for you would never endanger you that way."

"I know."

"I'm not inclined to feel any sympathy for him. He should have gone to the FBI with the shit he knew, not dragged you into it."

She loved that he was so protective of her. That he didn't have any doubts about right or wrong. And she didn't disagree with him. She'd tried to understand how Tony could have done what he'd done, but she couldn't wrap her mind around it.

For seven months, he'd known the truth. He'd watched her struggle with it, listened to her sorrows, talked about his own feelings of loss. She'd felt for him and she'd felt like he understood. He'd manipulated her to assuage his guilt.

"I'm furious with him," she said. "I'm not offering excuses for him and I don't forgive him for it. I'm sorry he died, though. It was senseless."

"So was Nicole's death."

Her throat was tight. "Yes."

"Sometimes, doing the right thing is painful. Tony didn't want any pain for himself. He wanted to assuage his guilt without getting his hands dirty. But he was too stupid to hide his tracks. The video he sent you was one he made himself. He was the one walking through the facility with Silva and the others. Recording the whole thing like some kind of James Bond wannabe. It was also why he ran that day—he knew they were onto him."

"Oh wow. How did you find that out?"

"Mal and Gem and Easy are here. They brought the news. Hacker and Bliss traced the video to the camera, then the camera to the IP—or some such shit like that. God if I know exactly how it works. Anyway, researching Tony's credit cards and travel records—he was in Mexico during the time frame, and he bought a body cam from a DC shop that specializes in espionage before he left."

"Holy cow."

"Yeah. With Tony, we might have been able to

connect Senator Watson to the organization, but now... Well, it's going to be a lot harder. But that's okay, we'll get him eventually."

She turned to gaze up at Wolf's profile in the dim light coming from the living room. She heard talking out there now. She'd assumed it was the television, but apparently it wasn't. "I want to thank them. Can you help me get dressed."

She could feel his hesitation. "You sure you're up for that?"

"No, but I think I have to move or I'll never be able to move again. I'm sore, but staying in one place isn't going to help, is it?"

"No, it won't." He eased away from her. "Let me get some clothes out of your suitcase."

She worked her way to the edge of the bed, watching him as he moved. He switched on the lamp and she blinked at the light for a second. Contentment settled in her soul as he tried to pull an outfit together for her. "Thank you, Wolf."

"For what?"

"For being you. For taking care of me. For supporting who I am and not trying to make me be who you want me to be."

He stopped and turned to face her. "Whoa, why would I do that? The best thing about you Haylee is *you*. I love you just as you are."

"I love you too. Just as you are... Well, maybe I love you naked and inside me too."

He snorted. "Yeah, I love me that way too. But

we've got time for that. Let's get you together so you can say hi to the guys."

———

THANKSGIVING

WOLF WAS the only man in the room. He felt the stares keenly, but he did his best not to high-tail it for the porch. If only he were a smoker, at least he'd have an excuse. But he wasn't and he wasn't about to start.

Haylee was helping her mom in the kitchen, though every once in a while she'd look up and catch his eye. They'd smile at each other and his insides would melt just a little bit more. They'd arrived yesterday, having driven down from DC. He'd talked to Haylee's mom via FaceTime before, but this was the first time he'd ever met her in person.

Lillian Bright was intimidating as hell. The woman was highly educated and, according to Haylee, not inclined to like men. Haylee had told him they didn't have to do this, that she could tell her mom she wasn't coming this year, but Wolf had insisted he wanted to go with her. So here he was, ensconced in a feminist enclave surrounded by Lillian's educated single friends, and feeling the heat just a little bit.

It meant a lot to him to show Haylee's mom that her daughter was important to him. Just like he intended to show his parents the same thing when he took Haylee home at Christmas. He'd endure any number of stares and grilling for Haylee. In the almost two months since Tony Davis had tried to abduct her, they'd moved in together and settled into a routine. He'd gone on a couple of missions and he could tell she was nervous when he did, but she had the other wives and girlfriends to talk to. She fit right in with them, too. He was glad for that. He didn't want her to be alone while he was gone.

His phone buzzed in his pocket and he started since he hadn't been expecting it. He'd already talked to his parents this morning. He fished it out and saw the California number. Excusing himself, he went out onto the porch and answered.

"Dean?"

"Cheryl—is everything okay?"

"Yes, it's fine. I just… I wanted you to know that I'm getting out of here soon. I've successfully completed the treatment. And I want to go home. I want to see Mom and Dad, and I want to hug my kids again."

Taylor and Jack had been with his parents for the past month. His parents had finally negotiated the thorny foster system and gotten temporary custody. They would get permanent custody eventually, especially since their senator had gotten involved. Having a United States senator on your side opened bureaucratic doors.

That was Haylee's doing. She'd told Grace

Spencer about his parents and their fight for their grandchildren at one of the HOT girls' nights. Grace was the president's daughter and she'd wasted no time. Of course Wolf had known who she was, and that Alpha Squad's Iceman was married to her, but he'd never thought there was a damned thing she could do to help. Turned out he was wrong.

"I'm sure they'll be happy to see you, honey."

"It's going to be different this time, Dean. I'm going to enter an ongoing treatment program back home. And I want Mom and Dad to have custody of my kids. It's for the best, and I know it."

His chest was tight. "I'll do anything I can to support you. You know that, right?"

"I do. And though I hate to ask, I was wondering if you could get me a flight home. I'll pay you back when I can."

"You don't have to pay me back."

"Yes, I do."

He knew not to argue with her. It was important for her to feel in control of her life. "Okay. Anything else?"

"If you could be there when I land—well, that would be great."

"I'll do you one better. I'll come and get you."

He thought she'd started to cry. "You would do that? After everything I've done? The lies and broken promises?"

"I love you, Cheryl. You're my baby sister. I'd walk through fire for you."

"I don't deserve you."

"Yeah, you do. You need to understand that."

"I'm trying."

"All right then. So text me the information and I'll make arrangements." He could get the time off of work if he had enough notice. And if something happened and he couldn't go, he'd ask Haylee. She'd be perfect for the job. He'd cross that bridge when he came to it though.

After a couple more minutes, he hung up and stood on the porch, staring at the quaint houses on the street and breathing the cool air in slowly. He didn't know if this time would take or if Cheryl would fall off the wagon again, but he damn sure intended to help her have the best chance of success he could.

"Hey," Haylee said, and he turned to see her stepping onto the porch, closing the door behind her. "Everything okay?" She wrapped her shawl around her and walked over to his side.

He put an arm around her shoulders. "Honey, everything is perfect."

"I know Mom can be difficult. I'm sorry if she's giving you a hard time."

"She's not. She's just worried about her baby."

She slipped her arms around his waist. "Well, her baby has never been happier."

"Neither have I. And maybe there's something more to be happy about."

He told her about Cheryl's call. Her face lit up with genuine happiness.

"Oh, Wolf. That's great. We both know it's a long road, but it's a start, right?"

"Yep. Hey, did you tell your mom about your article yet?" She'd worked hard to write the exposé about Oscar Silva and the Juarez Cartel, the bad drugs and the death of her friend. She'd shopped it around and a big New York magazine had picked it up. Her editor had mentioned the word Pulitzer in connection with it. Haylee was excited, but also realistic. It was her first big article and what she really wanted was to reach people, not win prizes. But he hoped she did both.

"No, I wanted to surprise her when the edition comes out next week."

"You should tell her, baby. Just tell her and then send her a copy. But let her have the joy of it here today with her friends."

"Maybe you're right," she said a touch shyly.

"It's up to you, but I think she'd be so proud. I know I am."

The door opened and Lillian poked her head out. "Dinner's ready."

"We're coming, Mom."

Haylee took his hand and led him inside. Wolf's heart was full as he sat down at the table with Lillian and her friends. His woman was by his side and he was in love for the first time in his life. That was a lot to be thankful for. If he died right now, he'd die happy.

But he hoped he had a lot of years with this

amazing woman. He intended to spend them all making sure she knew she was the most important woman in the world to him.

"Hey, Mom," Haylee said once they'd started passing the food. "I have something to tell you."

Shortly thereafter, the room erupted in cheers and exclamations of surprise and pride. Wolf sat back with his glass of sweet tea and soaked in the love in the room. Yeah, he was a lucky man. Saint and Hacker were right. Love was so worth the risk. Life with Haylee was going to be filled with it—and he couldn't wait to see what each day would bring.

Or what her reaction was going to be when he asked her to marry him later tonight when they were alone…

Epilogue

New Year's Eve

THE PARTY at Buddy's Bar & Grill was in full swing. People were laughing and drinking and having a good time. Echo Squad had just returned from a mission a few days ago and they were jubilant because they'd stopped a terrorist organization from blowing up an American military base on Christmas Eve. Yes, it meant they'd been away from their families, but they'd saved lives.

Add in the fact that Senator Frank Watson had just announced his retirement from the senate this afternoon and they were pretty damned stoked. No, Watson couldn't be officially tied to the Juarez Cartel, but the optics were so bad that he had no choice but to resign. It was rumored his wife was planning a divorce as well. Stupid bastard deserved it.

Mal nursed his beer as his HOT teammates caroused. Much of Alpha Squad was here, and the SEALs. A few Delta Squad members were there too, and some guys he didn't know yet. Best of all, Cage and Haylee were headed toward the pool table. Somehow, the guys had kept it quiet about Haylee. Cage had no fucking idea what was about to hit him. He even made the mistake of giving Haylee the break, same as Wolf had done in El Salvador.

The guys tried not to look too eager for the match. Haylee racked the balls and took aim. Those in the know got quiet and sauntered toward the table. Cage stood by looking unconcerned about the whole thing. Like he knew he had it in the bag.

His wife sat at the bar with her friends and shot looks toward the table. Did Christina Marchand know? And if she knew, had she shared that knowledge with her husband?

Haylee broke and the balls went flying around the table. She sank two right away. Then she chalked her cue and walked around the table, studying it. She looked hot as hell in a red sweater and black leather pants. Wolf was a lucky man.

Mal eased over to where Wolf stood, looking stony. "You upset, dude?"

"Hell no," Wolf muttered. "Trying not to let him see my glee."

Mal would have laughed, but he didn't want to tip Cage off either. Though maybe now was as good as any since Haylee probably wouldn't miss. Though she could. It was always possible.

"Make any bets?"

"Nope," he said. "I just wanted the satisfaction."

Haylee sunk two more balls before Cage started to squirm. By the fifth ball, Echo was done looking nonchalant. They were all around the table now, cheering Haylee on. Cage glared.

"You fuckers set me up," he said.

"Hell yeah we did," Easy hooted. "Haylee is going to cream your ass!"

Cage started to laugh as Haylee sank the next two. All that was left was the eight ball. She looked up and caught Wolf's eyes. Mal was standing right beside Wolf so he saw the weight of that look. The love contained in it caught him off guard. It wasn't for him, but he found himself wishing it was.

That thought stunned him. What the hell?

Wolf was his buddy. His teammate. Mal was happy for him. Damned happy. But, yeah, Haylee Jamison did it for him in a big way. He didn't know why. He didn't understand it. In fact, he pretty much hated himself for it. It wasn't cool to want another man's girl.

"Damn, look at her," Wolf said. "Magnificent."

"Yeah, she is." Mal didn't want to look, but he couldn't tear his gaze away as she bent over the table and lined up the shot. Her dark hair was a silky curtain. Her eyes glittered with happiness. The diamond on her left finger sparkled.

Haylee sank the last ball and Echo went nuts. Cage shook his head and laughed about the whole thing while some of the guys slapped him on the back. Haylee sauntered toward where Mal and Wolf stood. He could imagine, for the few seconds it took her to cross the room, that she was coming into his arms.

But she wasn't. She walked into Wolf's embrace. Her mouth met his and Mal felt like the lowest form of life on the planet. He turned away and headed for the bar. Time to find a willing partner for the night.

Because the woman he really wanted wouldn't ever be his. And he was so shook by that knowledge that he was going to have to bury it under an avalanche of alcohol and bad choices.

Happy-fucking-New Year to him…

Who's HOT?

Alpha Squad

Matt "Richie Rich" Girard (Book 0 & 1)

Sam "Knight Rider" McKnight (Book 2)

Billy "the Kid" Blake (Book 3)

Kev "Big Mac" MacDonald (Book 4)

Jack "Hawk" Hunter (Book 5)

Nick "Brandy" Brandon (Book 6)

Garrett "Iceman" Spencer (Book 7)

Ryan "Flash" Gordon (Book 8)

Chase "Fiddler" Daniels (Book 9)

Dex "Double Dee" Davidson (Book 10)

Commander

John "Viper" Mendez (Book 11)

Deputy Commander

Alex "Ghost" Bishop

Echo Squad
Cade "Saint" Rodgers (Book 12)
Sky "Hacker" Kelley (Book 13)
Dean "Wolf" Garner (Book 14)
Malcom "Mal" McCoy (Book 15)
Jake "Harley" Ryan (HOT WITNESS)
Jax "Gem" Stone
Noah "Easy" Cross
Ryder "Muffin" Hanson

SEAL Team
Dane "Viking" Erikson (Book 1)
Remy "Cage" Marchand (Book 2)
Cody "Cowboy" McCormick (Book 3)
Cash "Money" McQuaid (Book 4)
Alexei "Camel" Kamarov (Book 5)
Adam "Blade" Garrison (Book 6)
Ryan "Dirty Harry" Callahan (Book 7)
Zach "Neo" Anderson

Black's Bandits
Ian Black
Brett Wheeler
Jace Kaiser
Colton Duchaine
Jared
Rascal
? Unnamed Team Members

Freelance Contractors

Lucinda "Lucky" San Ramos, now MacDonald (Book 4)
Victoria "Vee" Royal, now Brandon (Book 6)
Emily Royal, now Gordon (Book 8)
Miranda Lockwood, now McCormick (SEAL Team Book 3)
Bliss Bennett, (Book 13)

Also by Lynn Raye Harris

The Hostile Operations Team Books

Book 0: RECKLESS HEAT

Book 1: HOT PURSUIT - Matt & Evie

Book 2: HOT MESS - Sam & Georgie

Book 3: HOT PACKAGE - Billy & Olivia

Book 4: DANGEROUSLY HOT - Kev & Lucky

Book 5: HOT SHOT - Jack & Gina

Book 6: HOT REBEL - Nick & Victoria

Book 7: HOT ICE - Garrett & Grace

Book 8: HOT & BOTHERED - Ryan & Emily

Book 9: HOT PROTECTOR - Chase & Sophie

Book 10: HOT ADDICTION - Dex & Annabelle

Book 11: HOT VALOR - Mendez & Kat

Book 12: HOT ANGEL - Cade & Brooke

Book 13: HOT SECRETS - Sky & Bliss

Book 14: HOT JUSTICE - Dean "Wolf" Garner

Book 15: Coming Soon!

———

The HOT SEAL Team Books

Book 1: HOT SEAL - Dane & Ivy

Book 2: HOT SEAL Lover - Remy & Christina

Book 3: HOT SEAL Rescue - Cody & Miranda

Book 4: HOT SEAL BRIDE - Cash & Ella

Book 5: HOT SEAL REDEMPTION - Alex & Bailey

Book 6: HOT SEAL TARGET - Adam & Quinn

Book 7: HOT SEAL HERO - Ryan & ?? ~ Coming soon!

The HOT Novella in Liliana Hart's MacKenzie Family Series

HOT WITNESS - Jake & Eva

7 Brides for 7 Brothers

MAX (Book 5) - Max & Ellie

7 Brides for 7 Soldiers

WYATT (Book 4) - Wyatt & Paige

———

About the Author

Lynn Raye Harris is the *New York Times* and *USA Today* bestselling author of the HOSTILE OPERATIONS TEAM SERIES of military romances as well as twenty books for Harlequin Presents. A former finalist for the Romance Writers of America's Golden Heart Award and the National Readers Choice Award, Lynn lives in Alabama with her handsome former-military husband, two crazy cats, and one spoiled American Saddlebred horse. Lynn's books have been called "exceptional and emotional," "intense," and "sizzling." Lynn's books have sold over three million copies worldwide.

To connect with Lynn online:
www.LynnRayeHarris.com
Lynn@LynnRayeHarris.com

49363773R00214

Made in the USA
Columbia, SC
21 January 2019